Silver Bullets

Dear Reader:

Fabulous at fifty! That's what four best friends—Queenie, Connie, Emma and Yolonda—are feeling. Now their goal is to work on spicing up their love lives.

Surely, every woman desires to find pleasure, however, author Suzetta Perkins takes the step to show how divas fifty and over, or so-called "Silver Bullets," as one character describes them, satisfy their romantic nature. It's an interesting view as we witness these silver-haired ladies who tackle the challenges as married, divorced and never married.

The overall message is that one is never too "old" to explore and get their freak on. From sex toys to five-inch stilettos, this eager quartet reconnects with their sensual side. The novel is like reality TV set in North Carolina; it's a never-ending adventure with added drama. Check out one of the author's titles such as *In My Rearview Mirror, Betrayed* and *At the End of the Day*. You're sure to find that the prolific author spins amazing tales, often filled with action and suspense.

As always, thanks for supporting the authors of Strebor Books. We try our best to bring you the future in great literature today. We appreciate the love. You can find me on Facebook @AuthorZane and on Twitter @planetzane.

Blessings,

Zane

Publisher
Strebor Books
www.simonandschuster.com

Silver Bullets

Suzetta Perkins

STREBOR BOOKS

NEW YORK LONDON TORONTO SYDNEY

SBI
Strebor Books
P.O. Box 6505
Largo, MD 20792
http://www.streborbooks.com

© 2014 by Suzetta Perkins

ISBN 978-1-59309-558-1
ISBN 978-1-4767-5620-2 (ebook)
LCCN 2013950691

First Strebor Books trade paperback edition April 2014

Cover design: www.mariondesigns.com
Cover photograph: © Keith Saunders/Marion Designs

10 9 8 7 6 5 4 3 2 1

Manufactured in the United States of America

For information regarding special discounts for bulk purchases,
please contact Simon & Schuster Special Sales at 1-866-506-1949
or business@simonandschuster.com

The Simon & Schuster Speakers Bureau can bring authors to your live event.
For more information or to book an event, contact the Simon & Schuster Speakers
Bureau at 1-866-248-3049 or visit our website at www.simonspeakers.com.

To my beautiful sassy sisters who are fine, fabulous, over fifty and still have it going on!

Acknowledgements

I'm ecstatic about the release of my ninth novel, *Silver Bullets*. There's no secret to being fine and fabulous when you reach the half-century mark. You are who you are. I thank God, my creator, for giving me the talent to create for you a memorable story that will make you laugh, smile, cry, and possibly remember a pivotal time in your life that helped to mold you into the person you are today.

To Zane, my publisher, and Charmaine Roberts Parker, publishing director for Strebor Books/Atria/Simon and Schuster, thank you for giving me the opportunity share my work once again. To Yona Deshommes, Publicist at Simon and Schuster, thank you also for the opportunities to make me better. A hearty thank-you to Keith Saunders of Marion Designs who always make my covers look wonderful. To Maxine Thompson, my agent, I appreciate all that you've done to maximize my literary future.

My children—Teliza and Gerald (J.R.), continue to be the wind beneath my wings. I couldn't have made it without you. To my cousin, Wanda Washington, you're a gem.

A special shout-out to DeSaundra Washington and Sharon Wilson of Let's Talk Book Club for supporting me each year with a book club meeting. I'd like to thank Nichole Redd of the Literary Divas, with whom I conducted a Skyped book club meeting while at a barbeque. I was overwhelmed that a book club in Iowa was reading my work.

I'd like to thank my awesome book club, The Sistahs Book Club, for their continued support. Thank you, LaTricia Smith and Mary Farmer for the great book release party you threw for me almost two years ago. From the awesome testimonies by Tara, Donna, Val, Bridget, Bianca, Pam F. and Pam G., Billie, and Alberta, to the delicious meal, the gifts, and the added fixture of my family who had arrived in town to be with me during my surgery.

When I began to think about all the book clubs I visited the past year and a half, my list was longer than I thought. First, Yvonne, my heart and my friend, thank you for hosting me with your ladies club—Sarah, Sandra P., Sydnell, DeNell, Wildena, Joyce, Lucille, and Dorothy—in Columbia. A special thank you to Thal Morris and the Girlfriends of Carolina out of Charlotte—Loretta, Marie, Leisa, Sheila, Estelle, Latarsha, Zelma, Phylis, Regina, and my friend, Deborah Miller. I had a great time. Thank you, Charlotte Adams-Graves and the Mu Theta Omega Chapter of AKA of Harker Heights, TX, for a wonderful literary event; I won't soon forget. Thank you, Connie Marks and the Sister Circle Book Club—Amy, Cynthia, Renee, Katrina, Rosie, Lucille, Margaret, Regina, Angela, Stefani, Alisha, and Cornelia—of Shreveport, LA for a first-class event. I had the pleasure of being the featured author at the Montgomery County Library in Troy, NC. Even though I was lost for two hours and arrived at the event almost forty-minutes late, this group was a joy. Thank you, David Atkins—Library Director, Anya Alsobrook, Sharon LeGrande, Pamela Alsobrook, Georgia, and Aaron for a splendid day. A special thank you to Mary DiRisio, Library Director at the East Regional Library in Cumberland County, who invited me to speak before a group of students. And to Emily Dickens and Wallace Sellars, thank you so much for giving me a place in your home to share my work.

I'd like to thank Juanita Pilgrim, my reader, for critiquing my work and telling me the truth. A big shoutout to Gilda Harris and Margo Pittman, my ultimate fans. A big thank you to Ray Thomas—The Brand and iBronco Radio staff at Fayetteville State University for my great interview. To Paula Hockaday, thank you for being a wonderful tour guide while I was in Texas. To Maxine Thompson, Gabriel Newsome, Lisa Muhammad, Joey Pinckney, Johnathan Royal, thank you for allowing me to express myself on your talk radio shows and your blogs.

A special thank you to Lasheera Lee, my publicist and dear friend, for her unwavering support and direction. I love you!

One For The Queen

Queenie Jackson threw her designer pocketbook on the pink, Queen Anne sofa, kicked off her black Manolo pumps, let out a sigh, and plopped down on the sofa next to her bag. She was exhausted from having to sing her solo part over and over again until she got it right during choir rehearsal at Shiloh Baptist Church. However, her exhaustion stemmed from a heated argument with her best friend and the choir director, Emma Wilcox, who said she'd seen her boo, Linden, slipping into Minnie Smith's house.

A squeaking sound came from the kitchen. Queenie jumped up from her seat and ran toward the kitchen in her stocking feet. She grabbed her chest when she saw Linden's butt, body bent over, extracting food from her refrigerator, as if he paid the bills at her residence. Linden was Queenie's on again, off again boyfriend. She was through with him—his fake brown contacts and perfect body, except for the slight limp incurred from his days of playing basketball—and didn't want to see him tonight or any other night.

"What are you doing here, Linden?" Queenie asked, her hands hugging her pleasingly plump hips. "You scared the hell out of me, and, furthermore, you can't ride up in here anytime you feel like it." Queenie shook her finger in his face. "I'm not that kind of sistah. This is my house, and you're going to respect my space. I want my spare key before you leave here tonight."

"Now hold your horses, Red. I don't know what's wrong with you, but I'm not going anywhere tonight but in your bed. I had a hard day at work. There's got to be something in this refrigerator that will give me a boost of energy so we can…throw down in the bedroom tonight."

Queenie stared at the six-foot, nut-brown, bald-headed brother, with the light-brown eyes thanks to his special brand of contacts. "I'm not in the mood tonight, sugah. You tail has got to go."

"Look, Red, I can whip it on you tonight. I've got the blue pills in my back pocket ready to rock-n-roll when you give the word. You might as well call that job of yours and tell them you won't be seeing them tomorrow. I'm going to be keeping you up all night long. Now give me some of that sweet, brown sugar."

Queenie slammed the refrigerator door shut. She tried to push her argument with Emma to the back of her mind. However, vivid images of Linden creeping inside Minnie's house formed in her head and wouldn't let go. "I don't care if you have red, green, pink, or blue pills, you won't be touching my sheets tonight. Give me my key and get your sorry-ass-behind out of my house now. Go to Minnie's since you seem to be so comfortable with her and she apparently has what you need. I'm nobody's stopover station."

The look on Linden's face didn't faze Queenie one bit. "I don't know what you're talking about, Red. Your old-ass, gossiping girl-friends run their mouths and tell lies every chance they get. Yeah, I was over at Minnie's…"

Slap.

Linden rubbed the side of his face with his hand. His eyes jutted out of his face like they'd been blown up with an air pump. "Hell, what you go and do that for, Red?"

"For fifteen minutes I stood in front of Emma and called her a liar—told her she didn't know what the hell she was talking about. Then she made me sing my solo over and over again although I was on key. And now you've got the audacity to stand in front of me and say that you were at Minnie's house?"

"Red, it wasn't like that at all. I went over to Minnie's house to connect her television cable. I didn't want to get caught supplying free cable to the sister. She's strapped for money and I said that I'd do her this favor but it had to be after the sun went down. Now you owe me an apology."

"It ain't that simple, Linden. Everybody's strapped for money. I bet you switched on her cable box all right."

"I'm telling the truth, Red. I love you, and if you weren't so damn stubborn, I'd marry you tomorrow."

Queenie softened a little. "Marry me? Did you hear what you said? Do you truly mean that, Linden?"

"Have I ever lied to you, Red? Girl, I'd kiss the ground you walk on and drink your bath water, too."

"You have a funny way of showing it. I've waited for an eternity for you to make your intentions known. You come in and out of my house like it's Home Depot…"

"Stop, Red, I'm serious about my love for you."

"I want to believe you, Linden, but you still have to go home tonight. There's a consequence for your actions. Next time, you'll remember to tell me before you step in another woman's home to do some housework. The argument I had with Emma tonight was no joke. Give me a kiss and my key. You can come by tomorrow; I have an early day at work…"

"You've got to be kidding. I'm horny as a…"

"Take a cold shower when you get home. My key, a kiss, and I'll see you tomorrow."

Wednesday Special

Before she could get the key out of the door, Emma Wilcox could smell the grease from the fried chicken her husband, Billy, had prepared for dinner. Every Wednesday night was fried chicken night. You could swear on your mother's grave that Billy was going to have crisp, golden-fried chicken sitting on a platter on Wednesdays—fifty-two weeks a year. Billy was a retired mess-hall cook for the United States Army where he proudly served Uncle Sam for twenty-four years.

Emma pushed through the front door and headed for the family room. She flung herself onto the sofa, which didn't protest her added weight. Even after three children, now adults, Emma was in remarkable shape. But it was her hazel eyes that defined her. With those and her processed bleached-blonde hair, she could still turn heads—from the young to the old ones. And if she wasn't so hung up on Jesus and Billy, she might have given a few of them a run for their money, especially since Billy was almost non-existent in the love making department.

As dutifully as always, Billy appeared in the room to take off her shoes and rub her feet. "You're tense, Emma. Those sisters give you a hard time at choir rehearsal tonight?"

"Only one sister was a thorn in my side tonight. I can't believe Queenie had the nerve to rock back on her heels, point her finger in my face, and call me a bold-faced liar."

"What did you say to Queenie to make her so mad? Queenie doesn't usually go off unless somebody hits her atomic bomb button."

Emma looked at her husband: fifty-six to her fifty-five; together since junior high; married the day after high school graduation. Having enlisted in the army right after, Billy had taken care of her for the next thirty-six years. He'd provided for her and their children as he moved up the mess hall ranks. He'd been admired and held in high regard as a cook, receiving many medals of commendation for his culinary skills in war and peace time.

Billy had been a little freak when they first got married. At one point, Emma thought they were going to have an army platoon full of kids. But she remembered her mother's words admonishing her to not let any man keep her barefoot and pregnant.

"A man will saddle you with a whole bunch of kids," Emma's mother had warned, "that you'll have to stay home and take care of while his tail run the streets behind some other young thing that has no baby bruises all over her body and makes him feel young. Take care of yourself—your appearance—and always be sure to make your man happy. That's how you keep them."

Emma's mother's words always resonated with her and she made sure that she took her daily birth control pill until she was ready to have another income tax deduction.

"I didn't say anything to her, Billy," she said now. "Queenie's an angry woman."

"I still say that you must have said something to her."

Emma eased off the sofa and laid her hands on her hips. "Yeah, I told her something that she needed to know."

Billy backed up. Although Emma was usually a gentle soul, he recognized this side of her.

"I told Queenie that I saw her man sneaking into Minnie Smith's house."

"Why did you go and do a fool thing like that, Emma? You knew Queenie was going to blow up in your face."

"She had a right to know. Linden Robinson has been sucking up all of her joy and great hospitality with no intention whatsoever to make an honest woman out of her."

"Well, it's none of your business, Emma. You need not stick your nose where it doesn't belong."

"Let me tell you something, Billy Wilcox. I'm a good looking black woman and I still got it. I see how the men at church watch me and how big Mike-next-door's eyes get when I go to close the blinds in my bra and panties. All I'd have to do is make one gesture, and they'd come running. But you're lucky, Billy Wilcox. You're lucky that I love the Lord and your sorry black behind that can't get his dipstick up and don't remember the first, middle, or last thing about pleasuring his woman. You're too happy frying chicken."

"You're wrong for that, Emma. Apologize now. I'll be damned if I'll have my wife belittling me in my home that I keep clean so she doesn't have to prepare every meal that she throws down in her belly, so she can relax and get off of her feet when she gets home from work at night. Yeah, I love to cook, but mess with me, sister, and this will be the last Wednesday you'll have fried damn chicken."

Billy was so mad he hadn't realized Emma had fallen onto the couch, laughing her head off.

"Billy, I think I lit a fire under your ass tonight. You are so cute when you get mad."

"Why did you have to go and insult my manhood like that, Emma? Why? I've been faithful to you all the years we've been married."

"Uhm-hmm."

"You can uhm-hmm all you want. I didn't say I never looked at anybody. I have. You're supposed to look at pretty things, but I always kept my hands to myself. The only place I've put my hands beside you is inside hogs, chickens, and cows to clean out their guts. And that wasn't even as much fun as making babies with you."

"Our babies are grown, Billy. That was a long time ago. The question is what have you done for me lately?"

"I clean your damn house, cook your dinner, and make your bath water. Dinner is served unless you don't want the Wednesday special. And if you don't want the Wednesday special, then you are plumb out of luck. Take it or leave."

If Emma wasn't a praying woman, she'd leave Billy and his fried chicken that very moment. Oh, it would be wonderful to feel the touch of a man who'd make her feel like a real woman. But after the foreplay and lovemaking were over, she'd want him to be gone. Emma was fifty-five and she didn't have time to babysit or play kindergarten teacher.

She'd keep Billy in spite of his shortcomings, no pun intended. He was a good man, who loved God and their children. She owed him. Maybe she'd surprise him one night—maybe on a Wednesday—and cook him up something special.

Looking Good

Queenie was glad it was Saturday. Her Monday through Friday job as an editor at *The News & Observer*—Raleigh, North Carolina's local newspaper—had taken a toll on her this week.

She had run herself ragged, verifying and editing stories that were serious headliners; stories that sold more newspapers in one week on the newsstands than the previous two weeks. That's how news went. Some weeks the papers were filled with fluff about old-money politicians and their thousand-dollar plate political fundraising dinners or Hollywood's bad kids gone further bad. Then a salacious story with all the makings of a major crime movie breaks.

Last week was last week. Today, Queenie set out for her favorite nail salon for her bi-weekly manicure and pedicure. There was nothing like pampering yourself. Queenie always came away with a euphoric feeling when her nails and toes were freshly scrubbed and polished. It made her feel as if she was on top of the world. She also enjoyed catching up with her girlfriends.

She hadn't talked to Emma since the incident at choir rehearsal the other night, but she'd be the bigger person and apologize. After all, Emma was half right. Queenie also looked forward to seeing Yolanda and her younger sister, Connie, as well as "First Lady" Jackie O'Neill.

Decked out in a pair of fuchsia capris that hugged her behind and wouldn't let go, a pair of five-inch, fuchsia stilettos, and a white frilly blouse with ruffles around the collar, Queenie plopped down in her red, Jaguar XK Coupe and hit the road. It was a beautiful spring day, exceptionally so for the last week in March.

The spa was located in the Cameron Village part of Raleigh. The ladies loved the area with all of its great shopping opportunities. The tree-lined streets and one-of-a-kind artsy shops, restaurants and cafes were what made the Village quaint and appealing. Queenie arrived at her destination and pulled into a parking space. She spotted Yolanda's Lexus a couple of spaces over.

Queenie latched onto Yolanda like a protective big sister. Yolanda was petite and sported a close-cropped hairdo.

"Hey, girl," Yolanda said, giving Queenie a big hug in return. "You're looking good."

"And so do you," Queenie said. She meant it too; Yolanda's silver and black mane complemented her dark brown complexion and she had a gym body with curves in all the right places. Not bad for a newly divorced fifty-six-year-old woman.

After releasing Yolanda, Queenie turned in Connie's direction and gave her a big hug.

"Hey, Connie, what've you been up to? Preston put a ring on your finger yet?"

"I love you, too, Queenie," Connie said, giving Queenie an extra squeeze.

It was an old joke between them. Connie Maxwell was knocking on a half century. The former pageant winner was still a natural beauty but had not been able to capture a man's heart the way she did those coveted rhinestone tiaras—that is until she met Mr. Preston Alexander.

Preston Alexander was the man of her dreams and came with a

pocket-full-of-money, a nice cushy job as a pharmaceutical rep for GlaxoSmithKline, and a three-bedroom cottage at Brier Creek Country Club Cottages. Foremost and of considerable importance, Preston had no baby mamas, no alimony, no child payments. Connie had been with Preston for the past three years, and while their relationship seemed to be at full throttle, there was yet to be a real conversation about marriage.

"Connie doesn't need to get married," Yolanda rushed to say, as they walked into the spa. "She's better off living the single life instead of getting her heart hurt over some man that'll cost her thousands of dollars later on when she decides that saying "I do" and becoming one ain't for her anymore. You see, I don't need a man; it's me and my Jesus."

"Don't hate on me, YoYo," Connie said. "It was you who allowed Eric to turn your happy home into an emotional, dysfunctional wreck. Whenever Preston decides to ask for my hand in marriage, that'll be fine with me. You busy bodies used and abused your exes and that's why they were happy when you threw them out. My man and I are fine, and he's going to be the father of my babies."

"Do you hear yourself, Connie?" Queenie asked, her face all bunched up. "Your eggs are going to turn to powder waiting on that man to propose to you."

Connie poked out her lips. "Come on, Q, that was a mean thing to say."

"All I'm saying is, if you really want to have a baby, there are a lot of orphans out there hoping that someone would love and adopt them. Look at Angelina Jolie and Madonna. Anyway, your biological clock is already doing a slow drag. Menopause is about to catch up to you any minute."

"I'm not trying to save the world, Q. I'm talking about one baby."

"I understand how my sister feels about having her own child," Yolanda said, rushing to defend Connie. "I wish I had more than one. All I'm saying is that she doesn't have to be married to have a baby."

"God don't like ugly, YoYo," Connie said. "I've waited all this time to have a baby with the man who I want to be my baby's father, and I'm not going to compromise my values because you all are operating on a high level of ignorance."

"A high level of what?" Queenie shouted as she looked at Yolanda. "Did your sister say we were ignorant?"

"We're telling you the twenty-first century truth, Connie," Yolanda offered. "I've known you all my life and you yearn for perfection. But if you think Preston Alexander is it, baby you've got it wrong. I like Preston, but you've got to put what Connie wants first. If you want a baby, adopt. Preston hasn't budged one bit when you hinted at marriage, which may be the reason why he's in his house all by himself and has never married. Do the math, sister."

"I think he's got something to hide," Queenie added. "He seems so secretive."

Connie twirled her finger about her head to indicate somebody was crazy. "As I said, someone is operating on a high level of ignorance."

"Saved by the bell," Yolanda said. "Here comes Emma and First Lady."

"Are you all ready for your pedicures?" the nail technician asked, interrupting what might have been a potential free-for-all at Connie's expense.

"Yes, we're ready," Queenie said. "You better be glad I'm ready for my claws to be manicured, Ms. Connie. I was ready to let you have it."

"Leave me and my man alone and we'll be good."

"What are you all so happy about?" Emma asked as she and First Lady Jackie O'Neill walked through the door and into the heated debate.

"Connie called Yolanda and me ignorant."

Emma began to laugh. "Connie had you pegged right, Queenie, but you're looking good."

"I'm not thinking about Connie. The only thing I'm thinking about is how these pretty nails of mine are going to be digging into Linden's back and have him purring like a big cat."

"You need Jesus, Queenie," Emma replied.

"Oh, baby, I holler for Him too. "Sorry about that First Lady."

"You are a hot mess, Queenie," First Lady said. "So that you know, I holler Jesus' name too."

Their laughter filled the shop as they continued their banter, got their feet and nails scrubbed and buffed, and their toenails colored. "I'm ready for lunch, now," Queenie said when they were done as she admired her nails.

"What about K&W Cafeteria?" Emma asked. "It's close by."

"It doesn't matter to me, but I need to go somewhere, as good as I look."

Doggie Bag

Queenie, Emma, First Lady Jackie O'Neill, Yolanda, and Connie filed into K&W Cafeteria chatting away about nothing. After everyone had filed through the line, they found a table large enough for the five of them to sit down.

"The chicken and dumplings are divine," Emma said in between bites. "I get so tired of Billy and his fried chicken."

"At least you have a man who cooks for you," Yolanda said.

"And cleans her house," Queenie added.

"That's a mighty fine man you've got there, Sister Emma," First Lady said matter-of-factly. "I'd keep him. If I could get Pastor to pick up a broom or put bread in the toaster, I'd be cooking with gas. I have to settle for him blessing the food." The ladies laughed.

"I'm going to keep him," Emma said with resignation. "If he should up and leave or suddenly keel over, I wouldn't get married again, though. As a widow of a retired military serviceman, I get free commissary and Post Exchange privileges, and a survivor's benefit check. Best of all is the medical. We pay a quarterly premium; but if I had to be hospitalized, the cost would be minimal. No, God wouldn't want me to mess with my military benefits fooling with another man."

"I hear you on that, Emma," Queenie said, giving Emma a high-five.

"Now, I didn't say that I wouldn't entertain a casual acquaintance every now and then."

"I hear you on that, too," Queenie said. "Look at me, Emma. My ex has been gone a long time, and I rather like the idea of having my own space. But when I want a little loving, I let Linden drop by and entertain me. Linden is where I go when I need an oil change and the tank is running on empty." Queenie licked her fingers.

The ladies broke out in laugher.

"Sorry about that First Lady, but the truth is the light. Pastor always told us to tell the truth."

"That's true, but I have no need to know what you and Linden do in your spare time."

"Tell me, First Lady, do you and Pastor O'Neill get your freak on?"

Jackie O'Neill laid her fork down on her plate, picked up her napkin, and wiped her face. "First of all, Queenie, it's none of your business what Pastor and I do in the confines of our bedroom or otherwise."

"She told you," Yolanda said, twisting her neck as Emma and Connie did the best they could to stifle their laughter.

"It's all right, YoYo. As long as we've been hanging out and talking trash, Sister Jackie O'Neill has been taking our golden nuggets of information back to the First Man and has shown him a few things. Yeah, they've been on their knees praying, but I bet that's not all they've been doing."

"That's blasphemous, Queenie Jackson. You're going down in Satan's fire."

"You're going with me," Queenie said. She burst out laughing and the others followed, unable to hold it in any longer.

"Emma, YoYo, and Connie, are you going to let this loud-mouth heifer talk about me like that? I'm a God-fearing woman…"

"Who gets her freak on," Queenie said, still laughing. "I'm not going to mess with you anymore, Jackie. I'm only having some fun, you old prude."

"I'm no prude. I'll have you know that Pastor and I role play. He's the devil and I'm Eve."

"Ohhhhh, I need some coffee," Emma said. "This is going to be good."

"Holy and righteous is His name," Queenie added.

"Let Jackie tell her story," Emma cut in. "We're all Christians, and we didn't get here by osmosis."

"There's nothing else to tell," Jackie stated. She wiped her mouth with her napkin and stared at the inquiring eyes that begged for more information.

"Jackie, you aren't going to take us to the threshold of discovery and leave us hanging," Emma said, after taking a sip of her coffee.

"Use your imagination. That's all I'm going to say about me and Pastor to you nosey heifers."

The ladies laughed.

For the first time, Connie finally spoke up. "Why does it always have to be about sex with you women? There's more to a relationship than having sex. Preston and I enjoy going to museums and Carolina Hurricanes hockey games believe it or not."

"Boring," Queenie said.

"Queenie, you talk a good game, but I don't believe you and Linden are getting it on like you say. My mother used to say that if someone has to talk about what they're doing all the time, nine out of ten they're lying."

"That's the second time today you called me out, Connie. For your information, Linden and I are in touch with each other's souls. We know how to keep our love fresh and strong. "

"So why was Linden creeping into Minnie Smith's house last

week in the dead of night?" Emma said with a sneer. "I'm with Connie; you talk a lot of trash, Q, but you're talking to someone else who's known you a long time."

"Linden was hooking Minnie up with free cable."

"I bet he was tapping those lines," Emma said. She broke out in laughter along with everyone else.

Queenie pushed her plate to the center of the table. She threw Emma a stare that would have scarred her for life if it was a lethal weapon. "Look, Ms. Emma Wilcox, don't try and make my situation look bad because your behind ain't getting none. Misery loves company, but you're going to be a miserable old woman all by yourself. Linden told me what he was doing, and I believe him. That's the end of it."

"Whatever, Q. It's your freeloading man."

Queenie rolled her eyes. "You all are haters. What Connie needs to do is take some advice from a woman who knows how to keep her love life spicy, give that Preston of hers something worth staying around for."

Connie was ticked off. "First, Preston loves me, Queenie. Second, I didn't ask you for advice. I don't need any gadgets, hoodoo or voodoo to make my man happy. He loves what he's got, and I love him."

She sounded less sure of that love though as she continued. "I'll admit he's dragging his feet about the 'M' word, but it'll come."

"Tell you what. You invite Preston over tonight and meet him at the door in a skimpy number or nothing at all. Get you a little whip; all men love women who play rough with them. You tear Preston's clothes off and show him what you can…"

"Queenie, do you have to paint the whole scene for us?" First Lady asked. "We get the idea and I'm sure Connie knows how to please Preston."

"Thank you, Jackie. Somebody is finally talking with some sense."

"Hold that thought, sister," Yolanda said. "I've spotted the man of my dreams and I'm going to get a doggy bag so I can take him home with me."

"What happened to 'it's only me and my Jesus'?" Emma asked. Yolanda ignored her.

The ladies turned to where a tall, golden-brown man, in his mid-to-late forties, with neatly pulled back dreads was setting his food tray down. He was two tables over and all alone, and he wasn't wearing a wedding band either..

"Jesus," First Lady said. "He is absolutely gorgeous."

"Drop dead gorgeous," Emma added. "Billy better watch out."

"I'm usually not this forward," Yolanda said, "but I must make his acquaintance."

"Go make your presence known, YoYo," Queenie put in. "I told y'all she couldn't live without having a side piece."

First Lady frowned. "I don't know about you, Q."

"Don't let Q get to you, Jackie," Yolanda said. "She's right about the side piece, though."

Yolanda retracted her lips. "Do I have any food on my teeth? Is my lipstick smeared?"

"Go on over there and talk to the man," Connie said. "We'll critique you later."

Yolanda smiled and got up from her seat. She sashayed over to where the gentleman sat and stuck out her hand. He shook it, smiling. They exchanged some pleasantries and before the girls knew it, Yolanda was seated and engaged in what seemed to be pleasant conversation. She put her arms on the table and gazed into the man's eyes while her girls looked on openly.

He noticed. "They seem to be very interested in what's happening here."

Yolanda waved at her girlfriends; they waved back.

"Yes," she replied. "They're my girls." She returned her attention fully to the hot man in the iridescent brown suit sitting across from her. "So, Illya Newsome, what brings you to Raleigh?" She'd already learned that he was a new arrival.

"My job," he said.

"Welcome to Raleigh. Are you here with family?"

"No, I'm a recent divorcée. I have two children, both girls, who have finished college and are doing things that have absolutely nothing to do with their degrees. One is in Hollywood. She believes she has what it takes to become an actress—she's my biology major, and my youngest wants to be a singer."

"Sounds like they know what they want to do."

"I could've saved all that college tuition I paid out of my pocket if I had known earlier.

"And what about you? Is there a man in your life?"

"Single and free."

Illya smiled. "How about leaving this joint and taking in a movie and dinner with me later? Or am I being too forward?"

"Not at all. Let me get my purse and tell the ladies that it's the end of the line for me and them for today."

"I'll be waiting."

Yolanda smiled and high-tailed it back to her seat. She picked up her purse and smiled at the ladies. "Doggy bag. I'll see you heifers later."

Let It Whip

Tonight would be the night she'd approached the subject of marriage with Preston. Connie couldn't conceive of not being with this man, a man she'd cultivated and groomed for a date with destiny—her destiny being that she would be his for the rest of their lives. There was no way she'd let her sister and crazy friends with their man-hating words destroy her faith in Preston and keep her from realizing the one thing she'd always wanted. She had to admit, though, that Queenie had some very colorful ideas about keeping her man interested. She might have to use one of those ideas to bring Preston down the home stretch.

Instead of driving home, Connie headed for her favorite naughty-nice shop. Occasionally, she'd go there and pick up a spicy piece of lingerie to add flavor to her steamy nights with Preston. She and Preston had separate residences, so she loved setting up seductive scenes when they got together. Now, she hoped it would bring them together permanently, fulfilling her dream of them purchasing a home together and living as husband and wife.

Upon reaching her destination, Connie jumped out of the car and headed into the store. She glided her hands over some of the displays while she picked up others. She toured the full length of the store before making her way back to an item that tickled her fancy.

Whips and chains hadn't been a secret desire of Connie's, but after Queenie painted the portrait of how she and Linden kept their romance alive, Connie was willing to give it a chance. For all she knew, Queenie was lying about her bedroom exploits. Still, the way she had colored it for the ladies had them sitting on the edge of their chairs.

Leather was one of Connie's favorite fabrics, especially if it was a soft, calf's skin. She poured over the leather outfit, that didn't amount to much, and imagined what she'd look like standing in front of Preston with her legs spread apart, a whip in one hand, and her free hand on her hip. Connie giggled at the thought.

"May I assist you?" the blond-haired sales associate asked, amused at Connie's attempt to seem uninterested in the leather contraption that consisted of a thong attached to a strap that intersected with another leather piece that wrapped around the breasts.

"I...I was only looking," Connie said, now a little uncomfortable with the sales associate looking over her shoulder.

"Trying to please your man?" the associate asked, now with a smile on her face. "If it makes you feel any better, this is a popular item. I sell at least two or three of these a week."

"You're kidding."

"Really. Ever since that *Fifty Shades of Grey* book came out, our sales of this outfit have skyrocketed."

"Well, I was looking at it. I'm not a real kinky person, but I wanted to do something different for my man...you know...spice up the bedroom."

The sales associate patted Connie lightly on the back. "Honey, make your man happy. I won't tell anyone if you don't; your secret is safe with me. There's nothing wrong with being a freak behind closed doors. We are all here on this earth because our parents had lust in their hearts and sex on the brain."

Connie laughed at the sales associate's attempt at humor, but it did relax her. "I'll take it and a pair of black fishnet stockings. And throw in a nice flogger...leather whip."

"Honey, that's what I'm talking about. Let it whip."

"I can't believe I'm doing this."

"Honey, you need to live a little; stop stressing over nothing. Think about all the fun you and your man are going to have tonight. Don't forget the champagne."

"I've already got a bottle on chill." She would do just that as soon as she got home.

"Well, let's ring you up, and if you feel like it, stop by next week to give me the four-one-one."

"Oh, you're naughty. A girl never tells."

"Honey, you should hear some of the stories some of these women come in here with. That's why we won't be going out of business anytime soon." Connie and the associate laughed.

"That'll be one-hundred and thirty-nine dollars and fifty-eight cents."

"Damn, that's a lot of money to get a man to say he wants to marry me," Connie said under her breath.

"I heard that. So that's what this is all about. I say whip his ass and make him beg for more."

Connie laughed. "Take my money before I change my mind. Thank you for making this a pleasant experience."

"The pleasure is mine. Now go on and have some fun."

Connie smiled and waved goodbye to the sales associate. She was going to do what the woman said, have some fun. She was always too safe and bottled up. It was time to live. She was going to get her freak on and turn Preston out. Connie laughed at her thinking, but it all had merit. Mr. Preston Alexander was going to come correct or she'd have to think about trading him in for a newer, more compliant model.

Arrest Me

Yolanda couldn't take her eyes off of the handsome gentleman that sat next to her in the driver's seat of the black Acura RLX luxury sedan. She'd had him pegged for a Mercedes man, but it didn't matter. He was a good looking piece of eye candy, dreads and all. His voice was smooth and velvety; hypnotic. Their conversation was casual and effortless and Yolanda was glued to every word.

"Thanks for the date," Yolanda said in a sultry voice. "I always enjoy a good Tyler Perry movie."

"It was quite a diversion from what I originally had planned," Illya replied, "but I'm glad I met you. I hope it won't be the last time we see each other."

"Well, you did promise to take me to dinner," Yolanda playfully reminded him.

Illya laughed heartily. "Of course, but surely you aren't hungry already."

"No, I'm not hungry yet. I was only hoping that our outing wasn't coming to a close so soon. I'm…I'm enjoying your company."

"You are a breath of fresh air. I haven't really dated since my divorce was final."

"How long has it been?"

"A year. How about you?"

"A year, three months, and five days."

Illya chuckled. "You've got it down to a science. My divorce was nasty, but now that it's over, I'd like to forget all the gory details. I've moved on and prefer a hassle-free life."

"I'm sorry that things weren't so easy for you."

"I'm beyond that now. Why don't we change the subject and enjoy the rest of the day?"

"I wholeheartedly agree. So what do you do in the Research Triangle Park?"

"My, you're so full of questions."

"Like the FBI, I have a very inquisitive mind."

Illya flinched.

"The truth is," Yolanda continued, "I usually don't jump into strange men's cars, especially at my age. So I have this need to elicit as much information about a person for the 'just in case' file."

Illya smiled. "You're a mess, Yolanda, but I like you. You can say that I'm in research."

"How exciting. Is it a new drug, a cure for cancer, or some research that hasn't yet been announced to the public?"

"None of the above."

"You're mysterious."

"So, how do you make your living, Ms. Morris?"

"I'm a healthcare administrator at one of the local hospitals."

Illya's eyebrow went up. "Healthcare? A commendable occupation."

"I wanted to be a nurse once but didn't quite go through with it. I've always been an advocate for causes and healthcare was one of them. My mother had a long history of health-related issues, and she and my dad had some very intense run-ins with so-called health professionals. They're both deceased. Because of them, I put all of my energy into understanding the healthcare system."

"I'm impressed," Illya said. "Let me ask you...ah, ah...have you seen a large climb in unethical behavior due to drugs?"

A severe frown crossed Yolanda's face. She studied Illya as she considered his question. "Why do you ask? Does it have something to do with the reason you're in North Carolina?"

Illya self-consciously flicked his ponytail over his shoulder. "I was merely asking." He hesitated then seemed to come to a decision. "However, since you asked, I'll say this. I'm here investigating a crime ring, specifically drugs. There has been a substantial rise in the number of drugs being pilfered from hospital pharmacies and hospital medicine cabinets; also corrupt doctors writing phony prescriptions."

Yolanda nodded. "And I wanted to know, right? However, to answer your question, yes, there have been cases of drugs being smuggled out of hospitals here in the Triangle, but my hospital has had a clean audit the past five years. I would know if we were in that kind of trouble."

He looked at Yolanda thoughtfully. "I like your confidence and the fact that you've got your hand on the pulse of what's going on where you work."

"I have to be; that's why they put me in charge."

She had an idea. "I could ask my sister, Connie, if her boyfriend has mentioned anything about a crime network."

"What would he know?"

"He works in pharmaceuticals. His ear would be valuable."

"Let's not take that route. I'm undercover and I've already divulged too much. I'd like to see you again, though, and Raleigh is growing on me, even if it has been only a few short weeks since I've arrived."

Yolanda finally relaxed. "Okay. If there's going to be any arrests made, I hope it's me," she joked.

Fishnet Stockings

Connie roasted a medium-size sirloin-tip roast and trimmed it with honey-glazed carrots, garlic mashed potatoes, a garden tossed salad, and potato bread rolls. When she was done, she plated individual plates and placed a stainless-steel cover over them. Then she sauntered off to her bedroom to prepare for the extraordinary night she'd planned for Preston.

A half-hour later her doorbell rang. The foyer and living room lights were dimmed. Connie took her time answering the door, and when she did, Preston was speechless. His eyes roved over her body.

"Come in, Preston. I've been waiting for you."

Preston smiled and shook his head. "Is it safe to come in? I don't know what your intention is with that piece of apparatus in your hand, but I hope it isn't for me—at least not tonight."

"Don't spoil the mood, Preston." Connie brushed her hand along her body as Preston came through the door. "I did all of this for you."

"Fishnet stockings turn me on and that leather number that you have wrapped around your body must mean dinner is delayed. Sorry, Connie, I've got a lot on my mind."

"Are you high on something?" The night wasn't progressing as she'd intended. Connie turned and walked into the living room.

"Hold up, hold up," Preston said, finally finding his groove. "Girl, let me slap those butt cheeks."

Connie turned around. "I want this night to be extra special. I love you, Preston, and I want to show you that I'm your girl for all seasons."

"Come here." Preston reached for Connie and pulled her to him. "You are my woman for all seasons, and I love you, too. I'm sorry if I didn't show you the appreciation you deserve when I came in. First, I was totally surprised to see you standing at the door half naked. It's so uncharacteristic of you. However, I'm a little preoccupied with a situation at work; but it's all good. You have my undivided attention."

Preston held Connie tight. He brought her hand to his mouth and kissed her fingers and then reached down and kissed her passionately on the lips. His hands dropped to her bare buttocks and squeezed until Connie moaned. He pulled back. "You don't mind if I get comfortable?"

"That is my intention."

Preston pulled off his tweed jacket and unbuttoned his black, silk shirt. His chest was smooth and taut; it rivaled any male model in *Vogue* magazine. "What were you planning to do with that whip? I haven't been a bad boy."

"I'm only going to tease you with it."

"You've been reading too much junk. During the course of my day, I've heard women talking about the erotic novel that woman wrote, although there are plenty of African-American authors who've already written that erotic story, much better."

"My, you're well informed, but what you say is true. I haven't read the book, but Queenie sure has."

"So, I have Queenie to thank for tonight's adventure. She fills you women's heads up with stuff she doesn't know the first thing about. I hear that Linden can't even get it up."

"That was wrong, Preston."

"He's tried to hit more than the Queen, and the women talk behind his back."

"And what women have you been talking to?"

"A couple of the women at work who know him. They say Linden pops those male enhancement pills like an addict on crack."

"Whatever." Connie stood at attention. "This night is about us. One little lick."

"Are you serious, Connie? Do you really want to hit me with that thing?"

"Yes, but not hard. It's part of the role play."

Preston sighed. "Okay."

"You've got to get completely undressed."

"So, you've become my lord and master."

"Oh yes, and you're going to do everything I say; otherwise no dinner for you."

"Those fishnets are hot, baby. I may need my dinner now so I'll have enough strength to endure what you're getting ready to put on me."

"No, that's not the plan. Now strip." Connie cracked the whip on the floor. The carpet dulled the sound, but Preston complied.

Still, something wasn't right. Connie couldn't put her finger on it. Preston's lackluster attitude had stripped her of any desire to continue the illusion she'd prepared for the evening. "I've changed my mind; let's eat," Connie said.

Pastor and First Lady

S hiloh Baptist Church was one-hundred years old. The red brick church was built by the blood, sweat, and tears of its early members and was considered an historic icon in the community. The congregation had seen its share of ministers come in and out of its doors. Pastor Franklin O'Neill was its pastor for the past twenty years and counting.

It was rare for Pastor Franklin O'Neill to not be at his office on a Monday morning. His body was exhausted after preaching both the eight and eleven o'clock services on Sunday. The services had been high spirited and the Holy Spirit had reigned supreme. Even Pastor O'Neill had worn a few holes in his shouting shoes.

Monday found him lying next to his wife and enjoying the serenity of the moment. Staring at the ceiling, a smile crossed his face. Good thoughts of his life with his family passed through his mind. Franklin and Jackie enjoyed a beautiful twenty-six year marriage. Their two children had gone to college, got a good education, and were now good citizens in the community. Their daughter, Kelly, had passed the bar on her first try and was now a practicing attorney. Their son, Franklin Junior, was a science teacher with aspirations to someday work for NASA.

There was a slight movement next to Franklin. He pulled his eyes away from the ceiling and turned toward Jackie, watching her as she stirred, stretching her arms and torso. A minute passed and Jackie's eyelids fluttered before she finally opened them.

Jackie turned and faced Franklin. She smiled at him; he smiled back.

"Good morning, baby. What's on that great mind of yours?" Jackie asked, touching his nose with her finger. "God give you a word for your next sermon?"

"He has, but in truth I was thinking about you…our family and how blessed I am…we are. God has blessed me with the most wonderful First Lady to be by my side, and I thank the Lord every day for it. How many times have we argued in our twenty-six years of marriage? Five…maybe six times?"

Jackie laughed. "You know it's been more like ten or twelve."

"That's not even one argument for each year we've been together."

"You're right about that, Franklin. We've been blessed."

Franklin kissed Jackie on the cheek.

"Franklin, I want you to be honest with me."

"Haven't I always?"

"Yes, but what I have to ask you is a little sensitive."

Franklin sat up. "Baby, you can ask me anything. Are you all right?"

"I'm fine. On Saturday, I went out with the girls, and Queenie called me a prude. She asked me questions about our bedroom playtime."

Franklin shook his head. "Those are your friends, Jackie, but it's none of their business what we do in our bedroom. That is sacred. Queenie needs to stand by the well like the widow woman and pray that Jesus walks by. The only problem is that she won't be trying to touch the hem of His garment."

"Don't go there, baby. God won't be pleased."

"That was my attempt at letting out a cuss."

Jackie laughed. She reached over, brushed her hand over Franklin's coarse beard, lowered her head and gave him a light kiss on the lips. "Do I still turn you on?"

"What kind of question is that? Baby, you know I love you. I still love that heart shaped behind that wiggles a little more than it did when we first met. It still turns me on. I love every inch of you, and you still mess up my mind. Come here."

Jackie moved closer to Franklin. He pulled her even closer and put his arm around her waist.

"Let's play Samson and Delilah," Jackie cooed.

"So you want to be the naughty seductress so you can con me into telling you my secrets."

"Think what you like, dear Samson. I'm going to blow your mind."

"God said to touch not His anointed."

Jackie whispered in his ear. "My dear, Samson, you are ruler over many."

"No, only the flock at Shiloh Baptist Church."

Jackie laughed. "You are so crazy, Franklin. Now assume the role of Samson and fall under Delilah's spell."

"Does this mean that Samson gets to make out with Delilah in the next few minutes? I don't have four hours to give before Delilah makes her move."

"The seduction of Delilah is foreplay. You enjoy the slow ride to euphoria and when you get to the top of the mountain, you scream like hell and let it all go."

Franklin stared at Jackie and laughed.

"I'm no prude, Franklin. I make my man happy in bed; I've got First Lady moves. I don't need toys, whips or chains to seduce my man."

"Is that the kind of stuff you women talk about?"

"Yes. Those women are afraid of getting old and losing their sex appeal. I don't have their problem."

Franklin giggled. "Honey, you are so funny. Why don't we forget about Samson and Delilah and play Pastor and First Lady? I want to make love to you, First Lady O'Neill, the twenty-first century way. Now, come and make Daddy happy."

"Be careful what you ask for."

"Who's your Pastor?"

"Who's your First Lady?"

Kiss My Grits

"Y ou're late," Emma she said, as Queenie strolled into the sanctuary fifteen minutes into rehearsal. She pointed at her watch. "Choir rehearsal starts at six o'clock sharp."

"Working on a big article that's coming out in next Sunday's paper. Sorry for the tardy, but you can now begin rehearsal."

Queenie wasn't going to let Emma get to her tonight. She'd sing and do whatever Emma requested of her, but she wasn't going to take any stuff off of anybody.

Truth of the matter, Queenie wasn't in a good mood. Ever since the night Queenie had told Linden to go home, he hadn't returned to her house. He had been obedient and returned her house key without a fuss, but that was the last Queenie had seen of him. She would have laid bets that he'd be knocking on her door before sundown the next day.

His absence only meant that Linden was laying his head down at Minnie's or some other woman's house, and that pissed Queenie off. Today her work had suffered for wondering where in the hell Linden could be. All that talk about loving her and drinking her bath water was a lie. Queenie had even pretended in front of the girls that Linden was giving her all she needed and that she was truly happy. *Why had she lied to herself?*

"Queenie, let's go over your solo for 'Take me to the King,'" Emma said, bringing her out of her daydream.

"And sing it like Tamela Mann," Yolanda shouted from the front pew, where the sopranos sat. Connie, sitting alongside, gave Queenie a thumbs-up.

Queenie got up from her seat and walked up to the podium so that she could sing into the microphone. First Lady O'Neill played the chorus on the piano accompanied by the church's faithful organist, Virgil Stubbs. With hands wrapped around the mike, Queenie stepped closer. She opened her mouth to sing but instead began to choke up. She threw a hand up and cupped her mouth like she was trying to keep from throwing up. Then she let it go, tears and all. In the next instant, Yolanda and Connie were on their feet. They rushed to a sobbing Queenie.

Yolanda held Queenie's chin. "What's wrong, Q? Are you all right?"

Queenie looked into Yolanda's eyes and shook her head back and forth. "No."

"Come and sit down," Yolanda urged, taking Queenie by the arm. Yolanda put her arm around Queenie's shoulder. "What's wrong, Q?"

"I can't talk about it now. Everyone is looking." Queenie wiped her eyes with the sleeve of her jacket.

"Why don't you go on home, and we'll get together this weekend."

"Okay." Before Yolanda could say another word, Queenie leaned over and whispered in her ear. "Linden is gone. He hasn't been back to the house since I told him to leave a week ago. When I asked him to leave, I only meant for the day."

"Are you and Yolanda finished with your sidebar conversation?" Emma asked. "You've already disrupted choir rehearsal for ten minutes."

Queenie rolled her eyes. "I'm going home." She threw her hands up. "Do what you want."

"You won't be able to sing on Sunday."

"Whatever."

Yolanda stood up and rolled her eyes. "You're mean, Emma."

"Are you going to talk or sing?"

Yolanda turned toward Connie and signaled with her finger. Connie followed Yolanda and Queenie out of the sanctuary.

Emma watched them leave and then opened her mouth. "If anyone else wants to leave, now is the time."

Queenie, Yolanda, and Connie stood outside in the church parking lot talking.

"I don't believe Emma," Yolanda said, rubbing Queenie's back. "She takes being the choir director much too serious. We've all been friends for years, and ever since Pastor O'Neill made her the head choir director, she's been a pistol."

"It seems she has something to prove," Connie chimed in.

"Ladies, I'm not thinking about Emma; she can kiss my grits. All I want is my man back."

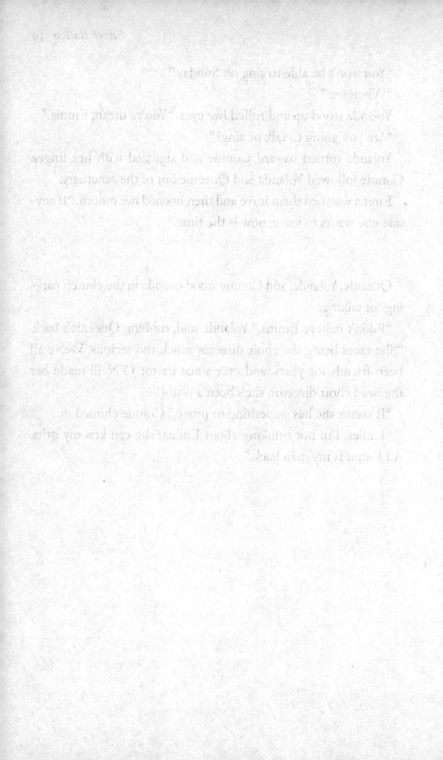

Surprise, Surprise

Yolanda's face lit up when she looked at her caller ID. The new man in her life was calling. Illya was a breath of fresh air. He didn't need tweaking—he already knew who he was, where he was going, and what life was all about. He was truly a specimen crafted by God, and Yolanda felt that she was the luckiest woman on earth.

"Hi, Illya, what's the good word?"

"You're the good word, Yolanda. These past few days have me somewhat confused."

"How is that?"

"I can't get you off the brain. I mean it in a good way. Since my wife and I divorced, I haven't allowed any other woman in. I've been consumed with my job, and that's kept me somewhat healthy and sane."

"To be honest, I've thought an awful lot about you, too."

"I'm glad I met you. I would love to see you this weekend; however, I have to travel out of town tomorrow for several days—work related."

"Oh, I'm disappointed, but I hope you won't be gone too long. Catching bad guys and taking them off the street is important."

"That's what I aim to do. What are you doing now?"

"I'm on my way home from choir rehearsal. I left a little early tonight."

"So you sing. I can't wait for you to sing me a song."

"Illya, you don't know what you're asking. I'm not a soloist; I accompany the melody although I should be singing it." They both laughed.

"Since you're already on the road, why don't we meet somewhere for coffee?"

"That's a wonderful idea. There's a neat little cafe near town that's open late."

"Tell me where and I'll meet you."

Yolanda rattled off the directions. For the first time in a long time, she felt at ease. Illya was a nice complement to her personality and wasn't needy like most of the men she'd met since divorcing her husband.

In fifteen minutes flat, Yolanda arrived at the café. She sat in the car until Illya's familiar frame exited the car that pulled into the parking lot a few minutes behind her. Like a true gentleman, he saw Yolanda sitting in her car and opened the door for her.

Illya couldn't take his eyes off of Yolanda. She was attractive, and for a middle-aged woman, well put together. He liked that she didn't color her hair—the silver stood out and accented her tapered cut.

Yolanda sported a two-piece, straight-leg pant set and denim jacket, with a red, lightweight, Lycra turtleneck underneath the jacket. Illya wore a black-and-white lightweight wool jacket, white turtleneck knit top, and black slacks. Illya wished Yolanda hadn't hidden her beautiful legs that he couldn't get enough of on their second date.

He placed his arm around her shoulder and they walked into the small, storefront café.

They sat at a table for two in a cozy corner. The room was dimly lit and provided an ambiance made for romance. Assorted pastries were displayed in the window at the front counter. Illya ordered coffee and a piece of key lime pie, while Yolanda ordered hot tea and a slice of pound cake. She couldn't keep the smile from her face.

Illya patted her hand. "I'm a lucky guy."

"I'm a lucky girl."

"Not as lucky as I am. I don't know what I'm going to do when I have to leave. I'm here indefinitely, but I won't be in Raleigh for long."

"So, what are you saying? It was nice to meet you, but it will only be a short-term relationship?"

"Not at all, Yolanda. Give me more credit than that. I'd like to know more about you—even take it to the next notch if the relationship were to go there."

"Wow, I'd like that too. I've been so tied to my job at the hospital..."

"There are hospitals in every city that are in need of good administrators. But I think we're getting ahead of ourselves."

"You're right. Let's enjoy the moment."

Illya smiled and took a sip of his coffee. "I agree. Let's enjoy the moment."

Yolanda took a sip of her tea and smiled back. Then she abruptly swung her head around. "Excuse me. That's my sister's fiancé. I wonder what he's doing here with the hospital CEO."

"What's his name?" Illya asked, suddenly interested in the duo.

"Who? The director or Connie's fiancé?"

"Both."

"Preston Alexander is sitting to your left. That's Connie's fiancé. Dr. Marshall Cole is the CEO of my hospital. I'm going over there and speak to them."

Before Illya could say another word, Yolanda was on her feet.

He watched as she crossed the room to where the two gentlemen sat. They were very much surprised to see her and seemed to offer some kind of explanation—for what, Illya hadn't a clue. Preston's hands were moving in all directions, his head tilting ever so slightly as he spoke. Illya made a mental note of the two and didn't ask any questions when Yolanda returned to their table.

"They're coming from a hospital board meeting," Yolanda said, as if Illya was expecting an explanation.

Illya said nothing but continued to watch the pair out of the corner of his eye. He took another sip of coffee and a bite of pie. "When are your sister and Preston Alexander getting married?"

"To tell you the truth, Preston hasn't officially asked Connie to marry him. They've been together for the longest, and Connie believes that Preston will pop the question soon."

"And if he doesn't?"

Yolanda looked at Illya perplexed. "What kind of question is that? My sister loves Preston and he loves her. Connie has never been married and is forty-nine going on fifty. She's anxious to be married before she turns fifty—she'd marry him today if Preston said let's go to the courthouse. But to answer your question, she'd move on with her life. I don't know why she feels she needs to get married. I was married for forever, and I ended up in divorce court."

Illya put his fork down and considered everything Yolanda said. Maybe she wasn't the one for him. Anyway, his line of work kept him moving, and it appeared that Yolanda wanted to stay put. But his real focus wasn't on Yolanda at the moment. The two gentlemen sitting across the way intrigued Illya.

Body Magic

Linden was still a no-show, but Queenie didn't care. In fact, she'd thrown him clear out of her mind. Tonight, she was going to have fun. She and her girls were going out to dinner and then to a jazz club to enjoy the music, dance a little, and maybe find a new play toy. She'd even entertain a younger man, if she could tame him. Summer would be here soon, and it would be nice to have a traveling companion on the Jamaican cruise Queenie thought about taking.

The night would be perfect if Emma was a no-show. She had called offering some half-ass apology that Queenie had thrown in the trash can. If Emma had been the kind of friend who wasn't up on her high horse and had been sensitive enough to find out what was wrong with Queenie during her moment of distress instead of waiting for someone to give her the four-one-one, then she wouldn't have had to apologize. But Emma was her girl, and she did interrupt choir rehearsal.

Thank God, First Lady O'Neill wasn't going to be tagging along to chastise them about fashioning themselves after the world; they wanted to hear some good music in peace. Queenie loved Jackie, but she was ready to have some fun.

Tonight, Queenie was going to wear her black Lycra dress that flared at the bottom but dipped low enough on top to show off her twin girls. Black was slimming. She hung her dress on the back of the bathroom door and laid out her black, shimmery stockings. They would jazz up her legs. She pulled out her black Body Magic from the drawer and looked at it. Her hips and pooch needed some help, and, if it would give her a flatter stomach, Body Magic to the rescue.

With her hair clipped high on her head, she bathed with her favorite Bath and Body wash. The floral fragrance permeated the room. The water was hot, like she liked it, eliciting *oohs* and *ahhs*.

Feeling refreshed, Queenie patted her body dry. She applied her favorite complementary Bath and Body Works lotion followed by a light splash of body powder. Queenie stepped into a pair of black, satin panties and a black, lacey, push-up bra that was filled to capacity with every inch of her 44DDD breasts.

Next, she picked up her Body Magic.

The Body Magic was for slimming her stomach and thighs and there was an art to putting it on. With the body slimmer in hand, she sat on the side of the bathtub and inserted one leg, then the other. Queenie placed her back against the wall and pushed a foot against the opposite wall and pulled the slimmer up to her crotch and repeated the task with the other leg. The real task was getting it over her buttocks and fastened. She sat lengthwise on the tub and placed her feet back on the wall, while she arched her back and tugged with all her might. She pulled and huffed until there was finally some give and the micromesh fabric made it over the hump in her rump. Blowing out air, Queenie counted to three and began the hard task of fastening the hooks that would pull her stomach together. She pulled, tugged and held her stomach in two or three times until she managed to get the first hook snapped. Queenie took a deep breath and repeated the process. Five long minutes passed before she got the second hook fastened.

"All for the sake of looking like the hot diva I am," Queenie said out loud to no one. "If I wasn't desperate, I'd take this crap off."

Queenie was able to get the next two hooks fastened without any problem. She was on a roll. Getting up from the tub, she went and stood in front of the big mirror in the bathroom and tried to fasten the next hook.

"Damn." Queenie screamed. Two of her nails broke off at the base of her nail bed. She kissed and sucked her fingers, while dancing around to will the pain away. A small tear escaped one of her eyes. Queenie was done. She pulled the straps of the Body Magic over her shoulders, fastened the top hook, and put her dress on. Enough was enough.

She continued to suck the tips of her injured fingers in between tossing her red weave up into a bun and putting on her black Louboutin heels. Regardless of what her nails looked like, she still looked fierce.

Divas

The ladies crowded into their favorite Italian restaurant. As bad as Queenie wanted to be mad at Emma, she couldn't after Emma told her how good she looked.

"You all look fabulous," Queenie said, taking a sip of her sweet tea. "Divas to the max. You don't know how close I came to staying home after I popped two of my nails trying to put on my Body Magic."

The ladies screamed with laughter.

"Only you, Q," Yolanda said. "But I'm not mad at you; you worked it, girl. And look at Sister Emma over there in her short, blue number. Billy didn't see her before she left the house tonight."

"You got that right, YoYo. Billy was out playing golf with some of his retired military buddies and I took off before he got home. I didn't want to argue with my husband about what I was wearing. He has it fixed in his head that I'm out trying to tease young brothers with my good looks. Just because I told him that Big Mike next door always waits for me to close the blinds so he could see me in my underwear." The girls laughed.

"Billy is going to surprise your behind one day and run off with another woman if you don't stop your wicked ways," Yolanda added. The girls laughed again. "But you do look divalicious in that dress."

Emma preened. "I bought this dress at Nordstrom today right

before coming here. I had the cashier cut the ticket off the dress before I wore it out of the store. And you know I keep at least three pairs of pumps in the trunk. I bought a dress that would work with at least one of the pairs."

"You are crazy, Emma," Queenie said. "That's why I can't stay mad at your behind. You make me laugh, and that's what I need tonight."

"Has Linden resurfaced?" Emma asked.

"No, girl. The brother has gotten ghost. And guess what? I don't give a damn. I've got a taste for something else...something delicious...a piece of eye candy. All the good brothers aren't in prison. Look, I don't mind being a cougar—showing the young studs how to satisfy a well-seasoned sistah."

"That's my girl," Yolanda said.

"So, you're going to step out on Linden?" Connie asked with a serious look on her face. She hadn't said a word in the last fifteen minutes.

"Stepping out on Linden? Where have you been all night, Connie? I've been emancipated, and the Queen Bee is ready to spread her wings. No one man defines me, and I'm not going to sit in a corner pining over one."

"But the other night at choir rehearsal, you said you missed Linden."

"I've come to my senses and have gotten over it, Connie. Take a sip of your sweet tea, and be glad I didn't ask how long you plan to wait for Preston to ask for your hand in marriage."

"That was wrong, Q."

"I'm only playing with you, girl. You love some Preston and he loves you. If he's worth having, I'd wait too."

Yolanda joined in. "Connie, I saw Preston the other night at the café with the hospital CEO. It was the night that we had choir rehearsal."

"You must have the wrong day, YoYo. Preston told me he had to go out of town on business."

"I clearly remember what night it was, Connie. I was on my way home from choir rehearsal when Illya called me."

"Ummm, now that is one hunk of a fine man," Queenie interjected.

"He sure is," Yolanda said in agreement. "Anyway, Illya called and asked me to meet him for coffee. I told him to meet me at my favorite café downtown, and after Illya and I had gotten comfortable sipping our tea and coffee, in walked Preston and Dr. Cole. I thought it was odd that the two of them would be together—after all Dr. Cole is the hospital's CEO and Preston is a pharmaceutical rep at another company."

Connie let her fork hit the plate a little louder than she had intended. "I don't understand what it is that you all don't like about Preston. He's a good man...an honorable man. And in due season, we're going to be married."

"Okay, everybody," Queenie said, commandeering the conversation, "we're supposed to be out having fun tonight. Let Connie and Preston be. After all, there's only one person here with a husband, and that's Emma. The rest of us don't have any room to talk about no one else; it's noneofourbusiness.com."

"Trying to sound like that Braxton girl," Emma said, as she and the others laughed.

"No, that was all me, the Queen Bee. Okay, are you heifers ready to have some fun?"

"Yes," Yolanda hollered. "I'm sorry, sis, if I upset you. I didn't mean to. I think Preston is a great guy."

"Thanks, YoYo. I appreciate you saying it out loud."

Yolanda smiled. "Love you, too. Now, I'm ready to hear some nice jazz, even though I wish my man was with me."

"Do you plan to take your budding relationship further?" Emma asked Yolanda.

"There's a definite possibility that there could be more. We'll have to wait and see. His job keeps him rather busy."

"What does he do?" Queenie asked. "I don't think you ever said what Mr. Doggie Bag does."

Yolanda hesitated. "He's in research," she said after a long pause.

"What kind of research, sis?"

"He swore me to secrecy, Connie. It's classified."

"Is he with the FBI?" Emma wanted to know.

"No, no, no. He didn't tell me what kind of research he was doing, no more than it was important. Look, all I wanted at the time was to have dinner with the dude—not have his babies or stroll down the aisle with him."

"Okay, enough," Queenie cut in again. "You all are killing my high. I was feeling good when I started this outing. Don't make me regret hanging out with you crazy women."

"I'm with you, Q," Yolanda said. "Let's have a good time tonight."

Divas To The Rescue

They looked like the Real Housewives of Raleigh as they strolled into the club, strutting what the good Lord gave them. Queenie was in her element the moment she hit the door. Her shoulders began to dance up and down to the soulful sounds of the live band, and her head fell back like she was in a drunken stupor. "The party is on," she declared.

Yolanda, Connie, and Emma followed Queenie to a table, their bodies moving with the vibrations of the music. Connie snapped her fingers and swayed from side to side, while Yolanda stood up and threw her hand at the band, encouraging them to continue the groove. Emma let the music float through her, her head swaying back and forth with her eyes closed.

A waitress sauntered to their table with a bottle of Moscato in tow. "Compliments of the gentleman sitting at the table to my left." The waitress pointed out the direction with her head, popped the cork, and poured wine into each of the ladies' glasses.

"This is what I'm talking about," Queenie yelped, nodding her head at the gentleman who looked in their direction.

"Jesus, he looks like the pimp that stole Christmas," Emma sneered. "Look at him grinning with all that gold in his mouth and still wearing a Jheri curl that has been outdated as long as dinosaurs have been extinct."

The ladies laughed, except Queenie.

"Of course, you would say that, Emma. But you don't mind guzzling down the wine he sent to the table."

"I was only stating fact, Q."

Queenie rolled her eyes as the ladies laughed louder.

"Look, I don't care what you ladies came to do," Queenie said. "I'm getting ready to party."

"So am I," Connie chimed in.

Yolanda, Emma, and Queenie swung their heads around in Connie's direction.

"You heard me. Preston has been acting strange...downright weird lately. I even listened to what Q said about getting freaky with my man. I went to my favorite store and bought a whip and a sexy outfit to put my man in bondage."

"You go, girl," Q said, holding her arm up in the air. "Put some spice in your life."

"Well, it backfired," Connie continued.

"Backfired?" Emma said, suddenly interested in what Connie had to say.

"Yes, backfired. Preston acted like I was some sleazy hoe and turned up his nose when he saw the whip. He told me that I wasn't going to hit him. All I wanted to do was please my man, and all he wanted to do was eat."

"Eat?" Emma asked, bucking her eyes.

"You're nasty, Emma. I'm talking about food—you know...like the fried chicken your husband fixes every Wednesday."

Their table once again exploded in laughter but Connie was not amused. "I don't know what you had on your nasty mind. Sometimes I'm not sure if you women are Christians, even if you do go to church, sing in the choir, and participate in all the church activities."

Emma was trying to recover from her laughter. "Sorry, Connie. You played into my hand and I went for it. Okay, the music is jamming, and I want to dance."

Before Emma could move, a tall, bald-headed, mocha-colored gentleman well dressed in a blue, linen blazer black slacks and a black dress shirt, stepped up and asked her to dance. No one heard Emma's reply, not vocally. But her answer was clear when she took the gentleman's hand and made a beeline for the dance floor.

Queenie spied another less desirable prospect approaching.

"'The pimp that stole Christmas' is moving this way," she announced. She tried not to look him square in the face, but when he put out his hand and asked her to dance, it was over. She'd come here to get her groove on, so she sashayed to the dance floor and did just that.

"It looks like you and I are stuck holding down the fort," Yolanda said to Connie. "I wish Illya was here, although I am having fun with my girls."

"You seem to be fond of him, sis."

"I like him a lot. It's only been a week, but there's something about him that I'm really attracted to. He seems to be the total package."

"You can surmise that in a week? You hardly know him. He's only let you see what he wants you to see."

"Well, I like what I see."

"He seems mysterious. Do you even know what kind of research he's into?"

"He's working on a drug case," she whispered.

"Oh, that kind of research. So he *is* FBI."

"I don't know if he's FBI, but he's working undercover."

"Be careful, YoYo. What if the bad guys catch on to him and try to take him out while you're with him?"

"If I was in any imminent danger, I'm sure Illya would protect me."

"You're foolish, girl. I may be younger, but you're 'coo-coo for Cocoa Puffs.' If Mama and Daddy were alive, they'd be giving you one of their lectures."

"I'm a grown-ass woman, Connie, and I do know how to take care of myself. Mind your business, and I'll mind mine. I'm not the one waiting for someone to pop the question."

"If you weren't my sister, I wouldn't sit up here and listen to your bull crap."

"But you are my sister, and I care about you."

"Save it until I ask for your opinion."

"Excuse me, sis. It appears that this good looking fellow coming toward our table wants to kick it on the dance floor. Hold down the fort."

Connie watched as her sister, Queenie, and Emma had a good time on the dance floor. They danced and danced until the band took a break.

"You all were having a blast out there."

"Whew, I lost at least thirty pounds on the dance floor," Queenie said, slapping Connie on the wrist and wiping sweat from her face. "My Body Magic even feels loose."

The girls laughed.

"I've got to go to the girl's room," Queenie said.

"I'll go with you," Yolanda said.

Queenie and Yolanda went to powder their noses, while Emma and Connie sat and listened to the piped-in music. Emma fanned her face with one hand and strummed the table with her other.

"That was so much fun," Emma said, still swaying slightly. "Billy doesn't like to go out like this and have fun. He'd rather sit in his man cave and watch football and basketball all weekend long or play golf when his buddies call. After thirty-six years of marriage, you become complacent and you live to survive."

"Do you think I'm wasting my time with Preston?"

Emma stopped fanning and looked at Connie with a serious look on her face. "I can't answer that for you. You're the only one who knows how you feel about your relationship with Preston. If all the signs are there that indicate you are both in it for the long haul, follow your heart. Sometimes women and men will ignore the signs that a relationship has cracks in it. They truly want to be with the person they've attached themselves to. Some have a hard time accepting and communicating that the relationship is over for fear of hurting their mate's feelings or they are a slow roller… and eventually they'll say what you want to hear. However, at some point, you have to recognize whether or not your significant other is adding value or stringing you along."

"I'm almost fifty, Emma. I want to get married and I still want to have babies, although that may not be possible now. All of my life I've been waiting for that perfect man, and I believe I found him in Preston. He loves me, Emma, I know he does, but I don't know what's holding him back. "

"Does he want the same thing you do?"

"I'm sure he does."

"Has he said it? If Preston wants to get married, Connie, he would be on the same page with you. Even if you didn't get married tomorrow, a ring and a date for the wedding would be in order. You are going to have to be straight up with Preston and let him know how you feel."

"I don't want to give him an ultimatum."

"Why? Are you afraid he'll walk away? If so, you need to rethink your relationship with the great Preston Alexander."

Connie sat without saying a word. Pursing her lips, she slipped into deep thought, only looking up again when Emma tapped her arm.

"Look, Connie. That's Linden Robinson with another woman, and it definitely isn't Minnie Smith."

"Queenie is going to have a conniption. Maybe I should go to the ladies room and warn her."

"Too late. Here they come. I hope Q doesn't see him before she gets to the table."

"Well, we don't have to worry about that now. Her dance partner is Johnny on the spot and ready to drag her to the dance floor, now that the band has started playing again."

"That was a close call, but what about the rest of the night?"

"What are you talking about?" Yolanda asked as she returned, grabbing a seat next to Connie.

"Girl," Emma began, "you won't believe who's in the club at this very minute."

Yolanda's eyes popped out of their sockets. "Who? Please don't tell me it's my ex."

"Not your ex. How about Linden Robinson, Queenie's boyfriend?"

"Shut your mouth, Emma. You're lying."

"She's not lying," Connie said. "And he's not here alone."

"Damn. Is he here with Minnie?"

"The woman doesn't look a thing like Minnie," Emma said chuckling.

"Preston said that Linden had been talking to a couple of women where he works."

"Queenie knew Linden was a dog," Emma interjected. "But she couldn't give him up."

"Look, this is what we're going to do," Yolanda said, taking the reins. "We are going to keep them apart. If we have to highjack Q and end her fun for the evening, that's what we're going to do. She's having a ball tonight, and no sorry ass Negro is going to spoil it for her. Agreed?"

"Divas to the rescue," Emma said.

Sunday's Best

Everyone dragged into church the next morning ready to do God's bidding. Not many hours had passed since they'd left the club, put their dancing shoes away, and headed home to get some sleep before Sunday service. And no one could tell the divas that they didn't look good this Sunday morning, dressed in their designer dresses and shoes.

Sunday school had come and gone, and Emma stood in the choir stand ready to direct the choir members down the aisles and to their seats. Yolanda and Connie stood in line with the others, waiting for Emma to give the signal. Queenie had looked forward to sitting in the audience after missing part of choir rehearsal and being told that she couldn't sing on Sunday. However, like the forgiving soul Emma could be, she invited Queenie to robe up.

The choir rocked back and forth as they advanced down the aisle, adding some fancy foot work as they sung a lively and upbeat song. The parishioners, feeling the music in their souls, clapped their hands and beat their tambourines.

Testimony service followed with different ones telling the church body how good God had been to them and their families all week. Minnie Smith gave the church announcements and the deacons took up the day's monetary collection.

Then it was the choir's turn. Emma stood, turned her back to the audience and raised the choir up with a swift motion of her hands. Queenie moved out to the front and was given a mike. "Sing the song, Queenie," someone shouted before she even opened her mouth.

Queenie waited for the introduction and then softly went into the verse of 'Take Me to the King'. The words rolled smoothly off of Queenie's tongue, so much so that it was almost seductive. After the second verse, she plunged into the chorus and had all of the worshippers standing on their feet, even Pastor O'Neill. First Lady Jackie O'Neill tickled the piano keys, the Holy Ghost oozing from her fingers. When Queenie was at the end of the song, she raised her hands to God and then lost it.

Everyone was shouting and praising the Lord. The divas were no longer in the club but in the house of the Lord doing the holy dance. Even Emma felt the spirit and began to shout, kicking up her heels.

The music died, giving way for Pastor O'Neill to preach the word.

Pastor O'Neill stood before the congregation in his white robe with its deep, rich purple panels on the front, embroidered gold crosses on either side. He thanked God for the day and looked over at Jackie, acknowledging his First Lady. Pastor O'Neill then went to the throne of grace and prayed that God would use him to preach the word to His people and that God would be glorified and that some lost soul would come to Christ.

"The text for my message today comes from II Samuel, Chapter 11," Pastor O'Neill began. "The subject is 'Lusting for the Wrong Thing.' I'm going to tell the truth, and you say 'Amen.'"

"Amen," someone shouted from the audience.

Queenie glanced in Yolanda's direction, but Yolanda looked straight ahead.

"We are all familiar with the story of David and Bathsheba. David was a man after God's own heart. He slew the giant, Goliath, when he was a little boy. He became king of Israel and ruler over many. He fought many battles and was victorious in most. David made a lot of mistakes, too.

"As the story goes, instead of going to war with his men this particular spring, David stayed behind. That was his first mistake. And in his idleness, as David strolled along the roof of the palace, he saw a woman bathing. She was beautiful and men, you know how you act sometimes when you see a pretty woman. You want to know who she is and whether or not she's available. Women, I can say the same for you when you see a handsome man."

"Amen," someone shouted. The congregation laughed.

"David summoned Bathsheba to the palace, and although he found out that she was a married woman and that her husband, Uriah, was far away in battle, he did the unthinkable. He slept with her. I'm not sure what kind of birth control precautions they had back in David's time, but the scripture says that Bathsheba became pregnant.

"King David was in trouble and had to cover up the act that he had committed. So he called for Bathsheba's husband, Uriah, to come home from battle in hopes that Uriah would get busy with his wife so that there would be no question of the baby's parentage. But things didn't go the way King David had hoped.

"Out of respect for his fellow soldiers, Uriah didn't sleep with his wife. He thought it would be unfair for him to enjoy his wife while his soldiers were off fighting in battle. After several days had gone by and Uriah had yet to sleep with his wife, David had Uriah sent back into battle and placed on the front lines where he would be killed.

"And as the story goes, Uriah was killed, but David's lust for Bathsheba was the beginning of his woes and that of Israel. Today, we often lust after things that are not only good for us but those things we know to be wrong without thinking about the consequences. You single men and women see a woman or a man that looks good to you, and in your mind you've got to have them. That goes for you married folks, too." There were snickers in the congregation. "You chase them down or get all dolled up in order to entice them to step your way. And when they do, you may find yourself in a relationship that is abusive. And for some, when it's too late you realize that you've made the biggest mistake of your life.

"Sleeping with Bathsheba was a blatant sin that David committed. God has given us commandments that we are to use in our walk with him. I'm sure you all are wondering why I'm coming hard with this subject today. It's a warning for God's people. The streets talk, and people don't mind giving me the four-one-one on my parishioners, although I do question their motives. Also, I've had several phone calls and visits from members who've been suffering through some bad situations and most could've been prevented."

Queenie jerked her head in First Lady Jackie's direction. Catching Jackie's eye, Queenie quietly snarled at her and Jackie smiled back.

"Church," Pastor O'Neill continued, "we must be careful in the decisions we make, especially if they aren't pleasing to God. Lusting for things that we know to be wrong will always have consequences. Every decision we make will have consequences, whether good or bad. You may be able to cover up a mistake for a minute, but like in the case of Bathsheba, who was with child after she slept with David, who was not her husband, an ugly truth was exposed.

"God forgives. He forgave David and eventually blessed the people of Israel. But let's not make the mistakes in the first place. God loves you."

Pastor O'Neill sat down and First Lady began to play *Yield Not to Temptation* on the piano. It wasn't an upbeat song, and the members of the church sang it like they may have been thinking about all the temptations they had yielded to recently.

Queenie wasn't amused and neither were Emma, Connie, or Yolanda who took turns giving First Lady Jackie a furtive side eye.

Butt Naked

Pastor O'Neill's sermon on Sunday stayed with Emma throughout the week. Even while at work, she thought about it; and now, as she headed toward home, she thought about it. Maybe she was convicted after having had such a good time at the club on Saturday. She hadn't danced like that in years, and it had felt good.

It was twelve-thirty in the afternoon, an early day for Emma. She was taking a half-day to surprise Billy—pay him a little attention and fix his dinner for a change. True, he wasn't going anywhere; he was content with his life the way it was. But in her heart, she knew she'd taken him for granted.

Emma went into the house, half expecting to find Billy preparing chicken for dinner, since it was Wednesday. But there were no signs of life. Everything was in its place—the furniture dusted and the carpet vacuumed; but no Billy and no scribbled note indicating where he might be. He'd probably gone out for a few beers with his buddies.

Retreating to her bedroom, Emma pulled off her wig and tossed it on the vacant Styrofoam head with the pins sticking out of it. She had to leave those synthetic wigs alone; they made her head sweat something awful in the heat. It wasn't that hot outside, but that's what you get when you went cheap.

A hot shower would do the trick. Emma hopped in. She felt like a new woman when she stepped out of the steamy room. Emma quickly dried off and put on one of her colorful caftans. Then she spotted the five-inch spiked heels she'd worn Saturday night.

An idea popped into her head. Queenie was always sharing different scenarios she'd used to turn Linden into a sex machine. If Linden was throwing down those blue pills like Queenie said he was, it didn't seem to Emma that he needed much help. But Emma rather liked the one about fixing dinner in her birthday suit. Billy was going to get the surprise of his life.

She wasn't going to fry chicken or grill any steaks. Emma called her favorite restaurant and ordered food to be delivered to her home. Tonight had to be special and she pulled out her best china and silver and set the dining room table.

It was close to four when the meal was delivered. She placed the food in chafing dishes to keep it hot. Maybe fifteen or twenty minutes had passed when Emma heard the garage door open and shut. She flew to her room and waited.

"Emma?" Billy called out her name. When she didn't answer he called out again.

Emma stood in the dining room just off of the kitchen. She was wearing her best Victoria's Secret push-up bra, a cute thong, and Billy's favorite heels.

She heard him rummaging around in the kitchen, heard his exclamation—"whoa"—when he realized dinner was waiting.

He walked into the dining room on cue, and when he turned around and saw Emma, his lip dropped to the floor.

"Damn, Emma, you're practically butt naked. You got a man in here?"

"Billy, don't be silly. I would be a fool to have some man up in our house. Don't you like what you see? "

"Yeah, yeah, I like it. Are you sure there's no other man in here?"

"Come on, Billy. I'm only trying to spice up our marriage."

"Look, if you don't want me to fry any more chicken on Wednesdays, it's done. But…"

"Stop talking and go and get cleaned up. You smell like the outdoors."

"What do you expect? I've been playing golf all afternoon."

"Billy, I didn't mean it as an insult. All I want is for you to hurry up so we can eat this scrumptious meal that I've prepared for you, and then we will retreat to our sanctuary for a little fun."

"You did this for us, Emma?"

"Yeah, baby, for us."

"Thank you. It's the nicest thing you've done for me in a long time."

"Sorry it took so long. Now hurry up. We've got a long night ahead of us."

"You can get butt naked for me every Wednesday night."

Ain't No Misunderstanding

The doorbell rang and Connie stopped in her tracks. Surely it wasn't Preston. He always called before he came, unless they had previous plans. Connie wasn't in the mood. It had been a long day at the job, and she was still frustrated and a little put out that Preston hadn't bothered to call or make an appearance since her attempt to seduce him.

Connie went to the peephole and peered through it. Standing on her porch was Preston, clutching what appeared to be a bouquet of roses. Opening the door, she pushed down her surprise and smiled at the man she loved. Preston smiled back.

"May I come in? And these are for you."

Connie took the roses, smelled them, and looked up at Preston. "Thank you. Come in." Connie wasn't sure why Preston had materialized in the middle of the week without so much as a telephone call. She stepped aside and let him in.

Preston followed Connie into the kitchen. She found a crystal vase, filled it with water and put the roses in. Preston draped his arms around her shoulders from behind and kissed her neck. "You're awfully quiet tonight, baby. Is everything all right?"

Connie pulled from his grasp, turned and met his gaze. "Yes, why wouldn't it be?"

Preston reached down and tried to place a kiss on her lips, but she backed away. "Okay, I'm not making this up. What's on your mind?"

Connie went and sat down at the kitchen table. Preston watched as Connie took her seat, and he followed suit. Connie squeezed her hands together, let out a sigh, and then looked into Preston's eyes.

"I love you, Preston. I went out of my way to do something exciting and romantic the last time we were together, but you blew me off as if I was some stripper at a cheesy strip joint."

"Connie, that's not true."

"Could've fooled me. I've never been witness to you not wanting to make love to me."

"I've told you over and over that I love you. Yes, last week I was preoccupied with something that's going on at work, but I didn't mean to minimize your efforts. Your fantasy really turned me on. However, you're being unfair. You should've realized that something was truly wrong, and while I wanted to be in the mood, I wasn't."

"Are you in some kind of trouble? Yolanda told me she saw you with the hospital CEO the other night. I hadn't seen or heard from you in several days, and I didn't know what to think. She thought it was strange that the two of you were meeting."

"People shouldn't make judgment calls about things they know nothing about."

"Why are you getting so put out?"

"Dr. Cole is a good friend of my father and he treats me like a son. He confides in me from time to time. That's all."

"It's not only that, Preston. I haven't heard from you in days. I feel as if you've put me away in a box, only to bring me out when you're ready to play. Like I'm some kind of whore that spreads her legs for you anytime you want me to."

"You said that, I didn't. In fact, I can't believe you even opened you mouth and uttered something that tasteless and ridiculous. Are you trying to end this relationship?"

"Why haven't you asked me to marry you? I've been waiting a long time to hear those words. We've given of ourselves so completely, and I haven't been able to imagine myself without you in my life."

"Is this what this is about—a marriage proposal?"

"Yes. Well, partially yes."

The look on Preston's face was one of bewilderment. "I don't believe you ran my blood pressure up with some foolishness."

Connie slowly stood up from her seat. "Foolishness? Really? Uhm...I have a vested interest in this relationship, and I thought you did too. So...does that mean I've been wasting my time?"

"You've got to be fair about this, Connie. We haven't even sat down and had a real conversation about marriage, let alone popping the question. If a ring..."

Connie raised her hand and threw it in Preston's face. "Hush. There's no need for you to say another word. My comprehension skills are tops, and I can read between the lines. No other words are necessary; you've said enough."

Preston got up from his seat and grabbed Connie's hands. "I love you, Connie Maxwell. It's evident that there's been some kind of misunderstanding." He held her shoulders. "I do want to spend the rest of my life with you, and if that's how you really feel, you should've conveyed that sooner."

"Really, Preston? How many more ways should I have conveyed it to you? I'm an open book...transparent. I've never misrepresented myself."

"Calm down."

"Don't tell me to calm down. I'm pissed off. I've waited my whole life for a man like you, and right now you're disappointing the hell out of me. I'm forty-nine years old, and I've never been to the altar. Did I miss God's signal?"

Preston drew Connie closer to him. He pulled up her chin and kissed her passionately on the lips. Preston held her tight and didn't let go. And then he withdrew his lips and looked into her eyes. "Connie, will you marry me?"

Connie was transfixed. She stared at Preston as if he wasn't real. "Don't play with me, Preston. My heart can't take it."

"Will you marry me?"

"You are serious."

"As serious as Barack Obama wanting to win the presidency. I love you, Connie; I've loved you for a long time. I've dreamed about life with you, but I'll admit that I've been slow to act. I don't have a ring, but you will have one by tomorrow. Please don't say anything to anyone until that rock is on your finger. Now answer the question, woman."

"Yes, Preston, I'll marry you."

Preston grabbed Connie and squeezed her tight; she grabbed him around the waist and held on. He looked down at her. "Let's not wait. As soon as I get the ring, let's go to Vegas."

Connie looked at Preston thoughtfully. "I did want a big wedding so that I could walk down the aisle at Shiloh Baptist, but I don't mind going to Vegas."

"I'm glad we had this conversation. You've been the bright spot in my life. I'll get through the rough space at work, as long as you're by my side."

"I'm here for you always; I love you, Preston."

"I love you, too, Connie Maxwell."

Undercover

Illya Newsome was on to something. He was a federal agent tracking the transport of stolen prescription and other illegal drugs up and down the eastern seaboard. The main source of the distribution was Raleigh, North Carolina from somewhere inside of a major hospital that had linked itself to a top pharmaceutical company. The search had been narrowed to three pharmaceutical reps, although they weren't the key suppliers. Preston Alexander had been targeted as one of the carriers.

Seeing Alexander and Dr. Marshall Cole together was more than coincidental. There had to be a connection—the pharmaceutical rep and a hospital CEO. The dossier on Cole didn't render more than his impeccable credentials: a Doctor of Medicine degree from one of the finest and prestigious medical schools in the country and document after document that demonstrated that he was a man of integrity who had earned his way to the top. There was nothing out of the ordinary on Alexander either, except that his clients weren't necessarily doctors and their meeting places were obscure, out-of-the-way places.

Something wasn't right, and Illya was going to find out what it was. He was to meet a couple of members of his team in a few hours. If Preston Alexander was a trafficker, he was going to bust his ass, and he didn't care if he was Yolanda's sister's fiancé.

He couldn't believe that he had complicated things so quickly by meeting a woman who knew his target. While he welcomed Yolanda's company and felt she would be a good distraction while he was in North Carolina, he hadn't anticipated being with a woman and having to watch everything he said around her. He'd let the scent of a good woman knock him off course—drop his guard. Even General David Petraeus, former Director of the Central Intelligence Agency and retired and decorated American military officer, had fallen because of a beautiful woman. He'd have to be on his p's and q's twenty-four-seven from now on.

A Lovely Day

The day was perfect. There wasn't a cloud in the sky.

But Preston was fidgety—jerking his head with every car that flew by, periodically squeezing her hand.

"Are you all right, Preston?" Connie asked.

"I'm fine, baby. I want this evening to be perfect for you…for us."

"Where are we going?"

"To a small, romantic, out-of-the-way place," Preston promised. He reached up and switched on the Sirius Satellite radio. Light jazz flowed throughout the car.

Connie smiled. This was the day that she would officially become engaged. She was excited beyond words.

"Do you love me, Preston?" She knew she sounded a little needy, but who could blame her; it had been a bumpy ride to this point.

"Yes, Connie. I love you with all of my heart."

She figured he was nervous, too.

They drove on until Preston finally turned off the road that led to a secluded cottage.

"Oh my God," Connie exclaimed. "It's the Knollwood House."

"I thought this would be the perfect place for an elegant lady— a beautiful English Bed and Breakfast Manor to formally propose to my future bride."

Connie couldn't believe her eyes. The drive was a little long, but it was worth it.

As Preston helped her out of the car, it was still light enough outside for Connie to see the holly trees, the long leaf pines, and the towering magnolias that bordered the property.

"I didn't bring a change of clothes or any personal articles like a toothbrush, toothpaste, comb, brush…and…and I have to go to church in the morning. I'm leading a song in the choir."

"It's okay, baby. I thought of everything."

"Preston, this moment is special. I will always remember it."

"There's more to come. Why don't we go in and register."

Preston took Connie's hand and led her to their room, one of only four in the main cottage. Connie was in awe of the place. Eighteenth and nineteenth century antiques; a large sunlit garden room with flowering plants and wicker furniture. She couldn't get enough of the place, and twirled around two or three times to make sure it wasn't a fantasy. Preston smiled.

"Why don't we go and get something to eat. I'm famished. There are also some quaint shops in town that you would love."

"If I had my way, I would stay in this room the rest of the evening. Preston, this room is so beautiful. All I want to do is take it all in and enjoy your company."

He kissed her; she kissed him back. "We can do that, too."

Connie smiled and kissed him again. She wiped lipstick from his lips. "I'm not totally selfish, and I am a little hungry. Let's go so we can get back; I'd like to walk around the place."

"We can do whatever you want to do. I only want you to be happy." Connie smiled and hooked her arm in Preston's.

The drive into town was only a couple of miles. Preston seemed to be more at ease, although Connie caught him on one occasion doing a quick scan, as if he was doing surveillance.

"Are you all right, baby?"

"Yes, I'm fine. Why do you ask?"

"You seem jittery."

Preston looked over at Connie. "Girl, you have nothing to worry about. I'm probably on pins and needles about how I'm going to propose to you again." He patted her thigh.

Connie took Preston's hand and squeezed it. "Okay."

They dined at Curt's Cucina and had a wonderful Italian meal. After dinner, Preston and Connie browsed several of the small shops closest to the restaurant.

"Let's go to the car," he said after a time. "I want to stop by the golf course before we turn in."

"All right."

Instead of driving to the golf course, Preston drove back to Knollwood, their B & B. A perplexed look crossed Connie's face. This time, she was aware of where she was but confused, as she distinctly heard Preston say he was driving to the golf course. He parked the car and guided Connie into the house. Still confused, Connie held her tongue. Preston led Connie to the garden that overlooked the fairway of the Donald Ross golf course. They were alone; Preston dropped to one knee. Holding Connie's hand, he looked up at her surprised face, and smiled.

"Connie, will you be my wife?"

Tears sprang to Connie's eyes. She clasped both hands over her mouth and let the tears roll down her face. Gasping for breath, she looked down at Preston, sniffled and tried to say something. Preston was no help as he continued to look at her with his deep, inquiring eyes.

"Yes, Preston Alexander, I will be your wife."

Preston got up off his knees and produced a black-velvet box. He opened it up and Connie's eyes bulged from their sockets and her mouth fell open and formed a large circle. A five-carat, princess-cut diamond ring in white gold stared back at her.

"Oh my God. It's…it's so beautiful, Preston."

"For the love of my life. I want to be with you forever, Connie. I don't say it often, but I truly mean it. I hope you will stay by my side through thick and thin."

"I vow to love you always, baby." Tears continued to flow from Connie's eyes.

Preston took the engagement ring out of the box and placed it on Connie's ring finger. Connie couldn't take her eyes off the ring. She reached up and kissed Preston who held her tight. More than a minute passed before they pulled back from their embrace.

"I will love you forever, Preston Alexander."

"I will always love you, Connie Maxwell."

Busted

Queenie was having the time of her life. She hadn't told the girls, but she had been out twice this week with the 'pimp that stole Christmas'. Never mind that Pastor O'Neill had preached about lusting for things that weren't good for you and making decisions that weren't as he called it, "not Christian like." Queenie had even missed choir rehearsal so she could be with her new fling.

His name was Joe Harris, and he really was a nice guy. He was sixty-years old and liked to have a good time; so did Queenie. He had already given her a beautiful diamond necklace and a Michael Kors handbag she had been admiring. Not once had she even thought about Linden Robinson. If anything, lusting after Linden would have been lusting after the wrong thing.

It was Friday night and Joe was taking her to the club where they'd met. Queenie knew that Joe wanted to get between the sheets, especially since he had given her those nice gifts. So far, she'd been able to keep him at bay, only allowing a few ripe hickeys to adorn her neck. She wasn't ready to give up her precious jewels—at least not yet, and she was going to ride the tide as long as she could.

Queenie jumped when the doorbell rang. She admired herself in the tall, vanity mirror and smiled at her reflection. Her dress was of blue stretch material with a bow around the bottom. She liked that it didn't accentuate her weight too much; liked it even more that Joe enjoyed heavy women. "The more to love on," he had told Queenie.

The doorbell rang again. Queenie rushed to get the door before her date became impatient. The other thing she liked about Joe was that he was punctual.

"Hey, Joe, you're looking mighty handsome tonight," Queenie said when she answered the door.

"Turn around for me, girl. You're rocking those hips in this dress. We're going to shake it on the dance floor tonight."

"I aim to do just that."

Joe's eyes zeroed in on the diamond necklace Queenie wore around her neck. "The necklace looks good on you. How about some sugah?"

"You're going to ruin my lipstick, Joe."

"Can't you put some more on? You're looking right tasty and smell good too."

Queenie slapped Joe on the shoulder. "I could, but if I let you kiss me, then my lipstick might smear across my face. I promise to give you a big kiss before the night is over."

"All right then. Let's go."

"I'm ready."

Queenie smiled as she let Joe escort her to his car. He was every bit the gentleman. When they arrived at the club, he ran around to her side of the car and opened the door, extended his hand and helped her out.

Inside, the band was playing a soft number and the room was dim. But there weren't many people on the dance floor. Queenie and Joe found a table, sat down, and ordered drinks.

Queenie bobbed her head from side to side, getting into the

groove of the music. Before another minute passed, Joe clasped a hand over one of hers. Queenie smiled.

"I like you a lot," Joe said, tickling her hand.

"I like you, too, Joe. We seem to have a lot in common."

"You like to dance and you like nice things. Most of all you like to be treated like a lady."

"That's it," Queenie said, tapping the top of Joe's hand.

"Let's dance. The band has picked up the pace. I love to two-step."

"You're on."

More patrons poured into the club as Joe and Queenie made their way to the dance floor. Joe was quick on his feet and Queenie was a definite complement. Joe held Queenie with precision as they continued to dance gracefully across the dance floor. Other couples joined them and before long the dance floor was full. After three more songs, Joe and Queenie took a break from the dance floor.

"The ice in my drink has probably melted," Joe said. "I need another scotch...water," he said to a passing waitress. Joe turned back to Queenie. "You sure know how to hold your own Ms. Queenie Jackson. You're a good dancer."

"And you must have magic shoes, Mr. Harris. The way you glide across the dance floor, I had to run to catch up with you." They both laughed.

"Would you like another drink, Q?"

"Yes, I would love another Long Island Iced Tea. I'm going to the powder room and I'll be back in a jiffy."

"Don't take too long, baby. My magic shoes are ready to take off again."

Queenie laughed. "You are so funny. I'll try to get in and out in no time flat."

"I'll be waiting."

Queenie dabbed her face with a napkin as she made her way to the powder room. As she was about to enter the restroom, she saw him, Linden, with another woman; hugging and kissing like there was no tomorrow. Queenie wasn't impressed. Although the woman had a nice shape, to Queenie she looked old enough to be Linden's mother. And then she recognized her. It couldn't be. It was her old friend from college, Drema D.

Instantly, Queenie hated her. She didn't move; waited instead for Linden to hold his head up and see her. And he did.

When Linden saw Queenie, he looked like a man who had been busted down to the white meat. He didn't acknowledge Queenie, but his date for the evening did.

"Queenie Jackson, is that you?" Drema D asked all snuggled up in Linden's arm. He smiled.

"Drema D, how long has it been? I didn't know you still lived around this way." Queenie wasn't the least bit interested in holding a conversation with her.

"After college, I left Raleigh and went to D.C. I worked in government for thirty-two years. I recently retired and came home to spend some time with my mother."

"I thought you had gotten married to that guy named Larry… something." Queenie snapped her finger.

"Girl, I've been divorced going on ten years. Linden and I met a couple of months ago. We've been dating, but nothing serious." Drema D pulled on Linden's arm.

Queenie stared Linden down. He didn't say a word but put his arm around Drema D.

"Well, it was good to see you again, Queenie," Drema D said.

"Yeah, likewise." Linden and Drema D moved on and Queenie pushed open the restroom door until it banged against the wall.

So Linden had been stepping out on her all along, and Minnie wasn't the culprit. Linden was a straight up, sorry ass dog…no a mutt, and Queenie was glad that she'd put him out of her house.

At first, Queenie sat in her seat and fumed; but when she caught Linden and Drema D in her peripheral vision, she grabbed Joe's arm and headed to the dance floor.

She shook her groove thing and two-stepped on every inch of the dance floor. Joe led and Queenie followed right along. Joe was an excellent dancer in his own right. Sweat poured from their brows, but they refused to sit down, and when Queenie was ready to sit, she got all up on Joe like they had been lovers for a long time.

"Q, you have mellowed out nicely. I like you when you're in the moment."

"I am in the moment, Joe. Why don't we lose this place and get something to eat…maybe go back to my place?"

"You've said nothing but a word. Your wish is my command."

"Do you know what else I'm going to do?"

"What is it, my Queen?"

"I'm going to get a tattoo tomorrow—a butterfly. I love butterflies, and I'm going to have it tattooed on my lower back, right across my hips."

"Are you sure about that?"

"Yep, I haven't been surer about a lot of things until tonight. Maybe you might want to tag along for moral support."

"Oh, baby, I'll be your moral support."

"Well, Joe, let's kick this joint, find some fish, go back to my house and we'll see what happens later."

"You do owe me a kiss, Q. I won't mind collecting."

"All right; let's go."

Tramp Stamp

There was a slight chill in the air. Queenie stirred under the down comforter, still in the midst of her daydream. All of a sudden her eyes flew open, now totally aware of where she was and what had transpired the night before. She eased the comforter down below her breasts and turned slightly to her left. It wasn't a dream. Lying next to her, nestled in the sheets, was Joe Harris, all cool and comfortable like he belonged there…as if he was sleeping on memory foam that had his name imprinted on it.

Queenie pulled the comforter up over her breasts. What had she done? The fog was so intense in her brain, she wasn't sure if she'd had sex with Joe or not. Hell, she had been mad at seeing Linden all hugged up with some other woman at the club, but she had no intention of letting Joe Harris, aka 'the pimp that stole Christmas,' share her bed.

She had to think fast. Lying there, Queenie couldn't come up with a good excuse to get rid of Joe, especially since he'd offered to go with her—and pay—for her tattoo. She'd laugh about this later, but right now she wanted to be alone.

An arm reached over Queenie's shoulder. She gasped at the sight of it, as if it was an alien intruder. Joe's head materialized and then he kissed her arm.

She could smell his morning breath—rotten fish laced with

tobacco—and knew this was the end of the road. But Joe wasn't ready to go. He kissed Queenie's arm again before reaching over to squeeze a plump breast. Queenie shuddered.

"Girl, you rocked my world last night." Joe smiled, showing all the gold in his mouth.

Queenie kept her face turned away from him. "I'm glad you enjoyed it," she said meekly.

"I could get used to lighting your fire every day of the week."

Queenie sat up. "Joe, you're moving too fast. I'm not sure I'm ready to be in a relationship."

"I can take it slow if you want me to. I'm the king of slow. And girl, I love healthy women. Healthy women have more to pleasure. Skinny women are disgusting to me. Nobody wants a bone but a dog."

"Well, I'm not so sure about that, Joe. I need to lose some weight, and…"

"Hush up, woman." There was a slight pause as Joe squeezed Queenie's buttocks. "Aww, that's what I'm talking about. I love a good ham bone."

Queenie turned and pushed Joe off of her. "What in the hell are you talking about? If you're hungry, there's a restaurant around the corner, but I'm nobody's ham bone."

"A figure of speech, baby; you're all that. Now, let a soul brother show you what he can do."

"I'm not sure this is a good idea…"

"Hush." Joe placed tiny kisses on Queenie's neck and slid down to the top of her breasts. She held her nose, although Joe didn't notice since his eyes were closed. "When I finish making love to you, I'm going to take you to breakfast. After breakfast I'm taking you to get that tattoo you want, and if you aren't tired, we're going to Jared to pick out a beautiful diamond ring to go with that necklace I bought you."

Jared? Diamond ring? Jared was one of Queenie's favorite jewelry stores. What the hell, Joe was already in her bed and maybe he wasn't so bad after all. But he had to do something with that breath; it was kicking.

"What do you say, Ms. Q?"

"Okay."

For a man in his sixties, Joe hadn't lost his touch. He touched all the right buttons and then some. Queenie relaxed, closed her eyes, and let Joe work his magic. He was gentle, smooth, and took his time making love to her. Queenie had to admit she loved the way Joe took control and made her body quiver. Maybe that was why she'd slept like a baby, waking to find Joe still between her sheets. He'd hypnotized her. She remembered how good she'd felt; and the encore felt mighty good.

Lying on the tattoo artist's chair, Queenie reflected on the morning. Joe had made sweet love to her and taken her out for breakfast. Now, she was ready to do something she had secretly wanted to do.

Queenie loved butterflies. She and Joe picked out a beautiful butterfly whose open wings were going to stretch out on either side of Queenie's hips. The hot pink and purple wings looked as if they were taking flight. Queenie was enjoying this moment with Joe more than she wanted to admit. It was nice to have a man who was attentive to her needs.

"Ouch," Queenie screamed at the first touch of the tattoo artist's needle.

Sunday Brunch

The ladies had a high time at church. Pastor O'Neill preached up and down the sanctuary and pricked a couple souls to get up out of their seats and come to Christ.

But it was time to eat, and the ladies were anxious to get a seat at their favorite restaurant. After all, it was hard work getting your praise on.

"Jackie, I'm glad you could join us this afternoon," Emma said, as they waited to be seated. "Sister Queenie Jackson says she has a lot to share with us today."

"I hope it's not gossip, especially after my husband put that good word on us today."

Queenie rolled her eyes. She loved Jackie, but now she would have to tame her conversation. Everyone knew that Jackie told the Pastor everything they said.

"I don't gossip, Jackie," Queenie began. Yolanda, Connie, and Emma put their hands over their mouths to stifle their laughs. "I was only going to give the girls my post-church testimony about how good the Lord was to me this week."

The ladies nearly choked with laughter.

"The buzzer is flickering," Queenie said, holding up the square gadget that was lit up in a blazing red. "Our table is ready, and it's time to eat."

The ladies followed the hostess to a booth in the corner and were seated. The hostess passed out menus, placed a basket of bread on the table, and took their drink orders.

"So what is your big news, Q? I can't wait to hear what the Lord did for you this week."

"Jackie, the Lord spoke to me this week and made me realize that it was time to move on without Linden."

"It's about time," Emma said, pointing her finger for the cause.

"Well, that's good, Q. I prayed and prayed that you would wake up and see the light."

"Thank you for your prayers, Jackie. Everyone saw the truth except me. How about you, YoYo…Connie?"

"I've given you the heads up too many times to count on that loser," Yolanda said. "I'm glad it wasn't too late."

Queenie didn't say a word. The waitress placed their drinks on the table and took their orders. "I'll have a Cobb salad," Queenie said.

"What's wrong with you, Q?" Connie finally asked. "I've never seen you eat a salad at any meal. Look, Connie and Emma were messing with you. Linden has some redeeming qualities, even if they are hard to find."

"It's okay. I'm over Linden; no regrets."

"Well," Connie cut in, "I have some news that I can't keep to myself any longer."

"So, did lover boy finally drop to his knees and propose?" Queenie asked with too much bass in her voice. "You better do what I did and let Preston go. That man will keep you hanging by a string and when you're not looking, he'll pop the question to someone else."

"What if I told you, Ms. Queen Bee, that my man not only proposed to me but he got down on his knees and laid a five-carat rock on my finger? Booya!" Connie threw out her hand and circled the table for everyone to see, the iridescent light hitting the ring just so. There was total silence as each lady examined the ring in turn, eyes wide in disbelief.

Yolanda looked at Connie, as she examined the ring. "How did I not see this earlier? I can't believe you kept this from me. I'm your sister for heaven's sake. I thought we were closer than close."

"The ring was in my purse and I just put it on. Wanted to surprise you doubters. Preston asked me not to say anything to anyone until he gave me the ring. I haven't been able to stop looking at it, except this morning during church and until this moment."

"So when did he propose?" Yolanda asked, still in a state of shock.

"He asked me on Thursday. And on Friday, my man wined and dined me before he dropped to his knees and asked me those four beautiful words again...will you marry me. Ladies, you should've seen my face when he opened the black box and presented me with this gorgeous engagement ring."

"You didn't have to twist his arm or do double somersaults to get him to propose?" Emma asked.

"Don't hate, Ms. Emma. No. No, I didn't have to twist Preston's arm nor did I have to get naked and do freaky stuff to him. He took me to the Knollwood House in Southern Pines to ask for my hand in marriage. It was breathtaking. We were in a garden overlooking the golf course. And, for your further information, we're going to Vegas to get married...in two weeks." There was complete silence for a couple of seconds.

"Oh hell no!" Yolanda shot back. "After waiting all this time, you're going to walk down the aisle at Shiloh Baptist Church and let Pastor O'Neill bless this marriage. And what's the hurry?"

"Please tell us you aren't pregnant," Emma chided, sitting on the edge of her seat clutching her chest. "Now, this is what I call juicy gossip."

"Slow your roll, Emma. I'm not pregnant. Preston and I want to get away by ourselves—away from you nosey, hating women. For your edification, our honeymoon will start as soon as we say 'I do' and the justice of the peace pronounces us man and wife, which means in plain English, we won't have time for y'all."

"Listen to my sister talking like she doesn't have any sense."

"I don't know about you, YoYo, but I'm getting a plane ticket to Vegas so that I can be a witness at this shindig," Queenie said. "You've got to have witnesses. Right, YoYo?"

"Right, but this isn't right at all."

"It's my wedding, sister dear," Connie insisted, "and I want to be married before I turn fifty."

"You won't turn fifty for another couple of months," Yolanda reminded her.

"If I get married now or in a couple of months, it won't change how I feel about Preston, YoYo. Preston and I talked about it, and we're going to get married now."

"You sound so desperate, Connie. Why are you rushing?"

"Look, you are my big sister and I respect your thoughts on the matter. But I'm a grown woman, and this is what I want to do."

"Well I'm going to be getting an airline ticket," Yolanda said. "You might as well get one, too, Emma."

"You all don't want me to come?" Jackie asked feeling left out.

"Sure you can come," Queenie said. "We'll get a large suite at the Bellagio."

"I've got to go shopping." Jackie pumped her fist in the air.

Connie pounded the table. "I don't want any of you to come. I'm sorry guys; my wedding day is for me and my man."

"Don't listen to that bull crap," Yolanda said. "We're getting on a plane to Vegas."

Connie shut her mouth.

The food came and the ladies ate, still reeling from Connie's news.

"Well, Q, whatever you were going to tell us won't compare with what Connie dropped in our laps."

"Maybe not, Emma, but I'll tell you anyway. I got a tattoo yesterday."

"A who…what, Q?"

"You heard me, Emma, a tattoo. Guess where it is?"

"On your shoulder," Yolanda guessed. "Trust me, it has to be a butterfly."

"You're partially correct. I do like butterflies, but I didn't get it tattooed on my shoulder."

First Lady Jackie O'Neill looked around the room. "I'm afraid to ask."

"Q is probably lying," Emma said. "She's afraid of needles."

"Do you want to see it?"

"Yes," Emma said, egging her on. "Show us this itty, bitty butterfly you had tattooed on your body."

Jackie was seated on one side of Queenie and Yolanda on the other. Queenie took off the jacket to her suit and let Yolanda hold it. Jackie and Yolanda's eyes veered down to where Queenie began to pull her blouse from her skirt. Queenie unbuttoned her skirt at the waist and pulled the top of her pantyhose down.

Jackie threw her hand over her mouth and Yolanda screamed. Emma and Connie pushed the others out of the way so they could take a peek.

"Damn," Yolanda shouted. "Sorry, First Lady. Q, is that a tramp stamp over your butt?"

"Tramp stamp? It's a tattoo, fool. It's a butterfly getting ready to take flight. You can't see it well, but it's beautiful."

"It looks like it's flying from the crack in your behind," Connie said.

"It's so…unChristian-like," First Lady added.

"What possessed you to do that?" Emma wanted to know. "I could have accepted a little butterfly on the shoulder, but that…"

"It's nasty, Emma," Connie blurted out. "Queenie has lost her mind."

"I wasn't by myself when I did it."

The ladies fell silent. They waited.

"Well," Jackie said. "Are you going to tell us who you were with?"

Queenie grinned. "No, that's my secret. You'd never guess anyway."

"We don't want to guess since we know that it wasn't one of us," Emma hissed. "And where were you Wednesday night? You definitely weren't at choir rehearsal."

"You heifers are jealous. You want to be like the Queen. Watch, you will all have your own tattoos before the week is out. You can't stand the fact that I have one. Now, I'm ready for dessert."

Illya Newsome

Illya sifted through his notes from two of his last surveillances. There was a common thread—Preston Alexander. However, Illya wasn't so sure that Preston was a willing participant in the illegal drug trade happening in this Southern town.

He reviewed with a critical eye the photographs taken at two of the drop off sites, photos now spread out before him. Each frame... each picture said a thousand words. It was all about appearances. The money men drove mid-size cars that didn't attract attention, usually white or black in color. Preston drove a blue, Dodge Dakota truck as if he had nothing to hide. Why would he expose himself so freely?

Then Illya saw it: the steel-barreled gun that barely hung below one money man's coat sleeve. Nerves were etched in Preston's face. Preston moved forward in each frame, all the while looking like he wanted to make a break for it. Only he never did. He resurfaced from inside the transfer station with a briefcase in hand, he and the money man going their separate ways. Illya noted that in both cases, there were always two money men to Preston's one.

Once the transfer was made, Preston always drove to a local Catholic church. He always entered with a briefcase and returned to his truck with a briefcase. Illya wasn't sure if that was another transfer point or a money deposit station. Since the drops were done in the middle of the day, Illya wasn't ready to blow his cover by following Preston into unknown territory without back-up.

Illya wiped his brow, got up and went to the refrigerator to get a bottle of water. He hated hotel living, but hopefully it wouldn't be for long. The only good thing about being in Raleigh was the distance it put between him and his ex who had extorted everything from him in their nasty divorce. For a moment, he thought about Yolanda. She was fun and vivacious. He could see them together for a short stint. Illya had already made up in his mind, though, that a woman would never again rule his heart, mind, soul, or body.

The FBI wanted a local reporter hovering nearby, and Illya hated it. News reporters were anxious for "the story" and never patient enough for the truth. Television had popularized renegade writers running with the police to solve crimes. Having the reporter ride shotgun made him play it safer. No need to jeopardize the headway he'd already made.

He liked the television show, *Castle*, but oftentimes, the bull-headed writer only got in the way. The Raleigh Observer reporter shadowing him was no different. He wanted to do a three-part series to get his name out there, he'd said. But Illya needed to be certain about Preston's involvement before meeting up with the reporter again. He would need Yolanda's help.

Illya took one last look at his notes and sighed. He looked up when his cell phone began to vibrate on the table. His team member was still out chasing an angle, but he smiled when he saw Yolanda's name light up on the caller-ID screen.

"Hello, Yolanda. This is a pleasant surprise."

"Well, I thought I'd call to see if you were back in town."

Illya hadn't been anywhere but here, chasing leads. However, there was no need to tell Yolanda. "Yes, I'm back."

"I see. Well, I'm calling about a proposition."

"A proposition? I'm not sure I'm ready for this."

"My sister got engaged this weekend and plans to get married in a couple of weeks."

Illya sat up straight and was all ears. "I see. What's her fiancé's name?"

"Preston Alexander."

"Yes, that's the guy we saw at the restaurant last week. So was it a sudden decision?"

"Obviously it was. I had no inkling they were even going to be engaged."

"Well, usually the parties concerned are the first to know."

"That's true, but yesterday at Sunday brunch, my sister blurts out that she's engaged and going to be married in a couple of weeks. I'm her sister; at least she could've confided in me. But no, I heard about the engagement at the same time everyone else did."

Illya laughed. "You're funny when you get wound up, Yolanda. I'm sure your sister had her reasons."

"Well, whatever they were, she didn't tell me. But you should've seen the ring on her finger. That was a massive five-carat rock."

"Five carats? He must really love her."

"Preston can afford it. He's been in the pharmaceutical business a long time and has done very well."

"So, what's your proposition?"

"The ladies and I are going to crash the wedding."

"Why would you do a thing like that?"

"The wedding is going to be in Vegas, and Connie said she didn't want us there."

"Maybe you should consider her wishes. After all, it's all about her and Preston. You don't want Connie to become one of those Bridezillas you see on TV."

Yolanda laughed. "You may be right but there's no way I'm missing this. See, Connie's wanted to get married forever. We've kidded her about being an old maid. Last week, she complained about Preston being unattentive; where did this marriage proposal come from?"

"Maybe he felt bad about how he acted. I'm sure your sister let him have it, as most women do."

"You're talking about your ex, aren't you?"

"Maybe, but I don't want to get into a discussion about her. She is off-limits."

"I'm sorry."

"There's no need to be. I have a proposal. Why don't we ask Connie and Preston out on a double date? That way, I can assess the situation for myself and I'll get to meet your sister. I'm sure she's as lovely as you are."

"That's a good idea but I thought you said something about compromising your cover?"

"What I do is private, privileged information. We don't discuss what I do. If they want to know, I'm doing research work."

"Okay," Yolanda said with some hesitation. "Let's say…Saturday. Is that okay?"

"That should work. Let's say we meet around five. You name the restaurant."

"That's perfect. This won't interfere with your research?"

"Not at all. If something should come up, I'll let you know in time."

"Okay. Thanks for making me feel better about this Connie thing."

"I'm not sure that I did, but I look forward to meeting Connie and Preston on Saturday. "

Yolanda hung up the phone. She had already shared too much; the dinner could get awkward if Connie pressed for information. She didn't want to look like a blabbering fool in front of Illya. She'd have to find a way to keep Connie from broaching the subject or better yet, make some excuse why Connie and Preston weren't available to meet them for dinner.

Preston Alexander

Breathing hard, Preston Alexander glanced down at the text message he'd received only moments earlier. His temples hurt. Taking the tips of his fingers he placed them on either side of his head and made circular motions with them, trying to ease the migraine that threatened to take up residence.

He'd gotten himself involved in some deep mess that had criminal implications, and he couldn't seem to find an immediate lifeline to pull himself out.

Thoughts of his impending marriage to Connie worried him. He loved her with all of his heart. There was no question that he wanted to marry her. The problem was whether or not he'd be able to protect his bride when a bullet was permanently aimed at his heart.

"Damn." Preston looked at the text again.

Meet 7 p.m. with package. Same place.

Preston sighed.

Getting up from the chair in his home office, he strolled to the wet bar and poured himself a drink. He swirled the cognac around in the glass before he took a swallow. The stress was about to kill him. He had to figure out a way to break free from his jailer, Dr. Marshall Cole.

Preston wasn't sure if Dr. Cole had been coerced into participating in the drug ring. In the beginning, he hadn't realized how vast the operation was, just that he was helping out a friend of his father; a friend who happened to be the CEO of one of Raleigh's leading hospitals. He was to deliver goods to a client of Dr. Cole's on one of his pharmaceutical runs. He was paid handsomely. It hadn't fazed Preston when the recipient of the package claimed to be the managing assistant to a medical doctor with impeccable credentials. But it all became strange when he had to begin meeting this person in out-of-the-way places. Then the players changed; enter the Colombians. That's when Preston panicked and asked for an out—an out that he was denied.

Dr. Cole had assured and reassured Preston that there was nothing to worry about. Without any answers he couldn't be sure of the implications, but Preston was well aware that it was illegal. He knew that whatever was going on, it was a ticking time bomb. He wasn't sure how many weeks, days, or hours he had left. And he didn't want to bring Connie into that world.

He looked at the text again and clicked the glass to compose a message. Preston stopped in the middle of his typing. He recalled the beautiful weekend he and Connie had had together. Preston could still smell her scent and see the smile on her face when he presented her with the engagement ring. A deep smiled crossed Preston's face. He loved his Connie.

A knock at the door startled him. Preston wasn't expecting anyone and rarely had visitors show up at his door unannounced.

Preston sat his drink down and rubbed the back of his neck with his hand. He waited, but there it was again. *Knock, knock.*

This time, Preston rose from his seat. He went through the foyer of his cottage and peeked through the peephole in the front door. Preston squinted at the strange dreadlocked black man who seemed to stare back at him. He frowned and backed up when the gentleman leaned in to knock on the door again.

Preston opened the door forcefully and stared at the man he didn't recognize. Then he squinted as if trying to remember something. There seemed to be a moment of recognition, but Preston wasn't sure. "May I help you?" he said gruffly.

"Yes, my name is Illya Newsome," Illya said, similar forcefulness in his voice. "I'm with the FBI." Illya flipped his badge for Preston to see.

Fear flew into Preston's eyes, although he tried to hide it. He could feel himself quivering in front of this man who represented his worst nightmare. He swallowed the saliva that had rushed to the back of his throat and spoke. "Again, how may I help you?"

"May I come in?" Illya asked. "I don't think you want me to stand outside on the porch and attract attention."

Preston's lips curled into a sneer at the man's smugness. The only reason Preston could deduce for the man's presence had something to do with the mess he was mixed up in. While he considered shutting the door, the only way he'd find out for sure was to entertain this visit. Preston scanned the area outside of his house to make sure there weren't any casual or suspicious observers. "Come in," he said. Against his better judgment, he stepped aside to let the gentleman pass.

Illya walked into Preston's space and surveyed the surroundings. Preston was both pissed and on pins and needles.

They sat across from each other, both analyzing the situation. Preston's jawbone locked in place while Illya continued to survey his surroundings like a human satellite.

"Let me cut to the chase," Illya began. "I'm sure you know why I'm here."

Preston could tell that Illya was sizing him up.

"You've been under surveillance for some time. We know of your involvement in a drug trafficking ring based here in Raleigh."

Preston's eyes bulged. His blood pressure spiked. He could feel himself beginning to sweat, could feel the way his heart tried to beat its way out of his chest.

Illya continued, "We know you're not involved voluntarily. So we're going to give you a chance to tell what you know, and if I'm right about you, it's possible that we can provide you with some protection—possibly in the Witness Protection Program."

"Witness Protection Program?"

Preston fidgeted.

"Why would I need to be in a Witness Protection Program?"

Illya's gaze was steady as he responded. "You're going to tell me all about the drug trafficking ring."

Preston was quiet and chewed on his tongue. "What do you know?"

"We know a lot. We've been clocking your every move. We've observed your rendezvous with known drug dealers. Is that enough?"

Preston stared at Illya with disdain. "Witness Protection Program. You mean to strip me of my identity."

"Yes."

"What about my job? I'm supposed to be getting married in a couple of weeks. How will I explain that to my fiancée?"

"Your job is what put you in this situation. As for your fiancée, you may not have an opportunity to explain things to her."

Preston rose from his seat. "So, you're saying if I cooperate, I may have to go immediately into the Witness Protection Program. And what if I don't?"

"I'm prepared to arrest you," the agent said. "But what the FBI really wants is all the big players, and you can help."

Preston's heart stuttered at the word arrest. Bravado kept him going. "If you've been following me and investigating the drug ring like you claim, what is it that I would say that you don't already know?"

"Tell me about Dr. Marshall Cole." Preston arched his eyebrows as he, finally, grabbed hold of the memory that had eluded him before. He took another look at Illya whose lips were drawn in a straight line. "I've seen you before."

"Anything is possible."

Preston moved closer to Illya. "Yes," he said, waving his finger, animated, "it was at the café a week or so ago. You were with my fiancée's sister, Yolanda. I'm right. I remember asking Yolanda who her new heartthrob was sitting all cool, calm and collected and wearing dreads. And she downplayed it as if it was a casual pick-up. Aren't dreads a little out of character for an FBI agent?"

Preston noticed that his words bothered Illya, if only for a moment. Illya seemed to collect himself before continuing.

"I'm undercover. And do you know why? I'm trying to save your ass."

"I didn't ask you to."

Truth be told, he was a bit relieved; even if someone was lurking and saw Illya come into his house, they wouldn't know he was FBI.

"Possibly I was wrong about you," Illya said. "You have only a few moments to make up your mind. Another agent can be put on the case, and you won't fare so well."

Preston looked at his watch. He had one hour to make the drop. He looked at Illya and spilled it all out.

Illya immediately contacted his head team member and gave him the information that he'd been provided. He clicked off his cell phone and turned to Preston. "A SWAT team will be deployed in a matter of minutes. That's how closely we've been working on this. I want you to act as if this conversation never took place. Your contacts will be arrested once you've made the transaction. You will also be placed under arrest and held in a holding cell for your protection. While that's going on, there will also be other arrests taking place."

"Dr. Cole?"

"He will definitely be one of them. We have others in our dragnet, but I'm not at liberty to say who they are. Your life is about to change."

Preston looked thoughtfully at Illya. He digested all that was said and was still not ready for the new reality he was about to face. There was no way he could leave Connie. She'd be devastated. The last thing he wanted to do was break her heart.

"It's time for me to leave," Preston said, looking at Illya who had gotten up and was ready to leave.

"This is an ordinary run; I've got your back."

Preston nodded his head and Illya was gone.

Fact or Fiction

Several days had passed since the ill-fated night when Queenie ran into her estranged college mate, Drema D, all hooked up in Linden's arms. As much as Queenie tried to let it go, to wipe the vision from her memory, it kept popping up. Linden was a loser, and she'd resolved to wipe her hands clean of him, but the more she tried, the more her inner self wouldn't let go. Joe was a great guy, even if he was still wearing a Jheri curl from the 1980s, but he wasn't Linden Robinson.

Queenie was seated at her desk, up to her ears, and didn't need to be thinking about either of them. She needed to concentrate on her work.

She opened the draft of an article sent to her inbox by one of the newspaper's lead reporters, Jock Atwater. It was marked PRIVATE and URGENT. Jock was working on a major, three-part story about a drug ring operating in the Raleigh/Durham area. It had been rumored that some high-level players in the city were involved with tentacles that reached as far north as New York and as far south as Latin America. The feds had taken up residence in the city, watching the movement of some of the foot soldiers in hopes of getting a solid lead on the ring leader.

Pushing her glasses up on her nose, Queenie took a sip of coffee and began to read the text. Queenie loved novels that were full of mystery, intrigue, and espionage; Jock's story had traces of each. She didn't know who the source was, but it was quite apparent that he had the goods, as the information reached deep into the bowels of Raleigh's underworld.

Ignoring the chatter around her, Queenie was consumed and entranced by the story. Then as if a bolt of lightning had zapped her, Queenie's head jerked back and her eyes bucked as she stared at the text. She changed the font size from twelve to sixteen and ran her eyes over the text again.

Federal agents followed pharmaceutical rep, Preston Alexander, to an undisclosed location in Raleigh. Five minutes later, two unidentified males, who appeared to be of Latin descent and dressed in expensive suits, entered the same premises. They were carrying a large, black briefcase.

Queenie's hands went to her face. "Oh my God. This couldn't be Connie's Preston…not the man who only this past weekend asked Connie to marry him," Queenie said out loud. She began to hyperventilate as she went back to the text. Other names were mentioned that she didn't know, but the only one that mattered at the moment was Preston's.

What was she going to do? Should she tell Connie?

Queenie stopped reading and looked at her surroundings. How could she be sure that the feds weren't watching her? Everything seemed normal; her co-workers were about business as usual.

Sighing, Queenie jumped up from her seat. She was an excellent editor and knew how to keep confidential reports under wrap until press time. But she needed to talk to someone—someone close. First Lady Jackie O'Neill would be the right person to talk to. Jackie was the pastor's wife, but she and Queenie had been friends for years. Although Jackie could be a busybody, she was the only person that she trusted at this moment. Queenie logged out of her computer, grabbed her jacket, strolled over to her boss' office and stuck her head in the door.

"Robert, I have an emergency and need to leave. I should be back in a couple of hours."

"Queenie, take all the time you need. I hope everything will be okay."

"Thanks, Robert. I sure hope so. I'll see you later."

Queenie waved goodbye.

She hightailed it over to Jackie's, running a couple of stop signs in the process. She couldn't wrap her brain around what she'd read, but it was there in black and white. The words were plain enough for a beginning reader to understand.

Queenie nearly jumped off the porch when Jackie snatched the door open.

"What's wrong with you that you had to lay on the doorbell, Q? Is this an emergency?"

Queenie pushed past Jackie. "Yes, girl, it is a dire emergency." Queenie blew air out of her mouth and fell into one of the chairs in the living room.

With hands on her hips, Jackie looked at Queenie as if she'd lost her mind. Jackie rocked her head a few times in the direction of her bedroom. Queenie looked puzzled.

"Getting ready to play Samson and Delilah," Jackie mouthed.

Queenie wasn't amused. "Sorry about that, girl, but what I have to say is more important than you getting your freak on with Pastor."

"You are so tasteless. I shouldn't have answered the door. Hurry up; you're interfering with my playtime."

"Jackie, this is serious."

Jackie turned her head and looked toward the bedroom, again. "Well, spit it out. Franklin is waiting on me."

"We have a dilemma."

"We?"

"Yes, we. I learned something today that's going to pierce Connie's heart."

Jackie sat down next to Queenie, anxious to hear what she had to say. "What is it, Q? Is Preston cheating on her?"

"In a way."

"What kind of answer is that?"

Queenie moved closer to Jackie until she was almost in her ear and whispered. "I was editing an article this morning and there in black and white was Preston Alexander's name."

"What's the big deal? And speak up so I can hear you."

"The big deal, Jackie, is that Preston is involved in a drug traffick-ing ring, and the FBI has been following him for days," she said, still whispering.

"Shut your mouth, Queenie Jackson. You're making that up."

"I wish I was, Jackie. My heart dropped to my stomach when I read it. So much so, that I dropped everything I was doing to come over and talk to you. We've got to warn Connie. She thinks that the man she's going to marry is on the up and up. All these years, he's been perpetrating a fraud."

"I do remember Connie saying that Preston had been acting strange lately."

"Yes, she did, and I believe this is the answer."

"How do we approach it?"

"I was hoping you'd have an answer. I'm only the transporter of the bad news. Maybe Pastor could speak with Connie."

"How do we know that there is truth in what you read? Isn't what you do sensitive material? Wouldn't you be violating the law by passing on information that the public isn't privy to?"

"You're such a scaredy cat."

"But I'm not the one who ran all the way over to my house with the news. Franklin won't touch this information with a ten-foot pole without it being substantiated."

Queenie sulked and sighed. "So, First Lady, what are we going to do?"

"We've got to save Connie from making a grave mistake. We've got to do our own investigation. What about her sister? Don't you think Yolanda ought to know?"

"Yolanda will go off on Preston the moment she hears the news. I can't risk my job."

"So how are we going to save Connie if you don't risk your job, Queen B? I say that you've already breached your confidentiality clause."

"You're right, Jackie. Right now, I could face dismissal without retirement. And I'm so damn close."

"Well, you need to make up your mind, but I'm down with you whatever you decide."

"Let me think about it and I'll get back with you; we can't wait too long."

They both turned around when they heard a swishing noise on the hardwood floor. Queenie bucked her eyes and then closed them when Pastor came into the room shirtless with only a towel around his waist.

"What's taking you so long, Jackieeee?" Pastor said, finally seeing Queenie parked next to his wife. "Hello, Sister Queenie. Please forgive my appearance." And Pastor O'Neill fled into the safety of his bedroom.

Queenie jumped up from her seat. "Girl, you were serious about Samson and Delilah. Honey, let me get up out of here so you can…"

"There's no need to say anything more. Yes, Franklin and I get it on, but it's time for you to go. Give me a call when you decide what you're going to do about Connie."

Queenie took a quick glance toward Jackie's bedroom and let out a howl. Seeing Pastor O'Neill close to his birthday suit was too much for her to swallow in one afternoon.

"TMI."

Jackie stood with her hand pointed toward the door. "Get your rusty butt out of here now."

Queenie laughed all the way to the car.

Bridal Shower

Yolanda was excited. Connie was finally going to marry the man of her dreams. Yolanda wished their parents, who'd already gone to glory, could witness Connie's big day.

She wanted to do something special for her sister before she got hitched. Although her idea was a little unorthodox, Yolanda decided she'd give Connie a bridal shower with a twist—a bridal shower intertwined with a Passion Party. A representative would come to the home and make a presentation with displays that included all kinds of sex toys, creams, and whatever else to add spice and pleasure in the bedroom. Everyone would have to bring a shower gift for Connie, but the entertainment would be the fun they'd derive from the Passion Party.

Time was of the essence since Connie and Preston planned to get married in two weeks. That only left the weekend. Yolanda got on her computer and accessed the Evite website and began to create invitations for Connie's bridal shower. It would be a group of Connie's closest friends, and she hoped that they all would be available on Saturday, although it was very last minute.

Pleased with herself, Yolanda contacted a caterer, decorator, and the Passion Party representative. She couldn't wait for Saturday to roll around. Yolanda was excited about the mere thought of having the extra element added to what might be a humdrum bridal shower. She was anxious to see what little goodies she was going to purchase for herself.

Yolanda pulled away from her daydream when her cell phone rang. It was her sister, and she was anxious to tell her about the shower, although she'd leave off the part about the Passion Party since Connie would more than likely object to the idea.

"What's up, baby sis?"

"Yolanda, I'm getting so excited. I can't wait to marry Preston."

"Well, this is what you wanted. You wore the man down, and now you're going to get your crown. Where are you going to live—his place or yours?"

"We haven't discussed that yet. He'll probably move in with me. My house is larger and I'm not ready to move my stuff anywhere until we find a house that will be ours."

"Stand your ground, sis. I've got a great surprise for you."

"I hope you aren't still planning to go to Vegas. I want to be alone with Preston."

"You're so selfish, Connie. I'll do my best to keep the ladies from buying airplane tickets, but I may not have much success."

"I'm sure. Knowing you, you'll be right in the middle of the pack." Connie sighed. "If you all show up, there won't be anything we can do." Then Connie laughed. "It might be fun to have you all as witnesses."

Yolanda smiled to herself. "Sis, you scared me for a moment. You know we've already purchased our tickets. I was holding my breath, but I'm so glad you came around. But that's not what I wanted to tell you."

"What is it? And by the way, I felt it down in my gut that you all had purchased airline tickets. You hussies are so brazen and disrespectful, but I love you. Now what were you saying?"

"This Saturday, I'm throwing a bridal shower for you at my house."

"For me? You shouldn't have, sis," Connie shrieked. "Thank you so much. I can't wait. Who did you invite?"

"Only your closest friends, and you're going to love what I've got planned."

"I can't wait, YoYo. I wish Mama was here."

"I do to. We'll have a moment of silence in memory of Mama."

"Sounds like a plan. Okay, I've got to call Preston. He's been under a lot of stress lately on the job. I'm so glad we were able to talk this past weekend. He put so many things into perspective for me—I understand where his head is. YoYo, he was so loving and attentive. We had the best time. He romanced me like I was his princess."

"You do love him, don't you?"

"I was always right about him. I didn't wait this long to find the man of my dreams to be mistaken. I love Preston Alexander with every beat of my heart."

"I'm happy for you, sis. In a couple of weeks, you're going to be playing those songs that we used to make babies, too."

"We already do that…but carefully. I guarantee we will be making love to each other morning, noon, and night. I'm going to be lovin' up on my man so much, the next-door neighbor will have to call the fire department to put out the three-alarm fire that we're going to cause."

"Shut-up, girl, that's what I'm talking about. After Saturday, it may be a four-alarm fire."

Yolanda and Connie laughed and laughed until they finally said goodbye.

Dragnet

The SWAT team was in place with the FBI safely monitoring the situation. Preston arrived at the usual place in the woods, parked his truck, entered the building and waited for his contacts to arrive. His nerves were on high alert; a thin veil of sweat covered his face.

Ten minutes passed, and Preston looked at his watch. It was only five minutes after seven, but his nerves were getting the best of him. Fifteen more minutes passed. Preston became antsy.

It was seven forty-five and Preston was past being worried. If his contacts didn't show, it would look as if he had pulled a fast one.

The tape that held the wires to his chest began to itch. Sweat formed around his neck and sent droplets to the listening device below. Preston had had enough. He picked up his briefcase and proceeded to walk out the door.

When Preston opened the door, his contacts rushed in, with black sunglasses hiding their eyes. They were dressed in black, silk suits and white, long-sleeved dress shirts.

"Where have you guys been? What took you so long? I've been waiting for over forty-five minutes in this hell hole."

"Shut up," the taller of the two Colombian men said in a heavy Latin accent. "Your job is to do as you're told. Do you have the package?"

"Yes," Preston said, letting go a sigh of relief. His eyes darted toward the door.

"What's up?" the shorter of the two Colombian men asked.

"What do you mean, what's up?"

The Colombian began to watch Preston more closely. "Is somebody squeezing your balls? You look like you've been kicked in the nuts." The taller Colombian laughed with a raspy tone in his voice.

"It's nothing," Preston said with a growl. "You should've been on time."

The shorter Colombian moved toward Preston. He backed up a few steps. "You wait as long as you have to wait," the Heavy said, his finger in Preston's face. "We take risks coming to this piss hole since your ass don't want to be seen in public. We pay handsomely for your services, so you shut up and do as you're told."

"You have the merchandise; now hand over what you owe me," Preston snapped.

The taller Colombian edged his way forward after making certain that the product—prescription drugs that included morphine, oxycodone, and Vicodin—was as it was supposed to be. It was, but he was still agitated. He pulled his Glock. "There's one thing I don't like and that is a cocky nigger," he said, pressing closer. "I ought to put you out of your misery."

Preston didn't like looking into the barrel of a gun. "I only want what's mine, and I'll be on my way."

The taller Colombian stood with his legs locked into place cocklegged and stared Preston down. "I ought to teach you a painful lesson on how you should conduct yourself," he said. "First, *viejo*, never ask dumb questions. Second, don't make demands."

Thug number one looked at thug number two. "Paulo, what do you think? Should I give him the money?"

Paulo sized Preston up and began to laugh. "He's a pussy. He's about to pee his pants. Give him the money." Paulo got up in Preston's face. "Next time, mind your manners or you won't have any fingers to grip a briefcase." Paulo slid the case to Preston. "Let's go, Luca, before our boy craps on himself."

Luca eased the gun down and returned it to a holster that was strapped to his long-sleeved shirt. "Remember what we said. Let today be a lesson to you; next time you might not be so lucky."

Preston didn't respond but watched as Luca opened the door and exited, followed by Paulo. Preston's nerves were unsettled. He wasn't sure how things were going to go down. In the thirty seconds it took Luca and Paulo to reach their car, gunshots rang out.

Preston hid in a far corner of the room and crouched down, while balancing on the balls of his feet. Several minutes passed before he heard what sounded like an army of feet approaching the house. All of a sudden, the door flew open and men dressed in all black with the letters SWAT emblazoned on their backs rushed him. Fear gripped Preston, unsure if they were friend or foe. His body began to quiver. Then Illya Newsome stepped inside, his familiar face giving Preston a temporary ease.

"Good work, Preston," Illya said. "We got everything on tape."

Preston stood up, still unsure about the other ten or so men in the room. "Are...are they dead?"

"One is dead and the other is in critical condition. An ambulance has been dispatched. We need your briefcase as evidence."

Reluctantly, Preston passed Illya the briefcase. Dr. Cole was going to be pissed.

"As I explained to you earlier, we will take you down to police headquarters...in handcuffs. You will be interrogated. You may retain an attorney, if you wish."

"I thought that if I cooperated, I would immediately be put into the Witness Protection Program."

"Yes, I did say that," Illya agreed. "But not right away. You must provide us with all the information on the drug traffickers as you know it before we grant you asylum. You provided me with some information this afternoon, but I believe you know more. You were great this evening, but this is only the beginning."

Preston looked confused as the police pulled his arms behind him and bound his hands together. He didn't bargain for this.

Shaking his head, he closed his eyes. What was he going to tell Connie? He had no intentions of hurting her, and now, she was going to suffer because of him. He thought back to the moment when he tried to break off their relationship. He was in deep and had wanted to save Connie from the repercussions. He couldn't do it, even then. Now he sat in the back of a patrol car, waiting to be transported to police headquarters. Hurting her was inevitable, getting out of the situation he'd got them both in was less certain.

All Hail To The Queen

The week flew by and Queenie was no closer to finding a way to warn Connie about Preston without compromising her job. Today would have to be the day since Yolanda had summoned them altogether for an impromptu bridal shower for Connie; the following weekend would be too late. Queenie hated to get a gift for a marriage that she didn't believe would take place, but for appearances sake, she'd play the role and would find the opportune moment to give Connie the bad news.

It was a beautiful April day. There were no rain clouds and the wind was calm. Queenie had taken the liberty to purchase, as a shower gift for Connie, a silk gown and robe—a short, sexy piece of lingerie that Connie could wear should there be a next man in her life.

Queenie swished her red weave from side to side and twirled around to look at herself in the floor-length mirror. She wore a pair of eggshell-colored slacks and a long-sleeved, red nylon blouse that buttoned down the front. Since it was a nice day, she wore her eggshell-colored vest trimmed in faux fur of the same color. Pleased, she retrieved her purse from the bed and headed for the door. She didn't want to be late, even if she believed this was a marriage—if it got that far—that was doomed.

Queenie picked up her gift, silver and black wrapping with a silver and black bow. Pleased, she set her alarm system and headed outside. She stopped short. Standing on her porch like a cocky son-of-a-bitch was Linden Robinson.

No words were spoken. The only thing audible was Queenie's heavy breathing.

"Aren't you going to say something, Red?" Linden looked Queenie over from head to toe. "I see you're in a hurry. You must have a hot date with that old dude who's still living back in the sixties."

"It's none of your business what I'm doing. You made your choice. Now go on back to Drema D and let her light your fire."

"Don't be so mean, Red. It's me, your lover man." Linden moved toward Queenie and reached in to kiss her.

Queenie pushed Linden out of the way and slammed the front door shut, realizing the alarm was about to go off. "Linden, I'm sorry. I'm going to be late."

"That ole geezer can't do for you what I can do."

"Who said I've got a date with him? However, for your information, he can get it up without the help of a blue pill that costs fifteen dollars a pop. And he knows how to treat a woman, more than I can say for you."

Linden ran his tongue across his teeth. "I'll give you that since it happens to be the truth, but you know that no one can handle you like me. Looking at me makes you wet."

"Shut the hell up, Linden, and get out of my way. I'm not your toy that you can pick up and play with whenever you like. I'm all woman, and I don't need you to fill a void. In fact, I've deleted you from my system. I'm done with your sorry ass. Queenie don't want ya."

Linden backed up a moment and sized Queenie up. "So it's like that, Red? You're gonna push away the best you've ever had? You know you still love me. I saw how you looked at me at the club the other night." Linden moved in closer. "I'm sure that if I touched you where you'd like me to touch you right now, you'd open the door lickety-split and I'd have you hollering my name in four seconds flat."

A smile appeared across Queenie's face. Linden smiled back. With her free hand, Queenie tickled Linden's chin. "You think you know me, don't you?"

"Everything about you," Linden agreed, confident that he had her, "how you like your coffee, your grits—milk, butter, and sugar… how you want me to make love to you."

Queenie laughed. "Contrary to popular belief, you ain't that good. Any woman that has to wait fifteen minutes or more for a man to get an erection without the blue pill is wasting her time." With her free hand, Queenie reached up and grabbed the side of Linden's face and pushed him away. "Don't want you. Go back to Drema D. And for your information, I like it slow, four-second man."

Without looking back, Queenie jumped in her red Jag and drove off. She took a peek in her rearview mirror and saw a perplexed Linden still standing on the front porch. Linden was partially right; she still loved him and she loved the way he made love to her. But he'd never know. He was dead to her.

What Kind Of Party Is This?

Queenie was the last to arrive for Connie's bridal shower. There were a little over a dozen women gathered for the shindig, but neither Connie nor Yolanda were anywhere in sight.

Queenie took in the gorgeously decorated room. Yolanda had outdone herself. In the middle of the room sat a large, wingbacked chair, draped in lavender toile fabric and blinged to the max with colorful rhinestones. It was fit for a princess or in Connie's case, a bride-to-be. In a prominent corner of the room sat a beautiful floral arrangement composed of calla lilies with white hydrangeas on a round, mahogany table with intricate designs carved onto its three legs. But what got Queenie's attention was another table, off to the side. It was covered with sex toys.

Seeing Emma, Queenie rushed to her side. "Girl, what's going on with that table over there?" She pointed in the direction of the sex toys.

"Yolanda is having a Passion Party," Emma explained. "She's using the shower for Connie as a disguise for what's really on her mind—sexing that new boy toy she's been seeing."

Queenie laughed, grabbing her chest. "Emma, you are wrong for that, but I don't blame Yolanda. That new man of YoYo's is so *phine*, he'd make a bulldog break his chain."

Emma boiled over with laughter. "Q, get away from me. I only put one panty liner on today, and my weak bladder won't be able to put up with too much of your crazy antics."

"You better go and see if Yolanda has something stronger. I can guarantee that this is going to be a jaw dropper of a day. There's Jackie. Lord, she's going to die when she sees all that filth YoYo has laying on that table."

Emma couldn't contain her laughter. "Q, bye. I've got to make a bathroom run."

Queenie laughed at Emma as she rushed to the bathroom. Out of the corner of her eyes, she spotted First Lady Jackie O'Neill and moved across the room to talk to her.

Jackie leaned into Queenie. "Have you said anything to Connie yet about you know what?"

"No, but if I'm going to say anything, I'm going to have to do it today. She's getting married next week, and it'll be too late if I don't."

"If you get up the nerve, wait until the shower is over, Q."

"I'm not crazy, Jackie. Yolanda would be some kind of pissed off if we ruined all of her hard work."

"Yolanda does have it decorated real nice. What did you get Connie?"

"Something she can wear with the next man in her life after she gets over Preston."

"That's so sad," Jackie lamented. "She may never wear your outfit."

"Finally, here are the ladies of the hour," Queenie whispered to Jackie, as Yolanda and Connie entered the room.

They were both wearing sundresses. Connie in an all-white strapless number that hit right at her ankles; Yolanda in a lavender and white floral print that hit right below the knees. Their feet and hands were well groomed, each with French tips on both. Yolanda's short, silver mane was gorgeous and sculpted to her face, and hints of gray were sprinkled throughout Connie's short bob.

"Where's Emma?" Jackie suddenly asked Queenie.

"I sent her to the bathroom."

Jackie looked at Queenie with a puzzled look on her face. "Is Emma sick?"

Queenie smiled to herself but decided against telling Jackie about the other part of Connie's bridal shower. She'd find out on her own. "No, she's not sick," she said before changing the subject. "Come on, Yolanda is waving for everybody to gather around."

"Thank you all for coming out to this special occasion for my sister, Connie," Yolanda began. She blew kisses to Connie who sat in the *blinged-out* chair. "My sister is getting married, y'all." There were claps all around while Queenie and Jackie pinched each other. "I see the gift table is filled with gifts, and I'm sure Connie is anxious to open them. But first, we're going to have a couple of games to see how well you know Connie and her intended."

"Uhm," Queenie whispered to Jackie. "Connie doesn't know her own man."

"Amen to that, sister." Jackie slapped Queenie's hand.

"After the games, I have a special presentation for you. We want to make sure Connie is well prepared for her life with her man. And, you, Connie's friends will also have a chance to take advantage of the special gifts that I'm blessing my sister with."

There were "ooohs" and "ahhhs" throughout the room. Some of the ladies were slapping hands.

"What are they talking about?" Jackie asked.

Emma sat down in a seat next to Jackie and Queenie. "Sex toys," Emma said. She laughed and gave Queenie a quick wink, then pointed to the table that sat next to the wall. "See that table over there?" Jackie shook her head. "Girl, it's full of stuff to help you get your freak on."

"I'm going to leave right after Connie opens her gifts. As a First Lady, this isn't the kind of setting I should be in."

"You aren't going anywhere," Queenie informed her. "You're going to sit your butt down and get a little education. Role playing as Samson and Delilah can get a little dull. Delilah needs some new tricks."

"You all are full of the devil," Jackie said with a huff.

Before Queenie could qualify Jackie's statement, Yolanda passed out paper and pencils to play the first game. The questions were created to see how well Connie's friends knew her and her fiancé, Preston. Some knew the couple well, while others didn't have a clue. The next game consisted of breaking into groups and creating a wedding dress with a roll of toilet tissue using one of the persons in the group as the model. There were some very creative creations, and Connie picked a winner from the four groups.

After the games, instead of having Connie open her gifts, Yolanda raised her hand to get everyone's attention. "It's time for the special presentation. If you haven't been to a Passion Party, you're in for a real treat."

"What's a Passion Party?" Jackie whispered in Queenie's ear.

Queenie cackled. "First Lady, you're getting ready to find out. Sit back and relax. This is the real show. Connie may not open up her shower gifts after this."

Silver Bullets

The Passion Party hostess stood in front of the group with a big smile on her face. She was an attractive, lean woman in her mid-to-late thirties. Her mocha-colored skin was smooth and satiny. Her hair was swooped up into a fake ponytail, and her acrylic nails were an inch long and painted fire-engine red. She stood about six feet and in her four-inch Prada stilettos that made her look as tall as a giraffe.

Her voice had a New York nasal sound. "Afternoon, ladies. My name is Taylor Chisolm and I'm your Passion Party representative. You're in for a real treat this afternoon. I promise, in the next hour, all of your inhibitions will be tossed to the wind. If at present you're not sure how to enjoy the body you were given, I'm going to show you how you can exact pleasure for yourself and your man, if you have one." The shower guests chuckled.

"I'm getting out of here," Jackie hissed at Queenie. "I thought I was coming to a bridal shower, not Sodom and Gomorrah. This is heathen worship."

"What are you talking about?" Emma asked, getting in on the tail end of Jackie's rant.

"This crazy mess Yolanda invited us to. I don't need anyone to tell me how to pleasure myself or my husband. And I certainly don't need some stupid apparatus to help me. This is sinful. I'm getting out of here."

Before Emma could say anything, Jackie was on her feet.

"Oh, we have our first volunteer," Taylor said, motioning with her hand for Jackie to come forward. Jackie froze and stood in the middle of the room with a dumb look on her face. "Don't be shy," Taylor said.

Jackie, feeling everyone's eyes on her, looked at the Miss Passion Party representative and pointed to herself. "Are you talking to me?"

"Yes," Taylor said with a smile. "Come on up."

"Oh, no," Jackie waved her hand. "This is not my scene."

Taylor stepped forward and held her hand out to Jackie. "Come on. You're going to be in for a pleasant surprise."

Not sure what else to do, Jackie moved forward and stood next to Taylor, her nose up in the air and her mouth twisted in disgust.

"What's your name?" Taylor asked.

"Jackie, First Lady Jackie O'Neill."

"First Lady, huh?" Taylor teased.

"Yes, I am First Lady at Shiloh Baptist Church in the city." There were snickers from the group.

Taylor smirked. "Oh, so this must be your first Passion Party then."

"I came here for a bridal shower not some crude display about pleasuring yourself. That's why I have a husband."

"I was a little put out, too, Jackie, but you know my sister," Connie interjected over the bubbling laughter of the other women.

"Hmph," Jackie said, rolling her eyes at Connie. "I can't believe you're buying into this nonsense."

Yolanda rushed to the front. "Everyone, excuse Jackie. She's new to the idea of taking care of her body, if you know what I mean. She'll be all right. Continue, Taylor."

Jackie stared at Yolanda as if she didn't have any sense. Instead of moving toward the door, Jackie stood in place as if she was glued to the floor. Taylor took her hand and rubbed a compound on the back of her hand that had a red shimmer to it. "What is this?" Jackie wanted to know, wrinkling her nose.

"It's an edible powder. Lick your hand."

"Are you serious? Jesus, keep me near the cross."

"Jesus doesn't have a thing to do with this," Queenie shouted.

"Trust me," Taylor said with a smile.

Jackie frowned, grunted, and gave Queenie the evil eye. "I need some hand sanitizer."

"This little bit isn't going to hurt," Taylor said.

"Lick it," Queenie shouted.

"Yes, lick it," Emma urged, snickering on the side.

Jackie continued to roll her eyes. She looked at the back of her hand and then drew it to her mouth. With encouragement from the audience, Jackie stuck her tongue out and licked her hand. "Uhmm, this has a nice taste to it."

Yolanda, Connie, Queenie, Emma, and the other ladies howled and clapped their hands.

"Go, Jackie," Queenie yelled.

Taylor took control again. "Jackie, wouldn't this enhance your lovemaking with your husband if you rubbed a little of this on him and licked it off? Double the pleasure?"

"Put it on him where?" Jackie wanted to know. "I'm not doing any freaky, nasty stuff."

The room erupted in laughter.

"Girl, you are too funny," Queenie said, slapping her thigh. "Go on and get your freak on. This is better than that K-Y Jelly stuff they advertise on television. You'll have your husband howling for days."

"I'd expect you to say something like that, Queenie Jackson. You're nothing but a freaky heathen."

"I sure am," Queenie hollered back. Everyone was in stitches, laughing at Jackie's expense.

"Okay, everyone, in all fairness to Jackie, especially being that this is her first time, let's cut her some slack. Jackie, this isn't about being freaky."

"That's a lie," someone muttered loud enough to be heard by the entire room.

Taylor continued. "It's about deriving pleasure for yourself and with your significant other. Romancing your husband in the purest form is an act of flattery for him and it certainly is for yourself if you chose to indulge yourself, and there's nothing wrong with that. Quite a few of our ladies don't have a significant other, so they derive pleasure from being in tune to their bodies. Our little demonstration only proved that you can heighten the emotion of your romantic interlude. It doesn't have to be crude or lewd."

A tear rolled down Jackie's face, and Taylor wiped it with her finger.

"You were brave to come up here. I want you to know that the products I'm going to show this afternoon aren't meant to minimize or exploit your sexuality but enhance your sexual experience." Taylor gave Jackie a hug.

"Most of you women here today are what I call Silver Bullets," Taylor continued. "You're over fifty, sporting your graying hair in the winter of your life, but you're still fierce and fabulous. You owe it to yourselves to do those things that make you happy. And if relieving your sexual tensions with or without a man makes you happy, I say go for it."

"I like that," Queenie said, "Silver Bullets."

"Me, too," Emma interjected. "Silver Bullets—women who are in their prime and still have it going on."

"I want to know about the other Silver Bullet," one of the other ladies hollered out. "You know what I'm talking about. Yeah, and if anybody wants to know, I am a true freak."

"Well, you probably have the Silver Bullet already," Yolanda chimed in.

"Girl, I need a replacement. I wore the other one out."

The room erupted in laughter. Several ladies held their sides from laughing so hard, while some gave each other high-fives.

"Taylor smiled and held up her hand. "We're going to get to that silver bullet. You can go on back to your seat, Jackie."

"God is going to punish me, but I need to find out what you all find so fascinating about this unholy stuff."

"Take a seat, Jackie," Queenie said under her breath while pulling on the hem of Jackie's dress. "Sit your ass down and learn something."

Jackie sat down and pouted for a few more moments but came alive as the demonstration continued. She asked question after question. Before the night was over, Jackie ordered the Cosmo Bunny, one of the largest vibrators in the catalog. "And I want one of those Silver Bullets. Delilah needs one of those in her toy box."

"Jackie has lost her mind," Emma said, laughing so hard she had to cover her mouth to keep from spitting her drink on everyone.

Queenie looked at Emma, then at Jackie. "Emma, this was exactly what Jackie needed. She's still a cave girl with primitive ways of making love."

"You are crazy, Q," Yolanda said, joining in on the laughter.

Jackie threw her hand up. "You don't know what I do behind the closed doors of my mansion, but know this Ms. Think-You're-the-Freak-of-the-Week, Samson is getting ready to be messed up."

There wasn't a dry eye in the house. The Silver Bullets purchased everything Taylor had in the catalog.

"This was the best bridal shower I've ever been to," Emma said.

"Why thank you," Yolanda said, taking a bow. "I wanted Connie's special day to be memorable. I feel sorry for Preston."

"Me too," Connie chimed in. "We're going to have to have a vacation from our honeymoon. Preston is going to be in heaven with all the toys I've got and the negligees that I'm sure are wrapped up in these pretty gift packages."

Queenie and Jackie looked at each other, but left it at that.

Witness Protection

Preston tossed and turned in the bunk he'd been provided at the county jail. He wasn't sure what was happening on the outside, but it had been a long night. Had the feds apprehended Dr. Cole? Who else was caught up in the sting? How long was he going to remain cut off from the real world? As much as his mind danced over those questions, Preston's foremost concern was Connie. Somehow, he had to alert her to what was going on. He needed an opportunity to explain everything.

He sat up when he heard muffled voices. Preston stood and walked to the bars that separated him from the outside world. In his mind, his incarceration wasn't what he'd anticipated for cooperating with the feds. He wasn't even sure about Illya, who was probably talking out of both sides of his mouth. Still, if Yolanda was really his girlfriend, maybe Illya would make a concession so that he'd be allowed to speak with Connie.

Illya and another man, who Preston didn't know, now stood in front of the cell. The deputy on duty opened it up, and the gentlemen entered. The deputy closed the bars behind them.

"How are you feeling this morning?" Illya asked Preston without any emotion.

Preston shrugged, hung his head for a moment, and sighed. "I feel like a caged man, although I'm happy to be freed of Dr. Cole and the drug ring." Preston looked thoughtfully at Illya. He hesitated before he spoke, but he had to ask the question that was burning on his mind. "Did they arrest Dr. Cole?"

"Yes, he was arrested last night. He put up quite a fight for an old guy. Let's say, he wasn't a happy camper."

Preston's nerves were rattled. "What did he say?"

"He claimed that he had no idea what we were talking about and that you must have been acting alone. By the way," Illya said, pointing to the white gentleman, "this is my partner, Scott Goldman. He's been working the case with me."

Preston nodded but didn't offer his hand.

"So what does that mean for me?" Preston asked with concern in his voice.

Illya held onto one of the bars of the cell. "Look, we appreciate your part in this, but the second stage of this investigation has only begun. You will be a target."

Preston slumped onto the thin cot.

"What about the Witness Protection Program?"

Illya's partner moved toward Preston and stood over him. "It's still available to you and is completely voluntary. If you opt to do it, you need to enter it now, which means you sever all ties to the life you once knew. You are permitted to leave the program at any time, although we discourage witnesses from doing so. However, Preston, you are the state's witness against Dr. Cole, and will have to testify. With your help we can put him away for a long time."

"What about the Colombians?" Preston wanted to know.

"What about them?" Illya asked, moving away from the bar and coming to stand next to his partner. "You were their transfer station—that's it. You weren't able to provide us with any information about them other than that you met them at the pre-determined location when advised. Dr. Cole was our real target."

Preston shook his head and tried to stand up, but was pushed back down on the bunk by Goldman. "You're still a suspect until such time as you're no longer considered one."

Preston rolled his eyes at Goldman. There was something about him that didn't sit well with Preston. In fact, if Preston could call it, Goldman would rather see him rot away in jail. He wasn't so sure about Illya, but considering his present situation, he'd have to depend on his situation.

Illya took note of Goldman's attitude toward Preston. Illya had no use for criminals. He'd witnessed his father getting gunned down in the street by some thug who thought that other people's hard earned money belonged to him. Although the thug and his accomplices had been captured, it hadn't brought Illya's father back.

Something about Preston spoke to him. Preston was a victim who'd been used by Dr. Cole. What Illya hadn't told Preston was that the feds already had information that Dr. Cole was illegally manufacturing drugs in the state and had a distribution network that had grossed close to $500 million. Of course, Dr. Cole wasn't acting alone; he was only one of the key players in North Carolina.

Yolanda spoke highly of Preston. He would do what he could to save him from the hell he now found himself in.

Exercise Your Faith

First Lady Jackie O'Neill had a glow about her as she played the piano—her fingers gently gliding over each key. It even appeared to Queenie that the reverend had an extra pep in his step this morning. Queenie smiled as she recalled all the fun they'd had the previous afternoon and the fun she'd had later that evening entertaining Joe Harris. She even allowed herself to reminisce about seeing Linden on her front porch, until Emma clapped her hands and raised them, instructing the choir to stand.

It was time to bring the tithes and offering into the storehouse. The choir sang as the church congregation rose from their seats and marched to the offering table to pay the Lord His ten percent. Pastor O'Neill believed that marching to the collection table was a good way to exercise their faith—exercise being the operative word.

Yolanda and Connie were notably absent from church. Queenie wondered what would happen to Connie when she found out about Preston's secret hobby. She'd decided it wasn't her place to say anything and had sworn Jackie to secrecy. It weighed heavy on her mind; she'd call later and find out how Connie was doing. After all, she had a ticket to Vegas for the weekend, and regardless of what went down the pipe with Connie and Preston, she was going to the city of lights and glam to have some fun.

It was time for the word. There was no doubt in Queenie's mind that her good friend, First Lady Jackie O'Neill, had laid a few moves on the pastor last night. The way he was smiling, you could see it and his pearly whites from miles away. Pastor O'Neill shifted his shoulders up and down like he was happy about something, and although it was less than three feet from his chair to the podium, he had a swagger on him that made you capitalize every letter in the word, *cool*.

"Church, I feel good today," he began, raising his hands toward heaven and taking a slight pause to turn toward his wife and give her a nod of approval. "God is good; He's faithful, church."

"Amen," the congregation shouted in unison.

"He woke me up this morning and started me on my way. He clothed me in my right mind and put joy down in my heart. The Lord gave me a helpmate who thought it not robbery to fix me a good breakfast this morning—and I do mean it was good, saints. But most of all, He gave me a mind that is stayed on Him."

Shouts of jubilation were heard all over the sanctuary. People raised their hands high and began to clap them in praise.

"Saints, God is love, and He loved us so much that He gave us His only begotten son who laid down His life for each and every one of you."

"Yes," hollered First Lady from the piano bench.

Queenie watched Pastor O'Neill as he took out a handkerchief and began to wipe his face. Yes, he was high on Jesus, and Queenie swore that that First Lady had something to do with it.

"My subject for today is feeling brand new in the Lord—an exercise in faith."

"Amen," someone shouted.

"What is brand new? It means to be made over again. You take off the old and put on the new. For some it could mean shedding pounds to become a brand-new person. For others it might mean getting a new set of teeth after all of the affected teeth have been extracted. For the man or woman with a bad heart, it could mean a heart transplant…for a person with a bad kidney, a kidney transplant. And for others, it could mean understanding the needs of your spouse and being receptive to new ideas…new things that will enhance your marriage. Whatever it is that you shed or get rid of, when you replace it with something that makes you whole or brand new, it is a rebirth…a fresh start."

Queenie smiled and looked over at Emma whose mouth was hanging open and who was giving Queenie the *"are you thinking what I'm thinking?"* look. Emma scratched her head and took the opportunity to glance in First Lady Jackie's direction. Jackie caught both Emma and Queenie staring at her. She smiled and raised her hand as if she was praising the Lord.

Emma and Queenie couldn't wait until church was over. Pastor O'Neill preached the house down and three souls came forward and gave their lives to the Lord. Normally, Jackie stood next to Pastor O'Neill at the entrance to the church at the end of service to wish the members a blessed week. However, Jackie was nowhere to be found.

Emma caught up to Queenie. "Girl, did you hear what Pastor said this morning? He looked like he had a fresh anointing on him. When he started talking about being receptive to new ideas as it concerned your mate, I almost lost it."

"I bet that's all you heard of the message."

"Queenie, you heard it like I heard it. I bet you were sitting right in that choir stand wondering how Jackie hooked up the pastor."

Queenie began to laugh. "Girl, you got me pegged. Sister Jackie exercised her faith with those new toys she bought yesterday."

"You need to quit, Q." Emma thumped Queenie on the side of her head. "You don't have a lick of sense. Let's find Jackie."

"We better get out of here before we get swallowed up in this holy ground talking about how Jackie sexed her husband."

The ladies rushed from the sanctuary to the Pastor's study. This was the one place they knew they'd find Jackie if she couldn't be found anywhere else. And they were right.

"Running away from us, dearie?" Queenie smirked while trying to control the laughter that begged to leap out.

"Why would I run away from you heathens?" Jackie said, looking between Queenie and Emma, as they stood in the secretary's office outside of the Pastor's study.

"Do you really want me to answer that? We know where that sermon came from that Pastor preached today," Emma said.

"You guys need to listen to the message instead of trying to put your own spin on things. Franklin's messages are all God-given, regardless of where the inspiration came from."

"So, you admit it," Queenie began, "that Pastor had a little help with the message."

"You dirty wenches," Jackie whispered.

"Say what you want, Jackie O'Neill, but we were with you when you made those purchases yesterday, vowing to get your money's worth," Emma said.

Jackie looked all around her to make sure there wasn't anyone in hearing distance. "Y'all, I put that yummy stuff on my husband's nipples and licked it off like Taylor told me to do, and the rest is history."

Queenie and Emma screamed.

"Oh my goodness," Queenie shouted, circling her face with her hand. "You have the glow all over you."

"Be quiet," Jackie said. She moved in closer to Queenie and Emma so that their heads touched. "And that vibrator…it shook every bone and muscle in my body. I've never felt anything quite like it…ever. I had to tell Franklin that it was prayer time; that man didn't want to leave my goodies alone."

"Oh my goodness," Emma shouted. "TMI—way too much information. Jackie is never going to be the same."

"Well," Queenie began, "Joe and I hit the top meter reading on the Richter scale. I left him in my bed this morning. I didn't want to hear Emma's mouth about not showing up to sing. Glad I didn't stay home since Yolanda or Connie didn't come."

"You need to get a husband," Jackie whispered. "What you're doing is sin. My romp in the hay with my husband is blessed."

"Check her out," Emma said, cracking up. "Ms. Jackie has become an expert."

"You might need to try some of those toys on Billy. May perk him up," Jackie said, resting her case.

"You've crossed the line, First Lady," Emma hissed. "Leave Billy out of this. I take care of him with my own brand of lovin'."

Queenie caught her chest to stifle a laugh. "Here's a fried chicken leg, Billy. Come and get it, Billy." Queenie and Jackie doubled over with laughter.

Pastor O'Neill walked into the office and looked at the women like they were conspirators. "What's going on in here, Jackie? Are you all having a hen party?"

"No, Pastor," Queenie rushed to say. "We were checking with First Lady to see if she wanted to go to brunch today."

Pastor took off his robe and hung it up behind the door to his office. "I'm going to take the liberty to answer for Jackie."

Pastor stared at Jackie with pure lust. "I'm taking my wife to Ruth's

Chris Steak House today. She deserves the best meal my money can buy."

Queenie and Emma traded glances.

"She does deserve a good meal," Emma said. "A woman who gets up and fixes her husband breakfast on Sunday morning deserves a medal."

"Last night's dinner wasn't bad either," Pastor O'Neill said, not noticing the look on either Queenie or Emma's face. "Tell Billy I've missed him. He needs to come back into the fold. Is he still frying chicken on Wednesday?"

It was Jackie's turn to laugh.

"Here's a fried chicken leg…" Queenie said but started laughing before she could finish her sentence. Jackie joined her.

"Have a nice lunch, Pastor," Emma said, pinching Queenie as hard as she could.

"We will, and keep today's message in your heart. There's nothing like being brand new in the Lord."

Queenie laughed and looked over at Emma. "He looks brand new."

"I'm not mad at First Lady; I'm not mad at all."

Something's Not Right

Connie looked at her lovely gifts. Her sister had outdone herself. Between the decorations, the food, and the surprise Passion Party, her bridal shower was sure to be tagged 'event of the season.' Not only had Connie gone away with a bundle of frilly and seductive outfits to wear when she and Preston got married, but all the ladies had benefited; their smiles proved it.

After all of the fun on Saturday, Connie opted out of going to church on Sunday. God knew her heart.

Besides, something else was weighing on her mind. Today was the beginning of a new week—the last Sunday that she'd be a single woman. However, it had been several days since she'd heard from her fiancé. All attempts to reach Preston had failed. The odd thing was he hadn't returned even one of her many telephone calls.

Concern shifted to panic. What if something happened to Preston? Surely he would've called. He'd never let several days go by without calling.

Connie rushed to her dresser and picked up her iPhone. She pressed the number for Preston and let it ring. After five or six rings, her call went to voicemail. Something was truly wrong.

Not wasting another moment, Connie pressed the number for Yolanda. A thin veil of sweat formed on her face, despite the fact that the temperature was only in the mid-sixties.

"Hey, baby sis," Yolanda said.

"YoYo, I need you to come to the house, now."

"What is it, Connie? Is something wrong?"

"Yeah," Connie said, feeling kind of spaced out. "Something is definitely wrong."

"Okay, I'm coming right over. Hang in there."

"Okay." Connie ended the call. She looked around the room, shook her head, and sighed.

No more than twenty minutes had elapsed by the time Yolanda's Lexus pulled up at Connie's house. It had been a mad, blind dash through the streets of Raleigh. Connie hadn't given any indication of what was wrong, but if it had to do with Preston, if he had hurt her sister, Yolanda was going to take a machete and cut off which ever part of him had caused her sister grief.

She feared the worse and braced herself for what she might find. She parked her car in front of Connie's house and leaped out like a fireman on his way to a two-alarm fire. Yolanda nearly ran the few feet to the door. Before she could knock, the door flew open with Connie standing off to the side.

"What's wrong, Connie?" Yolanda asked, noticing the tears that dripped from Connie's face.

Connie closed the door, grabbed her sister and held on. Yolanda held her for a long moment, feeling the way her body shook. Soon, she pulled back, wiping tears from Connie's face with her hand. Fresh tears replaced those as Connie stared at her with watery eyes. "I'm not sure, YoYo. My gut says something has happened to Preston. I haven't heard from him in three days, which is totally unlike him. We were in a good place. When we were last together, Preston talked about nothing but his love for me and how happy he was going to be when I became his wife."

"So," Yolanda began with caution, "what do you think happened to him? Has he said anything that would indicate that he's in some kind of trouble?"

Connie pulled away. "Something has been troubling him. He did tell me that he was having problems on the job. It was the reason he'd been so distant the past few weeks. But he told me not to worry, that he would handle it."

"Did he give you any indication what it was?"

"No."

Yolanda searched her mind.

"Remember the night I told you Illya and I saw him with Dr. Cole at the café?"

"Yeah."

"He wasn't himself that night. Preston was polite as he always is, but the more I think about it, he seemed tense. Did he mention anything to you, Connie?"

"Not a thing. Once I told him how I felt about his rejection, he apologized. Then he asked me to marry him. True, it was kind of sudden, considering we hadn't had an extensive conversation about it beforehand. And I was blinded by the big rock he gave me. So anything else that might have been going on I was completely oblivious to it."

Connie went into 'big sister' mode. "We've got to make some phone calls, little sis. You need to find out where Preston is hiding out...or if he's dead or alive."

"Don't say that, YoYo. If something has happened to Preston, I won't be able to go on without him."

"We've got to believe that everything is going to be alright, but in the meantime, we've got to find Preston."

"You're right."

One For Emma

"Look, I enjoyed lunch with you today, but I missed the rest of the crew," Emma said.

"Are you trying to say you were bored with my company?" Queenie asked, picking up a toothpick to dislodge some food that had entangled itself in her left molar.

"Naw, you know I love hanging out with you, Q, but it was like having a meal without the dessert and the sweet tea."

"I've never been compared to a meal before, but that was good, Emma." Queenie laughed. "I missed Yolanda, Connie, and Jackie, too. We laughed enough back at the church house to take us through the week. I still can't imagine Jackie getting her freak on with Pastor."

"Pastor Franklin O'Neill is no different than any other male. He puts his pants on the same way, brushes his teeth, goes to work and makes that long money for the family, and does what a man and woman do when they're making babies. Men of the cloth are usually known for having big families."

"You're right, although these modern-day ministers know that there's a recession going on. If church members weren't paying tithes like they should, pastors would have to go out and get a second job to feed a bunch of hungry mouths. Maybe I'm unconsciously jealous of what Jackie and Franklin have—a family. They have a beautiful love for one another and they love the Lord. They have two wonderful children who see about them. As much as I hate to admit it, Emma, I do want what they have."

"So how is your budding romance with Mr. Joe Harris? I see you like what he brings to the table."

"Girl, Joe Harris still has it going on. He bathes and massages me, and, girl, I've never hollered so much."

"You mean that moaning sound you make when it's feeling good to you?"

"Yeah, Emma, that's it. I believe Joe is trying to play for keeps. Now if I can only get him to cut that nasty Jheri Curl mess off of his head."

Emma fell out laughing. "Q, I remember when Billy used to wear a Jheri Curl. That man of mine thought he was *Superfly*. Billy would throw his head from side to side, throwing that Jheri Curl juice every which way."

Queenie laughed so hard, she almost choked on her own saliva. Then she got quiet.

"There's something I didn't tell you all yesterday."

Emma looked at Queenie with concern. "Something happened that we should know about?"

"Maybe…yes, I need to tell someone. Guess who showed up on my doorstep as I was leaving to go to Connie's bridal shower?"

"Who?"

"The Mandingo himself."

Emma's hands flew to her face. "No. You couldn't be talking about Linden."

Queenie was quiet.

"Isn't he with Drema D?"

"The sorry-ass Negro wanted some ass, and I wasn't going to give in to him. And the nerve of that trifling nigger to show up on my doorstep with the misconception that there was an open door policy at my place."

"But you wanted him." Emma search Queenie's eyes. "Didn't you?"

"Emma, I'm going to be honest. Yes, he was looking good and everything, but how he came to me made him look very ugly. Yes, for one second…maybe two…my heart was telling me to let the devil come in, let him wet my whistle. My heart is still strung out on the fool. I don't know what happened from one moment to the next, but common sense took over and thank God I made the right decision."

"So, what are you going to do the next time he blocks your doorway?"

"Emma, I haven't given it much thought, but…"

"But what, Q?"

"I've been thinking about letting Joe Harris change his residence to mine."

"That's crazy, Queenie. You just met him. What if he turns out to be an axe murderer or some kind of loony bird that you can't get rid of?"

"I've thought about it. Joe is different."

"He'll keep your sheets wet with that Jheri curl juice."

"Emma, only you would say something crazy like that."

"Seriously, Q, you're free to do as you please. But once the man gets his foot in the door, he'll start to make demands. 'What time are you going to be home? What time is the food going to be ready? Take my clothes to the cleaners.'"

"Is that how you feel about Billy after all these years?"

"Q, Billy is my husband. I've been with him nearly my whole darn life. We love each other, but we allow each other our space. We're like a ball and glove. We have history and a lifetime of memories. We have three wonderful children who've been the highlight of our lives. If something happened to Billy, no other man could take his place, and he certainly wouldn't be setting up camp in my place and getting the vajay-jay for free."

More than ten minutes passed without a word from either Emma or Queenie. Emma couldn't tell what Queenie was thinking; she could be so strong-minded sometimes. She had blown up when Emma had clued her in about Linden. Would she listen now?

Eventually, Queenie put her toothpick down and looked at Emma. "You make a lot of sense, Emma. She was up before Emma could get over the shock. "Let's blow this joint."

Missing

Connie and Yolanda weren't making any headway. Attempts to contact Dr. Cole failed. Yolanda dialed Illya's number and waited for him to pick up.

"Hi, Yolanda," Illya said. "You decided to play hooky from church today?"

Hearing his voice eased some of the stress. Yolanda grinned. "Guilty as charged," she replied playfully. "I was tired after hosting a bridal shower for my sister yesterday. In fact, I'm at her house now."

"Oh," Illya said. His voice was suddenly cool and detached.

"The reason I called," Yolanda began, proceeding with caution, "is a personal matter that involves my sister."

"Okay. How can I help?"

"You are…" Yolanda looked up and saw Connie waving her hands. She squinted to make sure she understood what Connie was trying to say.

"*No,*" Connie mouthed.

"What were you trying to ask me?" Illya pressed.

"Nothing, Illya, nothing that I should be bothering you with."

"It seemed serious when you began. Now, I'm curious."

Yolanda stared as Connie stood up from her seat and walked to within three inches of her. Connie shook her head no and touched the off button but not hard.

"Do you want to go to Vegas with me for Connie and Preston's wedding?" That was all Yolanda could come up with considering the groom was missing.

There was silence at the other end. It was Yolanda's turn to ask a question. "What's wrong? I'm not good enough for you to go to Vegas with me?" And then it came to her. Illya was recently divorced and going to a wedding was the last place he wanted to be—too many reminders.

"Look, you don't have to answer, Illya. I was being insensitive."

"Insensitive?"

"You know…being recently divorced and all."

Illya chuckled a little. "No, that didn't bother me. Where is your sister?"

"She's staring at me."

Illya sighed.

"What's wrong?" Yolanda asked, confused. "I'm not good with guessing games. I feel like I'm trying to figure out a phrase on the *Wheel of Fortune*." She looked up at Connie with her inquiring eyes and puffed up lips, looking like she wanted to cuss her out.

"May I speak to Connie?"

Yolanda frowned. She put her hand over the receiver. "Illya wants to talk to you?"

It was Connie's turn to be confused.

"Talk to me for what?"

"I don't know, Connie. He asked to speak with you."

Connie took the cell phone from Yolanda's hand. She looked at it as if it wasn't real. Breathing heavily, Connie lifted the phone to her ear.

"Hello?"

"Connie, this is a little awkward, but I think it's best that we have this conversation."

"A conversation about what? Are you asking for my blessing to see my sister? You have it."

"Whoa…slow down, Connie. Take a deep breath."

"Well, how do you expect me to act, acting all mysterious? Spit it out."

She knew she was being rude, but she couldn't help it; she was on edge.

Illya breathed heavily and let out a small sigh. "I have some…"

"Hold on a moment," Connie interrupted. "My cell phone is ringing." Connie rushed to her phone and answered it, although she didn't recognize the number. "Hello?"

"Is this Connie Maxwell?"

She didn't recognize the voice either.

"Yes, it is," Connie said.

"This is the Wake County Jail. Will you accept a collect call from Preston Alexander?"

There was a slight pause and then she swallowed hard. "Yes," Connie said, her hands shaking. Now, Yolanda was looking at her.

"Preston?" Connie squealed. "What's happened and why are you calling from the County Jail?"

"I've been arrested. It's a long story. I was caught up in a sting operation."

"A sting operation? What kind of sting operation?"

"Your sister's friend, federal agent Newsome, has been working on a drug case in North Carolina. I can't say much more. I need you to come down to the jail. I'll tell you all about it when you get here."

"I'm on my way." Connie hung up the phone, grabbed her coat and purse.

Yolanda pulled her arm. "What's going on, Connie? I still have Illya on the phone."

"Ask him. He can tell you all about it. I'm gone."

"Gone where?"

Connie threw her arms up in the air and let them fall. She walked out of the door without another word, her steps hurried.

"Illya, what's going on? Connie left here angry and in a hurry. It has something to do with Preston."

"Damn. Meet me at the Wake County Jail."

Ain't No Sunshine Behind Bars

Tears fell from Connie's eyes, so much so it clouded her vision, but she kept on course. Twenty minutes and she would be there.

Her heart beat rapidly and a barrage of thoughts ran through her head faster than she could catch them. How in the hell had Preston become involved in this madness? Why hadn't he told her what was going on? Why did this have to happen before one of the most important days in her life?

Connie wept openly. Nothing had prepared her for this moment. Was she being penalized for waiting all of her life to find what she believed was to be the man most worthy of her hand in marriage— the man whom she wanted to father her child, the man she'd love and wanted to be with the rest of her life? All of her adult life, she'd planned for this, and even though it came late, she felt that patience had won out.

Now she was a fool driving blindly through the streets of Raleigh to get answers...an understanding of why she'd suddenly been thrown a curve ball.

Connie found a parking space, turned off the ignition, and exhaled. She sat, closed her eyes, said a prayer, and sat some more. Finally, she wiped the remaining tears from her face and blew out a puff of air. She watched as cars whizzed by, and then out of nowhere, sprinkles of water appeared on her windshield.

The slight mist of rain began to get heavy, and without giving it another thought, Connie got out of the car. She ran across the street to the county jail. A chill went through her body as she walked through the glass doors. Straight ahead was the information desk.

With a steady gait and a sense of purpose, Connie walked to the officer sitting in the information booth. Calmly, she told the officer why she was there, and he dialed a number and gave a brief synopsis to the person at the end of the line. After the officer hung up the phone, he looked at Connie and pointed her to a waiting room. Thanking the officer, she headed in the direction he'd indicated; however, before she was able to take a step, she heard her name.

Connie abruptly whipped her head around and stared at Illya who held his hand up, signaling her to wait. There was no warmth on Connie's face as she stared at the man who'd call to give her the bad news. She was ready to cuss Illya out, but before he got a word out of his mouth, Yolanda came running through the doors.

"Connie," Yolanda called out.

Connie stared at both Illya and Yolanda. Her lips remained sealed, but her chest was heaving as her breaths came heavy, in and out, in and out, as if she was blowing up a balloon. She waited for Illya to offer an explanation.

"Connie," Illya began. "Let's go somewhere private so we can talk."

"I need to get to Preston. He needs to see me."

"I agree, but let me talk with you before you go to see him."

Yolanda stood next to Illya, and it irritated Connie. It was as if Yolanda was in perfect sync with Illya. *Had she known in advance about the sting operation?*

Connie wasn't making it easy for Illya. "Connie, there is a large drug trafficking ring operating in the State of North Carolina. Its nucleus is right here in Raleigh. I work for the feds. I was sent here as part of a team to follow up on some very important leads and hopefully put this operation to bed. An important tip led me to Preston Alexander. Of course, I can't give you any details about my investigation."

"Why Preston? What has Preston done to anyone?"

Illya sighed. "Being a traveling pharmaceutical rep, he was suspect. However, once we had him under surveillance, we uncovered a Trojan horse. What we believe is that Preston unknowingly was a pawn in a larger scheme, and when he realized what was going on, it was too late for him to bow out."

"So what are you going to do about it?" Connie asked in a cold tone of voice.

Illya grabbed his braids that were tied together by a band and lifted them off his back. "I'm going to take you to where we're holding Preston and let you talk, and then we'll talk again."

"I'll go with you, sis," Yolanda offered.

Connie held up her hand. "No, I want to see Preston alone. I have a thousand questions I need to ask...private questions, and I'd prefer to be alone." Connie exhaled and looked at Illya. "I'm ready to see Preston."

Wrong Place At The Wrong Time

It was a long walk to where Preston was being held, and it felt like Connie was never going to get there. She followed Illya in silence and refused to say anything to Yolanda, who tagged along anyway. Connie wasn't allowed to take any of her personals into the room where she would finally see Preston. Yolanda waited outside.

Connie braced herself before entering the room. Sitting at what appeared to be a conference table was her beloved Preston, looking worn and weary. The room was small and confining, but at the sight of him, Connie rushed forward and held him. That's when she noticed that his hands were cuffed.

He tried to put on a brave front, but all attempts were lost when Connie began to cry.

Preston looked at Illya. "Can we have a moment alone?" he asked.

"Sure. I'll be right outside."

Illya left the room and Preston turned his attention to Connie, pained that he could not take her in his arms, comfort her.

"How did this happen, Preston?" Connie asked gently.

"I was in the wrong place at the wrong time. You have to believe me, baby; I was blindsided by it all. Dr. Cole saw an opportunity to use me. He and my father had been good friends."

"But a drug ring?"

"Drugs are what I do, Connie. I sell drugs to hospitals...to doctors and private companies. When Dr. Cole approached me about some contracts he could send my way, I was forever grateful. I saw the dollar signs. Then everything happened so fast. It was like I had been hit on the back of the head with a brick and hadn't seen the perpetrator step from the bush with the brick in his hand. It wasn't until the players began to change and Dr. Cole began to dictate orders to me that I began to suspect something. I was worried, but then the warning came about what would happen if I had a sudden change of heart."

"There wasn't anything you could do, Preston? Couldn't you have gone to the police?"

"And be a dead man?"

"My God, and now you're going to prison for...and our marriage plans..." Connie began to cry again.

"Connie, I'm so sorry. Believe me, I wanted to tell you, but I couldn't. And it contributed to the mood I've been in. I love you, Connie, and I want to be with you for the rest of my life."

Connie looked down at the beautiful princess-cut diamond ring that sat shining on her finger and sighed. She couldn't look at Preston as her thoughts at the moment were that she'd have the ring but no husband, no marriage, no baby, and no happily ever after.

"Connie," Preston called. "Connie, please, baby, don't think the worst. I've got to think things through."

"What are you talking about, Preston? You're locked up in this God-forsaken place with cuffs on your wrists. The life that we planned together isn't going to happen. In fact, I'm pissed off at you. You knew this could be your reality, but you led me to believe that our life together was only a matter of days...right around the corner."

"Connie, listen to me. Illya is working to get me exonerated."

"Exonerated how? Why didn't you say so?"

"I didn't want to say anything so as not to get your hopes up. When I said I have to think things through, I was serious. I've been given some options, but they aren't the best solution for me."

"If it means you can get out of here, why not try? What is the option?"

Preston had a forlorn look on his face. Connie held his hand to reassure him that she was still in his corner.

"The Witness Protection Program."

Connie pulled her hands away and covered her mouth. "Witness protection? You mean going undercover where your family and friends won't have any knowledge of your whereabouts? Where I won't be able to talk to YoYo, Queenie, Emma or Jackie?"

Preston nodded. "That's the size of it."

Connie sat down in the chair opposite Preston. "I don't know if I can do that, Preston. As much as I love you, I love my sister more. The thought of not being able to see her is unfathomable. She's my flesh and blood."

"I wouldn't make you endure that, and I certainly don't want to put your life in danger. It would mean that we'd be separated... that we..."

"Please don't say it, Preston. I want to be with you."

"And I want to be with you. I don't want to live my life on the run. I've tried to convince the feds that I don't know anything about the drug ring operation. My only connection to this operation was Dr. Cole and the persons I made my distribution to. I didn't know anything about those people except they were my contacts."

Connie looked hopeful. "Well...maybe there's a chance you can get from under this and...and we can live a normal life."

"It will be difficult. There's going to be a trial and lots of publicity and..." Preston stopped when the door opened.

Illya Newsome walked through the door. "Time's up." Illya looked over at Connie. "I don't know when you'll be able to see Preston again. Maybe you'll want to consider getting married here since you had planned to do so this weekend. I can arrange for a justice of the peace."

Connie looked at Illya as if he was the one taking drugs. Then she swiftly turned her head in Preston's direction. She stood up, adjusted her clothes and tapped her forehead as if Illya's suggestion had merit to it. Connie turned to Preston and her lips moved. Then she spoke.

"That's not a bad idea—getting married here. I don't mind, Preston, if you don't. I want to be your wife."

"This isn't the place to begin our life together, Connie. Vegas is where we're going to get married. We shouldn't deviate from our plan except for the fact that it won't be this weekend. Go to Vegas with your girlfriends, but I promise you, Connie Maxwell, we'll go back—just you and me and do it right."

Connie smiled. "If we wait, I want to get married at Shiloh Baptist Church and let Pastor O'Neill officiate."

"I want whatever you want."

"Okay, we'll wait." Connie kissed Preston on the lips and said goodbye. Although her heart was heavy, she didn't feel like it was the end of the road.

Friendships Matter

Queenie sat in her cubicle, shifting back and forth in her seat. She had repeatedly called Yolanda and Connie yesterday evening, but neither of them had answered their phone nor had the courtesy to return the call. What could this mean?

A priority email flashed across her computer screen. It was from Jock Atwater who was writing the story on Preston and the drug trafficking ring. Queenie quickly sat up in her seat, and opened the email.

Ms. Jackson, disregard the article I sent you last week. I've had to rewrite the entire thing as a new turn of events has altered some of my information. I will send you a new article in a few hours. Please get it ready for immediate publication—Jock Atwater.

Queenie sat stock still. Something had happened over the weekend and she'd bet any amount of money that it involved Preston. She bet that was the reason she was unable to get Connie. She could feel her blood pressure rise and got up from her seat and walked around for a bit to try and ease her nerves.

Helpless, Queenie sat back down at her desk and dialed Jackie's number.

"Good morning, Jackie."

"Hey, Q, you're calling awfully early this morning," Jackie said with a smile on her face.

"Yeah, yeah. Look, something happened after we left Connie's shower on Saturday."

"What, Q? She's all right, isn't she? Please don't tell me Preston changed his mind. It wouldn't be fair to Connie."

"No, nothing like that…at least I hope it isn't."

"What do you mean, you hope it isn't?"

"Let me talk. I tried calling Connie and Yolanda last night, but they didn't answer and I haven't heard from either one of them. Then the reporter I edit for, you know the one I'm talking about, sent me an email this morning stating that he needed to can his first story due to something that recently went down. I can only imagine what it could be. And I'm sure Connie and possibly Yolanda are aware of something."

"Should I say something to Franklin?"

"No," Queenie admonished. "I don't have any facts yet. I was worried about not hearing back from the girls. We have to stick together."

"You're right, Q. Look, update me when you get some more news. Right now, I'm in the middle of something and I need to get back to it. Call me in a little while."

"Yeah, I'm sure you're in the middle of something." Queenie smiled and hung up the phone. The only thing she could do now was wait on the revised version of the reporter's article.

Working On It

Emma looked forward to going to Vegas this weekend. She'd already packed her clothes, took a couple of days off from work, and was ready to wish Connie and Preston well on their marriage. Weddings always made Emma happy. It meant new beginnings, and this new beginning had been long in the making for Connie. You didn't have to be a spring chicken to experience the joys of love.

All of the talk about the wedding and the fun time she'd had at Connie's bridal shower made her think about her relationship with Billy. They were like ships passing in the night—trudging along in the same body of water, but detached from each other. No one really cared what the other was doing, so long as there was companionship in knowing that each was nearby at the end of the day. But they were working on it.

Billy had been nothing but a wonderful husband to Emma. He adored her; she adored him. They raised their children to be respectable citizens. They paid their taxes, went to church—well Billy hadn't been to the sanctuary in a while, opting to hit the green and play golf rather than giving the Lord his time. Something had to change; she had to change. It was time to be a real husband and wife again.

Another World

Yolanda sat under the dryer at her favorite hair salon. Two days had gone by and she had yet to talk to Connie. Yolanda couldn't believe that Connie had clammed up on her like that. It wasn't her fault that Preston was a resident at the Wake County Jail.

"Hey, girl," Reecy, Yolanda's hairdresser, said, banging on the top of the hairdryer. Reecy pulled up the hood and felt Yolanda's hair. "You're good and dry. Let me put some pretty curls in your hair. I love your silver."

"Thanks, Reecy. You've kept it looking good all these years."

"Haven't I though. Let's go to the chair so I can work my magic."

Yolanda sat down in the chair, and Reecy went to work. Yolanda closed her eyes and let her mind wander to the day she'd met Illya and the fact that he was now somehow tied to her sister's fiancé. She wondered if Illya had been following her all along.

Looking back at how she'd been drawn to him like a magnet, Yolanda felt she had fallen into Illya's trap. Still, there was something about Illya that made her question this reasoning. It had to be coincidence.

"What's up, Yolanda? You're too quiet. Your mouth is usually running ninety miles-a-minute. You're somewhere else...in another world."

"I'm concerned about my sister."

"Isn't she getting married on Saturday? I heard about the Passion Party you threw under the guise of 'bridal shower.'"

"It was a hit. The sisterhood is now armed with the power to make themselves happy with or without a man."

"That sounds healthy, but you already know I've got a few toys tucked away in my toy chest."

Yolanda laughed. "Do you know what Taylor called us?"

"Who's Taylor?"

"The Passion Party rep. She said we were silver bullets."

"Like the Silver Bullet that makes women happy?" Reecy grinned from ear to ear.

Yolanda laughed out loud. "What Taylor meant was that we are still fabulous even though we've passed our prime. Every woman at the party was probably close to or over fifty, some with silver or gray in their hair, though they may have been hiding it."

"Your hair is so pretty." Reecy put the last bump in Yolanda's hair and smoothed it down with a comb.

Yolanda smiled, checking herself out in the wall to wall mirror. "Life isn't over at fifty," she said, as if speaking to her reflection. "Some women are only beginning to live. It's the new thirty. Or so I've heard people say."

Reecy's hands were still as she met Emma's eyes in the mirror. "Are you feeling lonely now that you and Eric have gone your separate ways?"

Yolanda laughed. "Reecy, I don't miss that knucklehead at all. I do have a new love interest though."

"A new love interest and you didn't tell me?" Reecy picked up a can of hairspray and lightly sprayed Yolanda's hair. She removed the towel from Yolanda's shoulders.

"My hair looks fabulous as always, Reecy. You must be vying for a double tip."

"I'll take it if you're blessing me with it. So tell me about the new love in your life."

"He's tall, handsome, and wears dreads."

"You're dating someone with dreads? He must've been the last crumb in the bag."

"When I say he's handsome, that word doesn't do him justice. He's drop dead gorgeous. Normally, I wouldn't be attracted to a man with braids in his hair, but this one could be a keeper."

"Sounds too good to be true."

"Well, like most men his age, he does come with some baggage. He is recently divorced, and from everything he's told me, it was pretty ugly. He has two daughters that are trying to make it in the world—one is trying to be an actress while the other wants to be a singer. They've both graduated from college."

"So he's not paying child support."

"That's a feather in his cap. The one drawback is that he works undercover…for the feds."

"A spy?"

"Something like that. Reecy, I don't know if I'd be comfortable being around a person all the time whose nature is to be suspicious, who snoops for a living. I'd be constantly looking over my shoulder."

"But if you truly love him, it won't matter."

"I'm not in love; I'm having fun."

"Oh, that's how it is. So what's up with your sister that you're so concerned about? I hear Preston knocked it out of the park with the ring he put on her finger."

"It's beautiful…"

"But …?"

Yolanda rose from the chair and brushed herself off. "I want my sister to be happy."

"You worry too much, YoYo. Connie is a grown-ass woman. She can take care of herself. Give them some space."

Yolanda smiled; it was all she could do. She gave Reecy a double tip and a sisterly hug. Though the conversation had left her unsettled as she'd been before, at least she looked good.

Headline News

Fresh from lunch, Queenie stretched her arms and settled into her seat. She swiveled back and forth in her chair, thinking about Connie and what she might be going through. In another breath, Queenie wondered why she was so concerned when neither Connie nor Yolanda had the decency to return any of her phone calls.

Queenie sighed and logged on to her terminal. She jerked her head when she realized that Jock had sent her another email. Queenie wasted no time pulling up the message and reading.

Last night, federal agents busted members of a drug trafficking ring in the Unites States. More than a dozen people, including several prominent individuals from the Raleigh area, were caught in a dragnet. They are reportedly major players in the ring centered in Wake County.

Dr. Marshall Cole, CEO of one of Raleigh's leading hospitals, is said to be one of the masterminds of the organization that runs as far north as New York and as far south as Bolivia. Several pharmaceutical representatives, acting as distribution agents for Dr. Cole, were also arrested. However, according to the Federal Bureau of Investigation, the reps may serve a minimal amount of time as it is believed they were unknowingly used as pawns to advance Dr. Cole's agenda. As more arrests are made and the bizarre details unfold, people will be calling this chapter in Raleigh's history, the Tale of Two Cities.

Queenie rubbed her eyes and reread the text. She proofed and edited, readying it for publication. When she was done, Queenie pushed back from her desk with the tip of her finger in her mouth. She wondered if she should warn Connie. Preston's name wouldn't appear in the text, yet, but once the story broke, there was no controlling what would happen. She sighed.

"What do I do?"

Queenie's work phone rang, breaking the silence and cutting into her thoughts. She picked it up on the second ring and was surprised to hear Yolanda's voice.

"What's up, Yolanda?" Queenie began hesitantly. "I've been trying to get up with you to make sure everything is on for this weekend."

"Yes, the trip is on. Let's get together this evening to discuss the details. I've spoken with Emma and she's on task."

Queenie rolled her eyes. After what she'd read only moments ago, why hadn't the wedding been called off? Surely, Connie was aware that Preston had been arrested. She didn't know it to be a fact but second sense told her it was so after reading Jock's article. "Sure," Queenie finally said. "Where do you want to meet?"

"Connie's house at six o'clock. You may want to bring your pj's; the pre-celebration is on."

Queenie stalled, her mind doing flip flops as she assessed and processed the information in her mind. "I'll be there. I don't know about all that celebrating since I have to be at work tomorrow."

"Loosen up, Q. See you at six."

Setting the receiver in its cradle, Queenie mulled over her conversation with Yolanda. Something was wrong, and she couldn't put her finger on it. Yolanda didn't seem herself. And why hadn't she asked the reason for Queenie's calls? There were no answers to be found in her office. The only thing to do was be at Connie's house at six.

What's So Urgent?

Queenie pulled up in front of Emma's house and waited for her to come out. She had been beating her head up against the wall since Yolanda called, racking her brain about the sudden invitation to come to Connie's. It would've been as easy to explain what they intended to do over the weekend on the phone. Something else was afoot.

Tapping the steering wheel with her thumb, Queenie watched as Emma kissed Billy on her way out of the house. For a second, Queenie thought about Linden. She couldn't understand how a loser like Linden could still be worthy of her thoughts. He was a cancer invading her body; every time she tried to rid herself of him, without warning he would come worming himself back into her life. He wasn't good for her. "I've got to get him out of my system," Queenie murmured to herself.

Queenie jumped when Emma knocked on the passenger car window. "Open up."

"Hold your horses, Ms. Emma." Queenie unlocked the door and Emma got in.

"What's the big emergency, Q? Do you think Connie called off the wedding?"

"Didn't Yolanda tell you the reason for the meeting?"

"She said it was to discuss this weekend. But who calls someone in the middle of the day about having a meeting, making it sound all urgent and everything?"

"You've got to ask questions, Emma."

"So…what did Yolanda tell you when you asked, Ms. Smarty Pants?"

"That we were going to discuss this weekend."

Emma turned and looked at Queenie. "For real, Q? Let's go so we can get the details."

Queenie smiled to herself. She loved getting Emma all worked up.

Connie's house came into view. Queenie became confused when she saw First Lady's car parked in the driveway and another on the street that she didn't recognize. She parked the car. As if reading her thoughts, Emma hit Queenie on the arm.

"I didn't know Jackie was going to Vegas. If Jackie's going, you know that everything that happens in Vegas isn't going to stay in Vegas. Everyone at Shiloh Baptist Church is going to know that we're some gambling Silver Bullets."

"You knew Jackie was going to Vegas. As soon as we said she could go, she went online and made her reservations. Lord, don't let me meet a nice young fellow. For sure everyone's going to know. In fact, I can bet money on it that Jackie will phone Franklin and tell him about our escapades before we land back in Raleigh."

Queenie and Emma laughed out loud. "Girl, I can hear Jackie now telling Franklin all of our business. We're going to have to lock her ass up in the closet while we have some fun."

"Emma, I was thinking the same thing. Girl, we think too much alike. Well, we better go find out what's going on."

"You reckon?" Emma and Queenie broke out in laughter as they exited the car and headed for the door.

Before either Emma or Queenie could knock on the door, it

opened. Yolanda stood behind the door and held it open to let them in. Both Emma and Queenie looked at Yolanda with quizzical eyes before following her into the living room, still trying to understand the nature of the impromptu meeting..

They stopped in their tracks. Not only were Pastor O'Neill and his faithful wife, First Lady Jackie O'Neill, present, but standing in the room off to the side was Preston and Yolanda's new boyfriend, Illya Newsome.

Connie was there as well, dressed in a stark-white dress, sleek but elegant. Queenie guessed Vera Wang. Preston was also dressed up; a black-tweed blazer, black slacks, and a white dress shirt. Yolanda wore a pretty pastel-pink chiffon dress that hit below her knees, and Illya wore a black suit over a pink polo shirt. Pastor O'Neill and First Lady O'Neill were dressed in matching beige-colored suits—Pastor O'Neill wore a cocoa-colored shirt with a tie that blended, while the First Lady wore a chocolate-brown-polyester brown blouse with a bow that tied at the neckline. Queenie felt out of place.

Connie's face was somber; so was the entire room.

Queenie didn't know what to think. Jock Atwater's article specifically stated that several pharmaceutical reps had been arrested, and although Preston's name didn't appear in the recent article, it had been in the first. What was going on? She looked around the room and then at Emma whose eyes were going back and forth, similarly assessing the situation.

Connie went to Preston and took his hand, intertwining their fingers. They moved to the middle of the group. Connie smiled. So did Preston. They then turned to the group who had gathered.

"Thank you all for coming on such short notice. I'm sure you're wondering why you've been asked to come here tonight. While we didn't see this coming, at least not at this moment, Preston and I have something to share with you."

Preston took over. "Connie and I are getting married. Tonight. Reverend O'Neill has graciously offered to marry us. We were going to wait, but since we already have our marriage license and we love each other," Connie smiled at Preston, "we didn't want to wait any longer."

Queenie's face went numb. When she recovered, Queenie chanced a look at Jackie, but Jackie's face was pointed directly in Connie and Preston's direction. Queenie then looked at Emma whose hand covered her chest, clueless and in utter awe.

Queenie was going to kill Jackie. Jackie knew this little shindig was going down and she should have had the decency to give her a heads-up, after all the sharing she'd done. Jackie was well aware of the trouble Preston was in. Yet, here she was, standing next to her husband while he made preparations to officiate a wedding Queenie'd had to learn about in the past few minutes.

Connie and Preston stood facing each other in obvious adoration. Their eyes never left each other as Pastor O'Neill performed the wedding ceremony. Yolanda served as Connie's Matron of Honor, while Illya stood close by Preston's side.

Pastor O'Neill went on and on with his sermonette about what a marriage between two people was and how they were to conduct themselves and so on and so on. Queenie's feet were hurting from standing the past twenty minutes, but they seemed rejuvenated by the time Pastor O'Neill asked them to repeat their vows.

"Do you, Connie Maxwell, take Preston Alexander to be your lawfully wedded husband?"

"I do," Connie said before Pastor O'Neill could finish his line.

"Well, all right then," Pastor O'Neill said. "Repeat after me. I…"

"I, Connie Maxwell, take you, Preston Alexander, to be my lawfully wedded husband, to have and to hold from this day forward, for better or for worse, for richer, for poorer, in sickness and in health, to love and to cherish, until death do us part."

Preston was next, reciting his vows with the same eagerness. Queenie and Emma looked on in utter amazement though for different reasons.

"I now pronounce you husband and wife. You may kiss the bride."

Pastor O'Neill stood back while Preston enveloped Connie in his arms and gave her the biggest, sloppiest kiss any of those present had witnessed at a wedding in a long time.

"They're acting like starving animals," Emma whispered. "They need to get a room."

"You're right about that, Emma, but I wonder where they're going live…whose house they'll be sleeping at."

"That's none of your business, Queenie Jackson. No one is saying anything about that Jheri curl wearing boyfriend you're sneaking around with."

Queenie's head snapped in Emma's direction. "So, who's been talking about me behind my back? You and you? Keep your nose in your house; you may look up one day and find Billy cooking fried chicken for someone else."

"You're a bitter old woman."

"You started it, heifer. The question we should be entertaining is why in the hell did Connie and Preston get married with a two-hour notice? She couldn't possibly be pregnant."

Emma laughed. "Q, you say some of the craziest things. Here comes Jackie."

"Ignore her."

"Why?"

"I said so."

"Hey, Q and Emma. Wasn't this a surprise?"

Queenie frowned and ignored Jackie's question.

"I certainly was surprised," Emma said. "Why didn't they wait until they got to Vegas?"

Jackie's eyes went straight to Queenie who refused to open her mouth.

"Well," Emma said, confusion written on her face. "Maybe the bride and groom will answer the question for us. They're coming this way."

Connie and Preston's arms were locked together. "Thank you guys for coming on such short notice," Connie said in a pageant voice.

"What about Vegas?" Emma asked. "I've got this non-refundable airline ticket…"

Preston jumped in to provide an answer. "Connie and I looked forward to getting married this weekend, but business has dictated that I stay in North Carolina."

"Uhm hmm," Queenie said under her breath.

"And," Preston continued, "since Connie already has her ticket to go to Vegas, I suggested that she go on and enjoy the town with you guys."

Queenie spoke up for the first time. "The reason we were going to Vegas in the first place was to be witnesses at your wedding. I feel like I got cheated. Yeah, I can still go to Vegas and have a good time but not for the reason intended. I spent my last dime on a gorgeous dress that I won't get to wear."

"Come on, Q," Yolanda jumped in, dragging Illya with her. "You can dress up when we go see Boyz II Men perform. I've got tickets for everyone. My treat."

Queenie sighed. "Well, I guess that won't be a problem since you're buying."

"Okay, everyone, since that problem is resolved, please pick up your champagne glass so we can toast the bride and groom," Yolanda chimed.

Everyone did as Yolanda instructed. She held her glass high. "To the bride and groom. To my sister, Connie, and her husband, Preston. Congratulations."

"Congratulations," everyone said in unison.

Silver Bullets

They all sat waiting to board the plane, including First Lady Jackie O'Neill. Freshly laundered at their favorite salon and spa, and dressed in colorful midi-dresses and fashionable sandals, they looked like yesterday's beauty queens. Everyone, excluding Queenie, wore their natural hair. Connie was the only one with ninety-five percent of her hair still black.

There should've been a lot of excitement about the trip, but they weren't their talkative selves. Yolanda seemed to smother Connie, acting like her guard dog, possibly to protect her sister from questions sure to come up after Connie's shotgun wedding to Preston.

"Good afternoon. In five minutes, we will begin boarding all passengers on U.S. Airways Flight 1164, leaving Raleigh/Durham at twelve-fifty p.m. with connections in Charlotte. We will pre-board all passengers who need assistance now."

"That's us," Connie said, trying to be cheerful.

"Yes, it is," First Lady Jackie said in agreement. "I'm looking forward to this trip. I even brought one of my toys from the Passion Party you had at the shower, Connie."

Everyone looked at Jackie with surprise and the word "stupid" written across their faces.

"What did you bring, Jackie?" Queenie wanted to know.

"My Silver Bullet. Ohhh, you guys don't know…"

"We know," Queenie said, holding her hand out for Jackie to stop. "We'll make sure you have some time alone. Ain't nobody wanting to be experiencing your pleasure moment."

The laughter broke the ice.

"I wouldn't have believed she said it if I hadn't heard it for myself," Emma said, scrunching up her nose in disgust. "Keep that stuff to yourself."

"You all are the heathens that introduced me to the products. Now, I'm supposed to be quiet? Shoot, Franklin and I have had some of our best days."

"Jackie," Yolanda gawked, although she tried to suppress her laughter. "TMI—too much information, girlfriend. Those are secrets that should be kept between you and Franklin."

"Yeah, Jackie," Emma said.

"Are you jealous, Emma? When was the last time you and Billy got your freak on? The only thing that man is a freak about is a fried chicken drumstick."

The crew had loosened up. Everyone slapped their hands on their thighs and tried not to strangle themselves on their saliva from laughing so hard.

"That was wrong, Jackie," Yolanda said, "but I could visualize it. Next time you'll keep your mouth shut, Emma."

"The hell with y'all. I'm getting ready to board this plane so I can go and have some fun. You won't be laughing when I hit the jackpot."

"They're only playing with you, Emma," Queenie said. "No harm intended."

"It wasn't at your expense, Q."

"Not this time. Okay, they're calling for our section to board. Let's rock and roll."

Queenie, Emma, and Jackie were in a row together, while Yolanda and Connie sat behind them.

"Our girl is awfully quiet," Jackie, who was seated inbetween her two friends, whispered to Queenie.

"I shouldn't even be talking to you. You left me high and dry the other night."

"How did I do that?"

Queenie pointed her thumb toward the row behind them. "You could've at least told me that Connie was getting married."

"I was in the dark like you were," Jackie whispered. "I had no idea what was going on until Franklin told me, and then we were already in the car on our way to Connie's."

"Jackie, you're telling a lie. Why were you and Pastor dressed alike?"

"He told me what to wear. He called home and told me we needed to be some place in a couple of hours and for me to be dressed and to have his clothes lying out."

"I'll excuse your behind this time. I hate to be out of the loop."

"You hate that you didn't know first; that's what this is all about."

"What are you and Queenie whispering about?" Emma asked, cutting in on their conversation. "We aren't going to have any of that crap on this trip."

"Gotcha," Queenie said, giving Emma a thumbs-up.

Confession Is Good
For The Soul

The plane landed safely at McCarran International Airport. Slot machines were scattered throughout the airport adding to the mystique of a city that was alive and full of adventure. The weather was balmy with a few scattered clouds in the sky. However, people floated past, dressed for the desert, as if they'd lived there all of their lives.

"The shuttle will be outside in a few minutes," Yolanda said to the group after placing a call to the hotel. "I'm ready to have some fun."

"Me, too," Jackie shouted, ready to explore her new-found freedom without the reverend in her back pocket. Everyone's head jerked around in disbelief.

"I can't wait," Queenie added, putting on her sun shades as they walked outside. "If I win some money, I may not be going back to Raleigh with you hyenas."

Everyone laughed.

"This was supposed to be mine and Preston's official wedding day," Connie finally said at last.

"It's a shame that his job wouldn't let him off for such an important day," Queenie added.

"I agree," Emma interjected. "Maybe he can still meet you, Connie."

"Not this trip, but we do plan to come out…alone."

No one said another word.

The shuttle arrived.

The women were whisked away anxious to begin their weekend of fun. When the driver pulled into the Bellagio, the ladies were mesmerized. The Bellagio was massive and towering, its arms outstretched, welcoming every visitor to its premises. A fountain that stretched the length of the hotel was breathtaking and the ladies couldn't get enough.

"They have a Fountain of Bellagio show throughout the day that we must do," Connie said, a little more upbeat and seemingly ready to enjoy.

"Wait until you see the room," Yolanda put in. "I've taken it upon myself to put us in the Lago two-bedroom suite. I didn't think we should have anything less."

The ladies paid the taxi while Yolanda handled the reservations. Soon they were following the bellhop to their suite. The ladies walked in and their mouths dropped to the floor.

"Lord, I've gone to heaven," First Lady Jackie said, twirling around in the room. "This is living."

Yolanda paid the bellhop and proceeded with giving directions. "Connie and I are going to take the master suite. The other room has two queen beds. It'll be up to you all to decide how you're going to sleep."

"I'm going to be in a bed by myself," Queenie said, not waiting for either Emma or Jackie's input.

"That's fine with me," Jackie said, scrunching her nose up at Queenie behind her back. "Nothing is going to stop me from enjoying this weekend."

"This place is magnificent," Queenie drooled, looking around and touching everything.

"We have a fully stocked refreshment center, a remote control for the Roman shades, jetted tubs, a fully furnished living room, flat-screen televisions, and for you, Q, the wool-throw blankets are four-hundred-count. The bathrooms are marble."

"How big is this?" Queenie asked. "It looks larger than the house I live in."

"It is one thousand, nine-hundred and forty-three square feet," Yolanda said. "As you can see, I did my homework."

"You did good, sister Yolanda," Queenie said. "I better win some money so I can pay for all of this finery."

Everyone laughed.

"I feel like Carrie Bradshaw in *Sex and the City*," Connie said, sitting down, but taking it all in.

Emma rushed to her side. "But you're married, Connie. Carrie Bradshaw didn't make it down the aisle, even though that girl was dressed to the nines. Remember, her fiancé, Big, got cold feet. But Preston put a ring on your finger and we were all witnesses to your happy day."

"Everybody, take a seat," Connie said. Queenie, Jackie, and Emma grew quiet. They took a seat opposite Connie, while Yolanda sat on the arm of the couch, seeming very concerned.

Connie dropped her head, sighed, and looked at everyone except Yolanda. "I have something I need to tell you. As my friends, I feel it's important that I share this with you. The weight of what I'm about to tell you is heavy on my shoulders, and in order for this to be a halfway decent weekend, I need to come clean."

"You're scaring me, Connie," Emma said.

"Let her talk," Yolanda said in a pissed tone of voice while waving her finger.

Emma looked at Yolanda as if she was crazy. "What's up with you?"

Yolanda didn't acknowledge Emma's question. She tapped her foot on the floor and looked straight at Connie.

"I love Preston Alexander with all of my heart. As I said earlier today, this was supposed to be our special day." Connie paused and looked up at Yolanda who looked away. "I'm sure you are wondering, with the exception of First Lady Jackie, why Preston and I didn't wait until today. I told you his job kept him away, and that's partially true, but it isn't the total truth."

Queenie pinched Jackie, who squirmed in her seat. Emma seemed distraught.

"Preston is in the custody of the FBI."

"Oh," gasped Queenie, pretending she didn't know anything. She threw her hands over her face for effect.

"Anyway, Preston was caught up in big drug bust that went down last week." The room was eerily quiet.

"I read something in the paper about a big drug bust," Emma rushed to say, " but I don't remember seeing anything about Preston."

Connie continued. "Well, he was a pawn in the operation, and initially didn't know what was going on. Some very big and prominent people in Raleigh...in the Research Triangle Park are being indicted as part of this drug ring. The involvement extends up the eastern seaboard and down to South America, I'm told. I'm surprised that you didn't know this, Q, since you work on the paper."

"I would've said something."

Connie didn't respond. She cut her eyes away from Queenie. Everyone was silent while Connie took her time composing her words.

"The feds believe that Preston wasn't a key player, although he took money on behalf of the person he was working for. For his testimony, Preston will serve a very light sentence and will then be put in the Witness Protection Program."

Tears began to run down Yolanda's face. She got up and went into the bathroom with Jackie at her heels.

"Wherever Preston goes, I'm going with him. It may mean that I won't see you all for a very long time. Preston doesn't want to go into the Witness Protection Program since he had no knowledge of the real big players, except for one, but if it means security for his family, and that includes me, then he may choose to go that route.

"The reason I chose this moment to tell you this was to put to rest all the questions, your opinions, and most of all your curiosity. You got it? I want to enjoy this weekend without reservations. Now that the cat has got everyone's tongue, I guess it's time to have some fun. Okay, I'm going to my room to shower and change. And I'm hungry. I'll see you in a few."

Queenie and Emma sat in the living room until Connie was out of sight.

"So you knew all along that Preston was in jail," Emma hissed at Queenie. "Yes, Ms. Newspaper Lady, Connie was talking about you."

"That damn Jackie can't keep her mouth shut for nothing."

"Oh, so Jackie was good enough for you to tell, but no, don't tell Emma. She'll tell the world."

"It wasn't like that, Emma. When I found out, I wasn't sure who to confide in. Jackie was the first person that came to my mind. I thought maybe if she told Pastor, maybe he would say something to Connie...you know, warn her. My job could be in jeopardy for sharing classified information with one person, I didn't want to make it worse by sharing with two. And I only shared in the first place as I was truly concerned about Connie."

"It's okay, Queenie. You did what you felt was best. I have to give you credit for that."

"You're not mad at me, Emma?"

"No, girl, I'm not mad at you, especially if you plot and plan with me to play a few fun tricks on Jackie."

"Emma, you know I'm good for it. Let's go change so we can paint the town."

What Happens In Vegas

The ladies emerged from the room as if nothing had transpired only an hour before. Connie was seemingly in a good mood, and Yolanda seemed to have recovered from her sister's announcement. Dressed in colorful sundresses that hit right at the knee, the group of five set off to discover Las Vegas. Tomorrow they would all luxuriate at the spa and salon that was offered at the hotel and round the evening out at a Las Vegas show featuring Boyz II Men. Queenie wanted to see Celine Dion. But since she wasn't paying for the affair, she'd go anywhere Yolanda's money said she was going.

They strolled through the streets of Las Vegas, although it felt like a sin to leave the Bellagio with its many attractions.

"On Sunday, we should go to Jasmine for the Fountain Brunch," Connie said. "The fountain dances to different music tunes that they set."

"That sounds wonderful, Connie," First Lady said, enjoying herself. "But right now, I'm ready to do some shopping."

"That's what this afternoon is all about, First Lady," Yolanda stated. "Maybe you'll find some pretty hats to wear on Sunday."

"I'm not looking for any hats. I want to buy some new dresses."

"You're going to pay a lot of money for them here, Jackie," Queenie said. "We can tell you don't get anywhere too often."

"Queenie, don't you worry about me. My boo gave me spending money, and I'm going to spend every dime."

"Whatever."

"Okay, Queenie and Jackie, I'm here for a good time. I don't want no mess out of either of you," Emma said. "In fact, this place looks like a great stop for eating and gambling."

"Lead the way, Ms. Emma," Jackie said. "I don't mind stuffing my face before I do a little shopping." The ladies laughed.

The ladies stopped at one of the local casinos and ate. After downing their meal, they went into the casino and dropped quarters in the machine until they had exhausted their limit. First Lady Jackie O'Neill loved pulling the black bandit, and she was the only one who went away with more than she came with.

"Let's go to the Venetian," Yolanda said. "The Grand Canal Shoppes at the Venetian will wet your taste buds. They have a Banana Republic and Ann Taylor there."

"I can't wear anything out of those stores," Queenie whined. "Take me to a real mall."

"Please," Emma said under her breath. "You could've stayed home and did that. Live a little, Q."

"That's easy for you to say, Emma Jean. Your butt can fit into a size ten."

"It's all about the fellowship, Q. We're going to make you happy too." Yolanda locked her arm in Queenie's; it made Queenie blush.

The ladies shopped, ate, and had tons of fun. By the time they were done, they were weary from their all-day excursion in the mall and only wanted to soak their bodies and go to sleep.

Fresh from a good night's sleep, the ladies readied themselves for the spa and salon. Their reservations had already been made, timed to make sure they would all be there at the same time; even if one or two of them had to wait a half-hour or so until it was their turn.

"I can't wait to get my Bellagio Signature Massage," Connie said. "I need the kinks worked out of my tense muscles."

"What are you getting, Yolanda?" Emma asked. "I'm getting one of the facials, but I don't remember which one."

"I' m having the Bellagio Signature Stone Massage and the Coconut Milk Bath. The stones are so soothing."

"It sounds expensive to me," Queenie said with a sneer. "I don't know why you guys are acting all bourgeoisie, like money ain't nothing."

"You've got money, Q, with your cheap-ass self," Yolanda retorted. "If I wasn't so nice, I'd let you pay your own way to the show tonight. Now shut your trap and don't spoil it for anyone else."

"Queenie isn't going to spoil anything for me," First Lady said. "I'm going to have one of those Brazilian and Beyond waxes that was listed on the brochure. I've always wanted to know what it would be like. I may even have a rose tattooed on the spot."

"Jackie, what in the hell are you talking about?" Queenie asked with a perplexed look on her face. "A Brazilian wax for what?"

"MindYourBusiness.com, Queenie Jackson. This isn't for you. And when I get finished, I'm going to put on my cute one-piece bathing suit I bought, and lay out in front of that gorgeous pool we have downstairs. Anyone want to join me?"

"That woman is crazy," Queenie said, twirling her finger near her head to further emphasize her meaning.

"Ohhhhhhhh, ohhhhhhh," sang Yolanda. "First Lady, you're bad. Give me five on that one."

Emma and Connie laughed.

"And what will Pastor Franklin O'Neill say about his wife…"

"Hold that thought, Queenie. What did you think I was going to do in Las Vegas? Sit up in the room and look out of the window while everyone else has a good time? Well, I've got news for you, Ms. Thing, who's dating a man still wearing a Jheri Curl from three decades ago."

Yolanda hit the floor, she was laughing so hard.

First Lady wasn't done. "I love the Lord and I love myself some Franklin. I'm a Christian, but I'm not dead. I've still got a gorgeous body that's going to rock this new swimming suit. You see, Ms. Queenie Jackson, I may turn heads even though no one is going to touch. And you can do that when you don't have titties that hang to the floor and look like metal detectors searching for loose change."

The women were busting a gut. First Lady had shut Queenie down.

But it wasn't like Queenie to let anything go. "You backsliding, supposed to be a Christian, little wench," she said.

"At least I'm sleeping with my husband every night."

"Okay, guys," Yolanda cut in. "Queenie, you started it, and I do believe Jackie finished it." Yolanda chuckled. "But...ooh Lord, you guys need to let it go so we don't miss our appointments."

"You all go without me," Queenie said, mad as hell.

"It'll be charged to your room as a no-show," Connie said.

Queenie picked up her stuff and headed for the door. "This is the worst vacation I've ever had. Stay out of my way, Jackie O'Neill." Queenie brushed past everyone and headed out the door. She wasn't about to pay for a spa appointment and not reap the benefits.

"You got her good, Jackie," Emma said, wiping the tears from her eyes. "I didn't know you had it in you."

"There's a lot you don't know about First Lady Jackie, but it doesn't matter right now. I'm on my way to get my Brazilian wax."

"You're all right with me," Yolanda said. And everyone gave Jackie a high-five.

The spa was serene. From the dimly lit rooms, to the tan-colored walls, wicker partitions, and large potted plants, you couldn't help but feel cozy.

"It's too quiet in here," Queenie said. She'd been hoping for a different kind of experience.

"Come on, lighten up," Jackie said. "Yes, I told Connie about the article, but my conscience is clear. Sorry, Q."

"Forget it, Jackie. I'm trying not to spoil anyone's time here. Go get your Brazilian Wax and leave me the hell alone."

Jackie went her way and left the others to their own devices.

They were done several hours later, and famished. Four of the five ladies opted for a quick bite to eat at the Race and Sports Book. Jackie went straight to the room, where she put on her new pink and lavender one-piece bathing suit with a matching sarong. She took one dip in the pool and sat on a lounger nearby and drifted off to sleep.

Twenty minutes into her lounging, Jackie's eyes fluttered. She sat up with a start, feeling as if something had come over her. That's when she saw a handsome man standing over her and staring.

"How are you pretty lady?" asked the ebony gentleman with the amber eyes and pretty white teeth.

Jackie jerked her head from side to side as if she was on neighborhood watch before pointing to herself. "Are you talking to me?"

"You're the prettiest lady I see for my miles," the handsome gentleman said.

Jackie made sure her sarong covered the meaty part of her legs. "Uhm, I'm fine."

"Are you here by yourself—no husband or boyfriend?"

Jackie covered her mouth with her hand and pretended to blush. She was embarrassed, if anything. She dropped her hand to her chest. "I'm here with my girlfriends, but I'm married." She flung out her hand with her wedding ring on it.

"As fine as you are, you don't need to be out here by yourself. You're working that bathing suit."

"This old thing?" Jackie lied, eating up the gentleman's compliments.

"Old or new, you look absolutely gorgeous in it. What's your name?"

"Jackie. And yours?"

"Shaw, Reuben Shaw. Do you mind if I sit next to you for a moment?"

Jackie looked frightened. The proper thing to say was *no, he couldn't sit there*. But in the midst of fumbling for the right words to say, Jackie opened her mouth and out came "no, I don't mind."

Reuben sat on the edge of the lounger and made small talk with Jackie. She rather enjoyed his conversation."

"I'm going to give you my card so that if you're in the area in the near future you can give me a call. I would love to have your number."

"I'm a married woman, as I've already said. However, I'll give you my number in the event you find yourself in Raleigh, North Carolina on a Sunday and want to stop by my church."

Reuben smiled and wrote Jackie's number on the back of one of the cards he'd fished out of his pocket. They had a few laughs, touched each other a couple of times, and when Reuben announced that he'd better be going, he leaned over and kissed Jackie lightly on the lips. She waved goodbye but kept touching her lips in disbelief.

The girls could never know.

"Was that Jackie kissing that man?" Emma asked as she began to sprint toward Jackie.

"Girl, First Lady has some explaining to do," Connie said.

"I love it; I love it," Yolanda said. "Jackie has flown all the way from North Carolina, got a Brazilian wax, and had some stranger kiss her on the mouth in twenty-four hours. That's barely a day. Go, Jackie."

"I wonder what the right Reverend Franklin O'Neill would say if he should by chance come into this bit of information? I can see the headlines: Minister Kills Wife After Learning of Las Vegas Affair."

"You're mean, Q," Yolanda said. "What happens in Vegas stays in Vegas. Think about your own headline if Linden Robinson finds out that you want to bring another man into your house to reside. Be careful where you throw stones; that's all I'm saying."

Silver Bullets

Emma, Connie, and Yolanda with Queenie trailing behind rushed to where Jackie still lounged and pounced on her. Jackie snapped to the upright position, pushing the sensations caused by the kiss deep down into her gut.

"Jackie, girl, we saw that handsome man put some sugar smacks on you," Emma said with a broad smile on her face.

Connie pushed Jackie aside and sat on the lounger. "We know you liked it. Look at you; can't even pretend that nothing happened. Don't try and fake it with us."

"Did you all see that honey bun sitting next to Diva Jackie? How in the world did that happen?" Yolanda wanted to know.

Jackie looked up into the faces of her girlfriends and let go of a smile. "You don't have any questions, Q?"

Queenie refused to buy into Jackie's moment. It might have been jealousy, but she wasn't going to give Jackie the satisfaction of boosting her ego.

"Well, it was nothing...really," Jackie said, ignoring Queenie's stares. "I was minding my own business when the nice gentleman stopped in front of me, said hello, and told me that I was beautiful." Jackie laughed at the memory.

"So how did he get to sit down and then plant that kiss on your lips?" Yolanda said. She pointed to Connie, Emma, Queenie, and herself. "All four of us saw it with our own eyes."

Jackie seemed flustered. "Well, he kept talking and asking questions...like what's your name and where are you from...and before I could blink, he was sitting down. But you better believe I produced my wedding ring and told him I was happily married to Reverend O'Neill."

"Sure," Queenie said with a frown on her face.

"I don't care what you think, Q, that's what happened. If you weren't so jealous about nothing, we wouldn't be having this conversation. Marriage is sacred, and the last thing I'm going to do is forsake my marriage to Franklin for a two-bit conversation with someone I don't even know. He was only admiring me. I've got it like that."

"Ohh, ohh, ohh, First Lady Jackie is getting bold in her old age. Give me some skin," Emma said.

"Look, Queenie, we came to have fun. That was a moment on our trip we will laugh about for years to come. I want to see the show tonight and maybe put a few coins in the one-arm bandit. Lighten up."

"You're right, Jackie. We came to have fun and lift another sister up. I owe all of you an apology," Queenie finally said. "I'm sorry to have put a damper on things."

"No, I think I did that," Connie said. "But last night I prayed, and God showed me that Preston and I are going to be all right, regardless of what things look like at the moment. Knowing that, I feel free to enjoy the rest of the weekend."

"All right, ladies," Yolanda said, raising her hands in the air, "let's drop the funk and have some fun. There are some shops in the hotel we can browse in and then get ready for the show."

"I'd like that, sis," Connie said. "Okay, bathing in the sun is over, Jackie. Let's go. We'll be talking about this for days."

Jackie smiled. "I'm sure. But what I took from this experience is that I've still got it. And it certainly helped the self-esteem issues I thought I had."

"You're the bomb diggity, girl," Emma said, giving Jackie a thumbs-up. "I could've used that hunk to make Billy jealous. You all know I'm not going anywhere, even if I have to eat fried chicken on Wednesday nights for the rest of my life."

The ladies erupted in laughter.

"I thought it was special," Queenie said to Jackie. "It was refreshing to see you out of your element. Emma and I had threatened to lock you in the closet."

"Why?"

"We thought you were going to be some kind of prude," Emma answered before Queenie could come back with something not so pleasant. "But you fooled us. Yes, it was refreshing."

The girls browsed the shops before heading for their suite. There, they showered and got all glammed up for the Boyz II Men concert at the Mirage.

They each wore sleeveless dresses, some dipped lower in the front than others and some of the dresses hit above the knees and showed off a little more skin. No one could tell these divas that they weren't fierce and fabulous.

"Silver Bullets out on the town," Queenie said, finally herself for the first time since arriving in Vegas. "I hope there are more hunks like the one Jackie caught this afternoon running around in Vegas. I'm not going back to Raleigh empty-handed."

"You better hope you hit the jackpot tonight," Emma said, cracking on Queenie.

"You're right, Emma. I do hope I hit some kind of jackpot."

The Boyz II Men show was sold out. Queenie felt good all dressed up in her new crepe dress that dipped so low in the front, it didn't leave anything to the imagination. But there were few single men. Everyone seemed to be paired, except for the occasional groups of women, like themselves.

The ladies took their seats and waited for the show to begin. They were twenty minutes early, so they watched the parade of showgoers take their seats.

"Look," Emma said, pointing in the direction of several attractive, black females. "There's those reality TV stars from *Sistahs with College Degrees*. They must be size twos."

"I call them black Barbies," Queenie interjected. "They wear teeny-weeny dresses; loud makeup; long, plastic hair pulled back into a ponytail; and have a gang of artificial friends."

"I heard that, Q," Yolanda said, giving Queenie a high-five. "Everything on me is real, and you all are my true friends." Everyone gave her a thumbs-up, although they knew in their hearts that Queenie wasn't ever going to give up her red weave.

Boyz II Men sang all of their original hits and some of their newer ones. They were like fine wine that had mellowed into perfection. Shawn, Nathan, and Wanya wore black tuxes and crooned out the ballads like they'd done when they first came on the scene. A symphony orchestra backed them up, and the audience was in sync.

"I wish I was a few years younger," Queenie said, holding her hands together while her body rocked back and forth. "They are so talented."

"Their music hits to the core, especially when they sing 'I'll Make Love to You'," Connie said. "I love you, Preston," she whispered.

The whole room was on their feet singing the words to "At the

End of the Road." It was the perfect song to end a perfect concert.

"Let's walk awhile," Connie said. "I want to take in the bright lights of the city."

"I'm game," Emma chimed in, "so long as I get my gambling time in."

"You have all night for that, Emma," Jackie added.

"I'm having a ball with my sisters," Queenie lamented, rounding off the pleasantries as the group found their way to the street. "Look at this city all lit up like an oversized neon sign. It's beautiful though."

"There's nothing like it. Eric and I used to come out here once a year to get away."

"I didn't know that, YoYo. That's why you know so much." Emma smiled.

"It's a fascinating city, Emma. It holds a lot of secrets."

"What are you talking about, YoYo?" Queenie wanted to know.

"I'll never tell. They'll always be my memories and mine alone."

"That's cheating, sis. You've got to share."

"No, I've got to keep that one to myself, Connie. If Mama had an inkling of what I did, she'd get up out of her coffin and whip my butt—even at my age."

"Lord, it must've been terrible," Jackie said, looking at Yolanda sideways. "Was it worse than being kissed by a gentleman you didn't know?"

"Much worse than that, First Lady."

"Look, I'm plain ole' Jackie out here. You can drop the First Lady until I get back to Raleigh."

"What did she say?" Queenie put her hand on her hip and stared at Jackie. "You've lost your mind. We've got to get her back to Raleigh quick before she loses it." Everyone laughed.

As the ladies were about to head back to the hotel, a bald-headed gentleman stepped in their path. "You all are the finest sisters out on the boulevard," he said. The ladies blushed. "Especially you," the gentleman said as he zeroed in on Queenie. She blushed as red as her hair and the lights that lit up the city.

"We aren't called the Silver Bullets for no reason," Queenie volunteered.

"I love it—Silver Bullets. I can see that in an ad campaign."

"I'm sorry, but that name belongs to my sisters and me."

"Excuse my manners; my name is Anthony Rutherford, and I'm a promoter."

Queenie swung her hair as the night air lifted it and let it swing like in the commercials on television. "My name is Queenie Jackson and these are my best friends—Connie Alexander, Emma Wilcox, Yolanda Morris, and First Lady Jackie O'Neill." Jackie crinkled her face at Queenie.

"Where are you fabulous looking ladies on your way to?"

"We're on our way to the gambling table," Emma said, not wanting to be distracted.

"Can I take you ladies out to eat?"

"Thank you for the offer, but we're tired and need to get to the hotel," Connie said, as an excuse to get away.

"How about you?" Anthony asked, turning his attention back to Queenie.

"I am a little famished. I wouldn't mind getting a bite to eat."

Queenie was left at the curb with the promoter.

"Let's have some fun, "Anthony said to Queenie.

"I'm game," she said, and they were off, arm in arm.

Two For The Queen

"Have you been to Pure Nightclub at Caesars Palace?"

"No, this is my first time in Las Vegas," Queenie said, blushing like a schoolgirl.

"Then you haven't discovered Vegas yet. I'm going to show you a good time and maybe you won't want to go home after tonight."

"I don't know about that, although, I told my girlfriends that if the city offers me something I can't refuse, I might have to cancel my flight reservation."

A broad smile lit up Anthony's face. "Hmph, there's something about you that drew me to you right away, Queenie."

"Besides my red hair?"

"That was certainly part of it. It's absolutely gorgeous. I love a woman's hair that hangs and bends at the shoulders. And I love a woman who is forceful but yet playful…and *phine*."

"You certainly are observant."

"That's what attracted you to me."

"Wow."

"We've been standing in the same place for the past ten minutes; let's go and get our party on. I'd also like to get to know you better."

Queenie blushed again. "We'll see what the night holds."

Anthony pulled out his cell phone from an inner pocket. He called a number and told the person on the other end that he would be arriving in fifteen minutes and to reserve special seating for him and his lady. Queenie was impressed and couldn't wait for this part of the evening to progress.

They took a cab to Caesars Palace. Many people were milling about, no doubt some of them leaving the Boyz II Men concert or another Las Vegas show. They passed several hotels that were dressed in neon lights. In less than ten minutes, they were at Caesars Palace.

Caesars Palace had a Roman theme running through it, and Queenie was in awe. But she wasn't ready for the Pure Nightclub in all its glory. It was stark white and made up of a labyrinth of rooms off of the main room. The place was crowded with people of every ethnicity, sitting at one the numerous bars or gathered together in clusters wherever there was a free spot, striking up conversations.

Queenie's eyes popped as Ne-Yo, the R&B singer passed in front of her. She'd only seen him on television, but he was handsome. Anthony held her hand and led her to an alcove within the main room where they could have some privacy but could also hit the dance floor if they felt the need to. Queenie continued to blush.

It was very expensive but Queenie felt as if she belonged; she was on cloud nine. Anthony had paid eighty dollars to enter and was told that their VIP space would be three-hundred and seventy-five dollars. Didn't she feel special?

"So tell me something about Queenie Jackson," Anthony said, after securing the best wine in the house and pouring them each a glass.

"There's not much to tell. I grew up in a little town called Youngsville, North Carolina, went to North Carolina A&T University, got a job at a newspaper, and have lived in Raleigh the majority of my adult life. I go to church, hang out with my girl-friends, and have a good time.

"What about you, Mr. Anthony Rutherford?"

"I grew up in Compton, California and went to the school of hard knocks. Having a stern father figure in the house, I was fortunate not to be consumed by the gangs. The real gang wars driven by drugs, especially crack cocaine, came after I was out of Compton. I went to UCLA on a football scholarship, went to the pros and was a steady for six years until I sustained an injury. I went back to college and got my degree in Business Management. I've always had a love for music and, with my football days over, one of my best friends in the industry pulled me into the game. That's kind of the gist of it.

"So, do you have a significant other waiting for you in Raleigh?"

Queenie took a sip of her wine and smiled. "No one that I'd call significant. I have a few acquaintances, but the single shingle is hanging over my door."

"Clever."

"I wasn't trying to be."

"I'm sitting here with a beautiful, attractive woman, and I can't believe that she's not seeing anyone."

"It's not far-fetched. The one person who I thought was my number one wasn't only entertaining me."

"Oh, I see. What a bastard."

"What a bastard indeed. I asked for my key and dismissed him. End of story. There's nothing to rehash."

"I feel you. What a shame he didn't know what he had?"

"I believe he realized it; he stopped by the house a little over a week ago to make amends, but I wasn't having it. After a while, you get tired of all the lies and games. All I want is peace, and if there's to be a man in my life, he has to come correct or not at all. What about you? I'm sure you have an arsenal of women waiting in line."

"I was married...not once, but twice. More married to my job than anything. I love what I do and I'm good at it. My clientele list contains several 'A' list entertainers. Sometimes the almighty dollar rules your life and you forget everything else. No time for the wife, no time to take the kids to football games..."

"So, you have children?"

"Yes, I have two sons. We're estranged. Their mother bad-mouthed me, but I don't blame her; I blame me.

"We're working on our relationship though."

"That's good to know."

"What about you? Have you ever been married...kids?"

"Kids? No. I was married once, but it was over almost before it began. I don't think I was marriage material. At least that's what I used to tell myself."

"But you don't really know; you weren't with the right man."

Queenie smiled. This man frightened her a little. She hadn't talked about her ex in years. Their only link was dissolved when she miscarried the baby who would've been their daughter. Queenie willed herself not to cry.

"Why don't we dance?" she suggested. "I love to dance."

"So do I," he replied, rising and reaching for her hand. "I understand that 50 Cent will be performing shortly."

"I'm not into rappers, but I'm not complaining."

"Why is that?" he asked, his hand at the small of her back.

Queenie looked over her shoulder, tossing her red weave. "I'm with you, Mr. Rutherford, and I'm having a great time."

Queenie and Anthony danced the night away. In between the

workout, they talked and talked, discovering new things about each other. And as they danced, they stole kisses, and before long, Queenie leaned her head on Anthony's shoulder.

After a lengthy stint on the dance floor, the pair headed back to the VIP section and sat down. Anthony poured them each a glass of wine, which they sipped. Relaxed, they enjoyed the music.

Queenie sat up with a jolt when she felt her cell phone vibrate. "It's my cell phone. I'm sure it's my girlfriends checking up on me." Queenie picked up her clutch, reached in and pulled out her cell phone, and looked at the time. "Oh my goodness; it's three o'clock."

It was Emma calling.

"Hey, Emma, what's up?"

"Don't you Emma me. Where are you, Queenie Jackson? We are worried sick."

"I'm having a ball, Emma. We're at Caesars Palace. I haven't been this happy in a long time."

"Well, you're going to have to cut your time short with Mr. Lover Man. Get your tail back to the hotel now."

"You're not my mother."

"Don't make me have to act like it. Have some consideration for the rest of us. You do remember Natalee Holloway who went to Aruba and never came back."

"Thank you for thinking about me, sweetie. I'll be home within the next hour."

"You better. Oh, guess what? I won big, Q."

"What?"

"I won one-hundred thousand dollars, baby girl, playing black-jack. Oh yes, we had a party of our own here at the Bellagio. Champagne and wine were flowing all over the place. Too bad you missed it. Even First Lady indulged. She's passed out cold."

"Oh, Emma, that's so exciting. I'll see you in a few."

"All right. Don't let Mr. Rutherford lead you astray."

"Go to bed, Emma. Love ya."

Queenie put her phone away and smiled at Anthony. "My girlfriends were checking up on me. I couldn't have a better set of friends."

"The Silver Bullets; I really like that."

"Yeah, it speaks of us—all over fifty, in the prime of our lives, but living life to the fullest."

"You are special, Queenie Jackson. It seems like your girlfriends had some excitement, too."

"Yes, Emma hit it big at the tables. They were celebrating."

"I'd like to celebrate us...our meeting. You know it was fate. If the wedding chapel was open, I'd take you there and get married."

"Why me? You hardly know me and I've heard that *if the wedding chapel was open* line one too many times. Anyway, I'm probably old enough to be your mother."

"Whoa, hold up, pretty lady. I'm forty-nine. And I like your bio you gave me earlier unless it was all made up. "

Queenie wasn't about to give up her age. "No, it wasn't. But I don't understand. You could be with any woman. All of these fake-ass, black Barbie dolls running around here, why not one of them? I'm a full-figured woman whose curves don't exactly rival..."

"Hush. I happen to like full-figured women; there's more to hold."

Queenie smiled. "That was nice of you to say."

"I'm sure you hear it all the time. You are a very attractive woman. Your red hair is beautiful and I must say that you're wearing that dress." There was silence for a moment. Then Anthony reached over. "May I kiss you again?"

Queenie searched Anthony's face and smiled. "Yeah, I'd like that."

Anthony took Queenie in his arms. They didn't care that they weren't alone; they locked lips and didn't come up for air.

"Would you like to spend the night with me?" Anthony asked after regaining his composure. His eyes searched Queenie's, begging for a "yes."

Queenie dropped her head and cupped her hand over her mouth. When she brought her head back up, she looked into Anthony's eyes, and said, "I like you a lot. I've had the best time tonight."

"So here comes the rejection."

"Hold it; let me finish. I would love to see you again, Anthony. I'm not accustomed to jumping into a man's bed when I first meet him. I'm better than that. Also, I came to Vegas to console one of my girlfriends; she's going through a rough time. While I should've been with her, I choose to go with you instead.

Anthony's eyes roved over Queenie's body. A faint smile formed on his face. "Classy and so eloquently put. That's why you're special. Let me get you a cab so that your girlfriends won't worry about you."

"Thank you."

"I had a fabulous time, and I'm going to give you my contact information. Hopefully this won't be the last time I see you."

Anthony took Queenie's hand in his and drew them to his lips. He kissed the back of her hand and reached over and kissed her again. "You don't have to believe me, Queenie Jackson, but you have tugged at my heart strings."

"If it's meant to be, it will be. Thank you for a wonderful evening."

Don't Hate, Appreciate

Queenie was giddy all the way to the room. She couldn't have dreamed up a better weekend. It had all the drama, passion, and fun any woman could've desired. She'd taken a chance, leaving her friends to be with Anthony, but something in her psyche had told her that he was a gentleman.

Queenie took off her shoes before swiping her suite key to open the door. She tiptoed through the foyer headed for the room when a light suddenly popped on. Queenie was momentarily blinded by the bright light and surprised to find she had an audience.

"Were you all waiting up for me?" she asked, looking around the room.

Yolanda got up from her seat dressed in a powder-blue, satin nightshirt. "You've got your nerve coming in here at four in the morning, working our nerves overtime worrying about your butt."

"I spoke to Emma."

"That doesn't count. Mr. Wonderful could have taken you somewhere, murdered you, and buried you in the hot desert sand. You've got a damn cell phone on you; be courteous enough to use it and put people out of their misery."

Queenie slumped down on the couch next to Jackie.

"Why are you sitting next to me?" Jackie asked. "My silence doesn't mean you're safe over here. I got a peck on the lips, what did you get, Queenie Jackson?"

"Oh no, you didn't," Queenie replied. "Ladies, Anthony was a true gentleman."

"Do you hear that, girls?" Connie asked, finally giving voice to the situation. "She called him Anthony. Only Queenie would be on first-name basis with someone she hardly knows."

"I'll be seeing him again."

"What?" It was Emma's turn to voice an opinion. "What about Mr. Jheri Curl or that sorry excuse for a man, Linden Robinson?"

"It's Joe Harris, not Jheri Curl, Emma."

"Whatever, Q. You can't be bouncing from this one to that one. It makes you look like a..."

Queenie jumped up and stood in front of Emma. "Watch it, Emma, before I knock the blonde out of your hair. Don't hate me for looking so good. Anthony appreciates a full-figured woman, and he said he wants to see me again. In fact, he told me if the chapels were open, he would have married me last night."

"Convenient. Listen to yourself, Q," Yolanda said, her hands on her hips. "Falling for some lip service is out of character for even you. Since when have you allowed a man to seduce you like that without getting the four-one-one on him? Please give me a break."

Queenie had had enough. "I'm going to bed. You heifers can't stand to see anyone happy except for your damn selves. Nobody said anything derogatory about First Lady being kissed by some stranger."

"She didn't stay out half the night or morning with him either," Emma replied.

Queenie turned around and looked at her girlfriends. "YoYo, didn't you say we came here to have fun? I was a stick-in-the mud initially, but I apologized and got with the program. I can't help that a handsome man came up to us and wanted to take me out."

"He asked to take us all out to eat. Did you forget that?" Jackie said.

"No, but he really wanted to get me alone. So, if you all are finished, I'm going to freshen up and go to bed so that I'll be ready for brunch tomorrow with my girlfriends. And by the way, Emma, I hope you're going to break me off a couple of dollars of your big win."

Everyone laughed.

"I got you, Q. We were worried about you; we didn't want anything to happen to you."

Queenie smiled. "Thanks, Emma. I love you all. I'm sorry if I got caught up with Mr. Anthony Rutherford. We had a grand time. I'll tell you all about it when you guys cool off. We had a mighty good time."

The rest of the trip went off without a hitch...almost. Mr. Rutherford was more than serious about seeing Queenie again. He showed up at Jasmine for brunch and paid for everyone's meal. Queenie enjoyed being with him, a little apart from her friends, gawking at the fountain as it was transformed into a romantic interlude accompanied by beautiful music.

The ladies were on their way back to Raleigh the next day with a ton of memories and promises for the future.

House Arrest

Connie came home to an empty house. She should've been enjoying her honeymoon with her new husband; instead, her future seemed bleak. She glanced through her mail, but there was nothing of note, only bills that needed her immediate attention.

It was four in the afternoon on a Monday. She wanted to call Illya to see what progress was being made in Preston's case. Instead, with a heavy sigh, she proceeded to empty her suitcase and prepare for work the next day.

Connie put a load of clothes into the washing machine and then went into the living room and sat down. As she waited, she reflected on her weekend. It was always great being around her girls, but in truth, it hadn't given her the satisfaction she was seeking.

Connie reached over and picked up a book from the nearest end table. The book was *Chosen* by Patricia Haley. Connie thought about her choices, and why she was chosen for her current journey as she opened the book and began to read. Before she finished the first paragraph, the doorbell rang, startling her. This was Monday and she would've been at work. Who could be stopping by unannounced?

Taking no chances, Connie looked through the peephole in the door. Her eyes widened and her sorrow lifted. She snatched the door open and welcomed her husband into her arms. Illya Newsome stood a couple of feet behind Preston.

"Hey, baby," Preston said, engulfing Connie in his arms. "May I and Mr. FBI come in?"

"Yes, yes, come in." Connie surveyed the two gentlemen—her husband and Illya. She prepared herself for the worst, even though Preston was a sight for sore eyes. "So...your being here means that..."

Illya spoke up for the first time. "It's good news, Connie, although temporary."

"What does that mean?"

"Preston is on house arrest. We have enough information and evidence to indict the masterminds of the drug ring. However, Preston is not completely off the hook, at least not yet. Not everyone is willing to believe that he wasn't involved in all aspects of the drug ring, especially since he is well connected to Dr. Marshall Cole, by way of his father. I'm confident that Preston will be released, but in the meantime, he's limited to where and how far he can travel. I hope this offers you some consolation on your wedding weekend."

"Thanks, Illya." Connie squeezed Preston's hand. "I'm happy to have my man here with me."

The man in question spoke up then. "So how was the trip since I had to relinquish my ticket?"

Tears rolled down from Connie's eyes. "It wasn't the same without you. I thought about you day and night, although I tried to have some fun."

Preston reached down and kissed Connie on the lips.

"I'll be leaving now," Illya said, backing up to make his getaway. "Preston, I'll be in touch. You'll have to testify. The powers that be are trying to schedule the trial date for early September. They feel that should be enough time to get the trial underway. There will be individual trials, but you will only be involved in the one for Dr. Cole."

"Thanks, Illya. Thanks for believing me and having my back."

"Given the pre-trial testimonies of all those people we interviewed who know you, you have yourself to thank."

Preston smiled and gave Illya the brother handshake.

"Remember, there's no taking off the device that's strapped to your leg."

"Gotcha."

And Illya was gone.

"Mrs. Preston Alexander, I'm glad to be home."

Judge Not

The story about the drug trafficking ring hit the newsstands with a bang. Extra papers were bought up by the inquiring minds of the city who were surprised to learn that Raleigh/Durham was a hub for the movement and illegal procurement of pharmaceuticals. While numerous names of prominent people were listed within the story, there was no mention of Preston Alexander. Queenie read and reread the article, and it was clear to her that Preston might have somehow been exonerated.

Her phone rang just as she'd moved on to another juicy tale, a double homicide involving transients in Durham's back alley.

"Hello," she said, agitated by the interruption.

"Q, this is Jackie."

"Is something wrong?"

"No, nothing like that. Did you hear anything else about Preston? Is he going into the Witness Protection Program?"

"Slow down, girl. Jack's article didn't mention Preston at all. Besides, if Preston went into the Witness Protection Program, they'd whisk him away faster than you could blink."

"Well, I hope it doesn't impact Connie too much. The real reason I called you…"

"Oh, so now we're getting to the purpose of this phone call. Are you feeling some remorse for letting that stranger kiss you in Vegas?"

"Queenie, stop it. It was all very innocent."

"Could've fooled me. It looked to me like you invited his attention." Queenie laughed.

"Why in the world did I call you?"

"You knew that I was the one friend who'd listen without judging."

"You're full of crap. All you did was judge me from the time we got on that plane until now."

"Jackie, you're my girl. I'm here for you. What's up?"

"Look, I had the time of my life in Vegas, but I don't want Franklin to get a whiff of what went on."

"So, now you're worried that Franklin may find out. There's no need to worry; your secret is safe with me."

"Thanks, Q. Franklin's been asking all kinds of questions."

"Like what?"

"He noticed my bikini wax."

"He, he, he, he, he, he, heeeeeeeeeeeeeee. Girl, Franklin would have to be blind not to notice how clean your fur patch was."

"You're nasty."

"I'm not the one who had the Brazilian wax, trying to be all twenty-first century. What did you expect, ding-dong?"

"I shouldn't have put it on him so strong. It was as if I had a new zest for life. I only wanted to please my man and let him know how much I appreciated him."

Queenie couldn't stop laughing. "It looks like Samson and Delilah stepped it up a notch."

"Oh, it was on. But I don't want Franklin thinking that I went to Vegas and went crazy and wild. I am the First Lady after all."

"Let me stop you right there, First Lady. I do recall, and my recall is good, that you asked us not to call you First Lady while we were in Vegas. Am I right?"

"You know why I said it. I wanted to be known as Jackie—one of the girls. I didn't want people looking at me as if I was some holy roller that got lost in the desert. Church folks have conventions in Vegas all the time."

Queenie snickered. "Girl, you worry too much. Franklin isn't going to find out a thing unless somebody tells him. It's not going to be me, nor do I think any of the other ladies would be so self-righteous to do a low-down thing and say something to Franklin. They'd have to tell on themselves, also."

"Okay, I feel better."

"Your conscience is eating you alive, isn't it?"

"Maybe, but I had the time of my life."

"Well, you'll have to hang out with us more often. You know your limitations; exercise it."

"I can't believe I'm getting advice from you."

"So why in the hell did you call me?"

"You're the only person who knows me well enough that I could confide in like this."

"Precisely. Now, go on and enjoy the rest of your week and keep your private thoughts to yourself. Remember, 'what happens in Vegas stays in Vegas'."

Jackie laughed with Queenie. "Whew, I can breathe again."

"Until the next time. Have a good afternoon, First Lady."

A Virtuous Woman

The week slithered by without incident. Even choir rehearsal was dull and monotonous. Queenie had avoided all six of Joe Harris' telephone calls, but she hadn't heard from Anthony since returning from Vegas. She was starting to believe that all the words blowing out of his mouth, about wanting to see her again, was a bunch of bull.

Something was in the air; things didn't feel right. With the exception of First Lady Jackie O'Neill, she hadn't heard anything from Connie, Yolanda, or Emma since they'd returned from Vegas. Not one of them showed up for choir rehearsal, and Emma was the choir directress. First Lady had had to play and direct.

It was youth Sunday, and Queenie was glad for the distraction. She loved dressing up and she out did herself today. Easter Sunday wasn't until the following week, but Queenie didn't care. She wore a wide-brimmed, peach-colored, netted hat over her red weave and rocked a two-piece, peach-colored suit with white piping bordering the lapels. Her off-white, scoop-neck blouse was accented by an eighteen-inch, two-strand, white, cultured-pearl necklace and matching pearl earrings. Peach-colored pumps adorned her feet.

Queenie sashayed halfway down the aisle and parked her behind in the middle section of the church at the end of the pew. After plopping her handbag onto the seat next to her, she looked up and saw First Lady pointing. Queenie leaned forward and was surprised to see Connie and Preston along with Yolanda and Illya. So Preston had been released. Was it a secret?

Recovering from her discovery, Queenie looked up and saw Emma standing in the aisle, waving her hands for her to move down. Reluctantly, Queenie moved from her comfortable perch on the end so that Emma could sit down.

"Guess who's here?" Queenie whispered, wanting to get Emma's reaction.

"Who? Do we have a guest speaker?"

"Look ahead and to the left. Connie and family are here in force."

Emma moved her body forward and looked in the direction Queenie had indicated. Emma put her hand over her breasts and made a large 'O' with her mouth. "Preston is here. Does that mean he isn't going into the Witness Protection Program?"

"I don't know. I haven't seen or heard from any of y'all this week. Where have you been?"

"Working hard." Emma patted Queenie's hand. "Quiet. Pastor is looking in our direction."

The children's choir sang two numbers and had the congregation standing on its feet. Minnie gave the week's announcements followed by the collection of the offering. And then it was time for the spoken word.

Pastor O'Neill rose from his seat and walked to the podium. He had an angelic glow about him. He placed his Bible on the podium, looked out into the congregation, and smiled.

"It's so good to see so many of you today, especially Sister Connie Maxwell, who is now Sister Connie Maxwell Alexander."

There was a gasp from the congregation followed by the clapping of hands.

"Sister Connie," Rev. O'Neill continued, "was married in a private ceremony last week by yours truly. Sister Connie and Brother Preston, please stand. We're so glad to see you both in the House of the Lord." Connie and Preston waved their hands and sat down.

"I see that Sister Yolanda is accompanied by a friend." Yolanda waved her hands signaling no, but Rev. O'Neill moved forward. "Maybe, we'll be hearing wedding bells from her sometime in the near future." Yolanda sat with a blank look on her face. "It's great to have you worship with us today, Mr. Newsome." Illya nodded his head.

"Yolanda didn't seem amused by what Pastor said about getting married," Emma whispered in Queenie's ear. "If left up to Yolanda, calling another man her husband isn't going to happen in this lifetime."

"You're right about that. However, she seems to be digging this guy a little more than she's let on."

"Uhm hmm."

"Marriage is a sacred institution, church," Pastor O'Neill stated. "I've been married to my wife for over thirty years and I love her as much as I did when we first got married."

"What do you think he's getting ready to talk about, Q?" Emma whispered.

"How am I supposed to know? I'm sitting here listening to the man like you are."

"Young men, when looking for a wife, look for a virtuous woman—a woman who is pure of heart."

"Ohh, ohh," Queenie whispered to Emma. "Franklin is on to something."

"The book of Proverbs, Chapter eighteen, tells us that a man 'whoso findeth a wife findeth a good thing and obtains favor from the Lord.'"

"Hell is getting ready to open up, Q. Look at First Lady fidgeting at the piano and sweating it out."

"Emma, keep it down. I feel you, though."

"I found a virtuous woman in First Lady O'Neill. She's been nothing but a model wife, mother, and lover."

Church members were eyeing each other out of the corner of their eyes, wondering where the pastor was going with his sermon.

"Here it comes, Q," Emma whispered. "This might get ugly."

"If you look at Proverbs thirty-one, beginning at verse ten, it gives you the traits of a virtuous woman. The good book says that 'her price is far above rubies...the heart of her husband doth safely trust in her. She will do him good and not evil all the days of her life.'

"That's what you want men and women when you decide to settle down for life with a mate. 'Her husband is known in the gates, when he sitteth among the elders of the land. Strength and honour are her clothing; and she shall rejoice in time to come. She openeth her mouth with wisdom; and in her tongue is the law of kindness.'"

"What are you thinking, Queenie? Do you think Franklin knows something?"

"How in the world could he, Emma? He'd have to have been in Vegas to spy on her, and I doubt that he would do such an idiotic thing."

"Maybe he did."

"Listen to what the man is saying, Emma: His wife is virtuous and does no wrong."

Emma scratched her head. "I don't think we're listening to the same sermon. Yes, I hear what's rolling off his tongue, but I bet you your next paycheck that he's saying something else. I'll agree that it would be stupid of him to send a spy, but don't you think his message is a little odd, today of all days, especially since it's been only a week since we were in Vegas and we know what happened there?"

"Maybe you're on to something, Emma. Now be quiet; I don't want to miss anything he's saying."

"Saints, I want to tell you this morning, that the world is in turmoil," Pastor O'Neill continued. "Satan is busy, trying on every hand to destroy the sanctity of marriage. We're bombarded with television ads about erectile dysfunction..." the congregation gasped. "Visions of how your sex life can be enhanced with certain lubricants and oils are thrust before our eyes."

"Shut the monkey up," Emma whispered, beating Queenie's thigh with her fist. "I'm telling you, something's got Franklin wound up this morning."

"Emma, I'm not passing my check over to you, but I think you're in the ballpark on this."

"Sometimes a spouse may feel invigorated, sexy, on top of the world and may want attention elsewhere. A spouse who doesn't know any better, may become blind or complacent, going along, clippity-cloppity, without recognizing the changes in their spouse. The changes are subtle at first but may become downright bold as the spouse becomes more confident.

"What changes do you ask? Things like new underwear or a change in the style of dress. And then there are all those crazy things people are doing to their bodies such as getting a tattoo that people think no one at church will see or getting a Brazilian wax—the new way of removing unwanted hair from your body on places I won't describe."

"Oh my God, Emma. Our First Lady is in trouble."

"And some of you still don't recognize the changes until a bomb is dropped in your lap and wakes your closed eyes up."

"Aww hell, Q. The crap has hit the fan."

What's On The Agenda?

Emma and Queenie couldn't wait for church to be over. They had to know firsthand what Franklin's sermon was all about. At the end of service, they made a desperate attempt to get to Jackie. However, they weren't successful. People blocked the aisle and made it impossible for them to move forward. Everyone wanted to give Connie and Preston their well-wishes.

When the rush of people cleared, the Pastor and First Lady were nowhere in the sanctuary.

"Do you think we should go to the Pastor's office?" Emma asked. "I'm pretty sure Jackie wanted to get away before she was bombarded with questions."

"My thoughts on that, Emma, are that we better give the First Lady and her spouse some room. Mark my words; Jackie will come clean with what's going on in due season. Franklin got wind of something and he is mad as hell."

"Shoot, it's almost felt as if he was in Vegas with us."

"Ain't that the truth? We'd better go say something to Connie and Yolanda before they start wondering why we're avoiding them."

"Are you trying to avoid them, Q?"

Queenie wrinkled her nose at Emma and led the way to where people were still congregating around the newlyweds.

Yolanda held out her arms as Queenie and Emma approached. "How are you guys doing?"

"How are you doing?" Queenie asked. "I haven't heard hide or hair from any of you birds all week. You could've told me Preston was released from prison."

"Hold your panties, Q. A lot has gone on this week, but I think you need to ask Connie about what she and Preston are doing. You do realize that she was supposed to be on her honeymoon, and may have wanted time to herself."

Queenie hugged Yolanda. "No harm done, YoYo. "I missed you guys after we got back from Vegas."

"So has Anthony called you?"

"No, not yet. It's only been six days since we last saw each other. I'll give him some time."

"How are you doing, Emma?" Yolanda asked, turning to give Emma a hug.

"Fabulous, but I'm not sure about First Lady."

"That sermon was suspect," Yolanda added.

"It was almost as if Pastor was in Vegas himself, sitting on a side street spying on us."

"Queenie, you're a mess," Yolanda said. "We'll probably get the four-one-one sometime later. Look, do you guys want to go to dinner with us? Preston has to…."

Queenie looked from Emma to Yolanda. "You want to go?" Queenie asked Emma.

"Sure, why not."

"We're going to P. F. Chang's. Illya loves it."

Queenie shrugged her shoulders. "Illya loves it, huh? We'll meet you there."

As Queenie drove toward P. F. Chang's with Emma in tow, the car's Bluetooth announced that she had a call. She looked at her cell phone and saw Jackie's number. "Be quiet, Emma. I'm going to see what Jackie wants."

Queenie hit the Bluetooth button to connect the call. "Hey, Jackie. You must've run out of the sanctuary; we couldn't find you after church."

"I didn't run, Q, but I'll admit I was in a hurry to get out of there. Where are you headed?"

Queenie looked over at Emma. "I was headed to P. F. Chang's to meet up with Yolanda and Connie. What's up?"

"Look, I need to talk to someone right now. Can you stop by my house and pick me up?"

"Well, uhh, I've got Emma in the car with me."

"Hey, Emma."

"Hey, First Lady."

"Look, it's okay, Q. You and Emma go ahead and call me later."

"No, Jackie, I'll drop Emma back at church so she can pick up her car…"

"No, don't do that. Y'all get over here. I need you both."

"Okay, we're on the way, Jackie. It should take me no more than twenty minutes."

"I'll be waiting."

Queenie deactivated the Bluetooth and turned her head slightly in Emma's direction. "Sounds as if we're on a rescue mission," Emma said. "We better call Yolanda and tell her we won't make it."

Silver Bullets To The Rescue

Queenie put the pedal to the metal as she flew her red Jaguar XK Coupe through the streets of Raleigh. She turned onto Glenwood Avenue with its beautiful dogwood and magnolia trees lining the streets. Continuing west and driving like a bat out of hell, she passed Crabtree Valley Mall, one of her favorite shopping centers.

"Are you trying to kill us?" Emma asked, holding the emergency handle inside the car with all her might to embrace the impact of Queenie's last minute effort to stop at a red light and what could've been a near collision with a car that had already started into the intersection. "Damn, it's not like First Lady is going to die if we don't get to her in time."

The light turned green, and Queenie put her foot on the gas, ignoring Emma's concern. "I don't care what you think, that was a call for help. Who knows, whatever had Franklin in an uproar this morning during Sunday service, he may be taking out on Jackie."

"You've got a point there, Q. But please exercise some restraint with that foot of yours. I want to live so that I can help Jackie. There's no need to speed."

"Emma, you have no sense of urgency." Queenie paused. "No, this couldn't be."

Emma turned around and snickered. "Five-o, huh? Your behind will slow down now. And guess what?"

"What, Emma, what? The last thing I need is a damn speeding ticket."

"You better call Jackie and tell her you'll be detained for another thirty minutes."

"Damn, damn, damn."

The police officer appeared at Queenie's window. She handed him her license and insurance information without giving him a passing glance. He stood near the car door and examined her documents and then looked through the glass of the window that Queenie had already pulled up.

Knock, knock, knock.

"What in the hell does he want?" Queenie asked annoyed. "He needs to call the information in and give me my ticket so we can be on our way." Queenie hit the automatic window button and looked at the officer, who was hidden behind a pair of expensive sunglasses. He was tall, dark, and looked good in his uniform. His muscles weren't obscene, but large enough that it warranted another look.

"Ma'am, do you know why I stopped you?"

"I could guess, but why don't you tell me?"

"We have a smart mouth. Umm. Don't you know that I hold the key to whether I'll issue you a ticket?"

Queenie took a good look at him. Something about him seemed familiar, but it was probably her imagination. "Look, I'm sorry officer. I was in a hurry to get to a friend who needs our assistance."

"You were going sixty in a thirty-five miles-per-hour zone."

"I'm guilty."

"So you're Queenie Jackson."

"What's that supposed to mean?"

"You're very familiar with my brother."

Curiosity got the best of Queenie. She looked the officer over but couldn't find a resemblance to anyone she knew. "Who's your brother?" Even Emma was trying to get a glimpse of the officer.

"My name is Richard Robinson, Linden Robinson's younger brother." Richard took off his sunglasses.

"Jesus," Queenie said, tapping Emma on the arm. There was no mistaking the family resemblance, although Richard was a much more handsome version of Linden. "Richard? I don't recall Linden ever talking about you."

"That doesn't surprise me. We don't have the same mother, but our father's genes are very strong. We've been estranged, especially not growing up in the same household and there being a fifteen year difference in our ages. But I do believe you were at one of the family reunions I attended."

Queenie smiled. "Well, I didn't know that Linden had such a *phine* brother. It isn't a secret. Linden and I are no longer an item."

"Oh…I'm sorry. I didn't know."

"There's no need to apologize. Do you have any more brothers… like yourself…who are older?" Queenie winked.

Richard smiled. No, only my sister and me. I'm happily married with two children, and life's been good. Look, I'm going to give you a warning this time, but next time it'll be a big, fat ticket."

"Thanks, Richard. I appreciate it. I promise to be a good girl."

"See that you do; it was nice meeting you."

Queenie took off and grinned while doing so. "Can you imagine meeting Linden's brother at a traffic stop? If he had been older, I would've offered to have him put my hands in handcuffs."

"You're lying. I wonder why Linden never told you about Richard."

"Linden is trifling; I was aware of that when I first met him. Emma, the truth is I was lonely. Linden came along and said some nice things to me and I fell for it like ants at a picnic."

"That's until you smelled the *RAID*."

"That was funny, Emma. I should've exterminated his ass a long time ago. I'll admit the sex was good, whenever he was able to get it up, but it wasn't worth it. Being in my fifties, I felt that life was over."

"So you saddled up with the first cockroach that came around the corner."

Queenie laughed. "Emma, I'm not going to share any more of my thoughts with you, but that's about the size of it. No more."

"What about Mr. Anthony from Vegas?"

"I could see something smoldering with him, but the truth is he hasn't called since we left Vegas. My hopes were high especially after he told me he liked healthy girls."

"It's not the end of the world, Q."

"Yeah, yeah; I have self-esteem issues. Well, we're here. Let's put on our smiley faces for Jackie."

Your Sins Will
Find You Out

It didn't take a rocket scientist to know that First Lady Jackie O'Neill was under great stress. Her eyes were red and bloodshot from crying. She reached out to both Queenie and Emma when they came through the door and held them close to her bosom.

"Have a seat," Jackie said, when she pulled back, wiping her eyes. "We're by ourselves."

"What's going on?" Queenie asked, cutting to the chase. "Emma and I were worried about you."

Jackie sighed, catching her breath once or twice. She blew air from her mouth, wiped her runny nose, and sat limp in the chair. "Franklin found out about Vegas."

"Found out what?"

"Yeah," Emma said, following Queenie. "You were minding your own business when an admirer saw you lying on the chaise, bent down, and kissed you. There was nothing in that."

"Even so, how in the hell did Franklin find out?"

Jackie looked from Emma to Queenie who sat forward on the couch across from her, waiting for an answer. She wasn't sure that she could tell her friends that she was the biggest fool on the planet, but she had to tell somebody. "I messed up big time."

"Okay...," Queenie said, praying that Jackie would hurry up

and spit it out. "We had the firsthand account on what happened, and I can understand Franklin being jealous, but how in the world did he find out?"

"I gave Reuben my phone number, and he called."

"You did what?" Emma shrieked. "That's the dumbest thing I've ever heard. What in the world were you thinking?"

"He gave me his number and I gave him mine so that if he was ever in the area on a Sunday and wanted to come to Shiloh Baptist, he'd have my number. It's called winning souls for Christ."

"I'm with Emma, Jackie. That's about the dumbest and stupidest thing you could've done. That man was out on the beach canvassing women and going to church in Vegas or Raleigh was the farthest thing from his mind. Didn't you even stop to think that the man might call? He calls and Franklin answers. Is that how it happened?"

"I called you all over for moral support. You've done nothing but make me feel like Bozo the Clown."

"Have you forgotten your bold talk about getting a Brazilian wax and lying out in the sun for all to see?" Queenie inquired. "That's when you didn't want to be called First Lady…didn't want anyone to know that you were a pastor's wife. But you see, holiness doesn't mean wearing a long white dress; it doesn't mean anything if you can't keep the white dress down."

Tears once again began to flood Jackie's face. If looks could kill, Queenie would be dead.

"That wasn't called for, Q," Emma said with a scowl on her face.

"The truth is the truth, Emma."

Jackie jumped up from her seat. "And I suppose you're exempt from the Lord's wrath. I'm not jumping from one man's bed to another…"

Emma had to run interference. "Calm down, Jackie. I'm not condoning what Queenie said to you, but… for God's sake, you're a married woman…a pastor's wife. You broke the rules. You can play, but you don't invite anyone to participate in the after party. That phrase about 'what happens in Vegas stays in Vegas' loses meaning when you create mayhem by doing what you did."

Jackie sat down. Queenie hadn't said anything in the past few minutes. "Look, guys, I was wrong. I don't know what got into me. I hadn't felt that free in years, and I let the lure of the city swallow me up and take away my good sense. I only have eyes and mad love for my husband. Even after all the years we've been married, raising kids, and working in the church, Franklin O'Neill is still my heart. I never meant to hurt him."

"Where's Franklin now?" Queenie finally asked.

"He's staying at a hotel for the night. He said he had to go to God in prayer and consecration and he wanted to be left alone."

"Franklin isn't going to do anything stupid, I hope."

"Emma, his feelings are hurt. He said I betrayed his trust. Having another man call his wife at home was a blow to his heart. Franklin said some choice words to me, and he didn't want to hear it when I tried to explain it to him."

"Do you blame him, Jackie?" Queenie asked. "I wouldn't have believed that nonsense either. Though it does sound like you."

"Q, Franklin knows me. In my wildest dreams I hadn't expected that man to call. Why would I give him my home phone number if I was trying to hide something?"

"Lord, this woman needs some blessed oil," Emma said. "You can't be that naïve, Jackie. I don't care how innocent you thought giving your home number to that man was, no man wants another man calling his house asking for his wife. And I'm sure the joker told Franklin he met you in Vegas."

Jackie looked over at Queenie and Emma. "I look like that big a fool?"

"Big, huge," Queenie said, throwing her arms wide. "Look, Jackie, I'm sorry if I came on too strong. Sometimes it's hard to get stuff through your thick skull. I love you like a sister, and I only want the best for you."

"That's the kindest thing you've said to me all day."

"Why don't Emma and I take you to get something to eat?"

"Let's go some place good," Emma chimed in. "I didn't want to go to P. F. Chang's anyway. I think Jackie needs some food for the soul."

"Girl, I was thinking the same thing. I don't feel like bamboo shoots or some crazy mixed-up noodles," Queenie said. "Give me some meat, potatoes and gravy."

"Let me get my purse." Jackie stopped in her tracks and turned to look at Queenie and Emma. "I love you guys. Thanks for coming to my rescue."

Family

"What happened to Queenie and Jackie?" Connie asked after an hour had gone by. "Didn't they say they were going to join us?"

"They did, although they didn't seem too excited about going to P. F. Chang's," Yolanda replied.

"Actually, I'm glad they're not here," Connie said. "I wanted this to be family time and drama-free."

"I say amen to that, sister. So, Illya, have they arrested everyone connected to the drug trafficking ring?"

Illya smiled. "Yolanda, I can't divulge everything."

"Baby, are you all right?" Connie asked Preston, who hadn't said a word since entering the restaurant.

He placed his arm around Connie's shoulders and squeezed. "Yeah, baby, I'm fine. I just want to sit here and listen to you talk, smell your fragrance and hold you tight. I love you."

Connie leaned over and kissed Preston. "I love you too, baby."

"I have an announcement," Illya began. "I'll be leaving in a few days."

Yolanda's face seemed to lose color. "Where are you going?"

"I can't share that with you as it would jeopardize my investigation. I'll be away for approximately two months but hope to return to the Raleigh/Durham area. Raleigh was only meant to be a temporary stay, but I'll have to admit it has grown on me."

"Will you keep in touch?" Yolanda asked, her emotions getting the best of her.

"Of course, I will." Illya rubbed Yolanda's shoulders. "You're part of the reason I want to return."

Yolanda blushed. "Okay. But I've got to share something that's been on my mind."

"What is it?" Illya asked perplexed.

"Was our meeting a coincidence or…or was it a set up?"

A severe frown formed on Illya's face. "Is that what you thought?"

"Yes," Yolanda said in a hushed voice.

"Our meeting was purely coincidental. I had no idea who you were when you walked up to my table and laid that sexy smile on me."

Yolanda smiled. "I feel much better now. When you leave, I want to hear your voice every night so that I'll know you're all right."

"Okay," Preston said. "It's getting too mushy in here for me. I believe the waitress is bringing our food now."

Connie picked up her glass of water. She raised her glass and said, "To family, friends, and good times ahead."

Everyone picked up their glass of whatever they were drinking and took a sip without another word.

I've Been To
The Mountaintop

The day ended better than it began. Queenie, Emma, and First Lady Jackie O'Neill enjoyed a scrumptious meal at the Braza Steak House in Brier Creek, recounting their Vegas vacation. Jackie's spirits were lifted, especially after receiving a call from Pastor O'Neill, asking her to come home.

Queenie smiled. While Jackie's marriage seemed to be on the mend, she was still a lonely, fifty-eight-year-old woman. Men had been in and out of her life, but she wanted to settle down with someone she could be with for the rest of her days. More than twenty years had passed since her divorce, and the only thing stable in her life now was her job at the *Raleigh News and Observer.*

As was customary when she entered her house, Queenie kicked off her high-heel shoes and plopped down on the sofa. She turned on the television before going to her room to take off her Sunday clothes. She hung up her suit, put away her hat, went to the bathroom and stood before the mirror.

Queenie looked at herself for more than a minute. She was still an attractive woman. Maybe she should try Weight Watchers and see what Jennifer Hudson was talking about in those television commercials. She could stand to lose thirty or forty pounds.

After another minute had gone by, Queenie pulled a comb through her red, flowing weave. It was time for her to get rid of it and go natural. Her natural hair was as silver as a Kennedy half-dollar. She raked her hands through her weave, and, after framing her face with it, made a major decision. She was going to get her hair cut, shaped, and wear it in its natural form. It would be a carefree look and easy to manage.

Decision made, Queenie went to the kitchen and brewed herself a cup of tea. Satisfied, she sat down in her family room to enjoy the Sunday line-up on television. She took a sip and before she could place her cup on the coffee table, her doorbell rang. She'd seen everybody there was to see already today. Who in the world was trying to disturb her time to herself?

Dressed in a pair of black, silk lounging pajamas, Queenie headed for the door. God, she hoped it wasn't Joe Harris.

Standing in front of the door, Queenie peeped through the peephole. She couldn't believe her eyes. There stood Linden Robinson as bold and brazen as he wanted to be. Queenie was closing that chapter of her life.

Before Queenie was able to step back, Linden began to bang on the door. "Red, I know you're in there. Let me in."

Queenie moved away from the door and let Linden bang away. After about five minutes, all was silent again.

But not for long.

Queenie's phone began to play Linden's song. She let it play; but when he hung up, he dialed all over again. This went on for the next five minutes. Then Linden began banging on the door again.

Enough was enough. Queenie marched to the front door, pulled it open, and assumed a ninja pose. Linden had been leaning on the door so hard he almost fell when she yanked it open.

"It's about damn time you opened this door. How does it look having your man knocking on the door for twenty minutes?"

"You're not my man, Linden. Not now, not ever. So whatever it is that you're trying to sell, you better try the house next door; I'm not buying."

"My brother told me he ran into you...no...he stopped your flying behind from killing somebody."

"And..."

"Look, Red, all I want to do is make conversation with you. Can a brother come inside for a minute?"

"I have company."

"I don't believe that lie, although you do look mighty comfortable in those silk loungers, showing off those healthy curves of yours. Anyway, Richard told me you asked him this very afternoon if he had another brother that was available. I'm available. I'm here to rock your world."

"I don't need anybody to rock my world, Linden. I'm happy in the place that I'm in, and I don't need any losers, two-time hustlers, or an erectile dysfunctional man to impede my progress."

"Now you're making me mad, Red. I came in peace."

"Not by the sound of the pounding you gave my front door."

"Maybe so, but you made me go there. Look, I'll only take up a few minutes of your time. Can we talk, Red?"

Queenie looked at Linden as if he was the last person she wanted to see. "Ten minutes; that's it."

Linden grinned as he squeezed his way past Queenie. Her eyes were on his back as he headed to the family room like it was familiar territory. Queenie stopped when he stopped and turned around.

"Where are you sitting?" he asked.

"I'm sitting on this couch and you can sit in the chair over there." She pointed. They sat. "So whatever it is that you've come to say, spit it out. Your time is ticking."

"Come on, Red. We're better friends than that."

"Are we? Where's Drema D tonight? Is she out of town and you figured you'd take the opportunity to see what Red was doing?"

Linden held his lips together, smacked them, and then stared at Queenie. "Drema D and I don't have anything going on. I ran into her at the supermarket after you kicked me out. She agreed to go out with me, and you and your lovely date ran into me. That's the end of the story. I've only seen her twice since that night."

"Well, I'm sorry about that, but that's not my problem."

"It's not mine either."

Linden rose from his seat and walked over to where Queenie was sitting. Queenie held out her hand.

"What are you doing? I let you in here so you can talk; nothing more."

Linden ignored Queenie and sat down next to her.

Before Queenie knew what was happening, Linden was holding her face in his hands. He pulled her to him. His lips fell hard upon hers and sucked them until there was no life left. He used his tongue and parted hers, gently teasing and stroking the nerves of seduction. Linden felt the tension in Queenie's body, the tension that tried to resist but was on its way to giving in.

Linden savagely tongue kissed Queenie, allowing his raw emotions to get the best of him. He kissed, slurped and entangled his tongue with hers until he pulled back from exhaustion. Then he looked Queenie straight in the eyes, as his begged for forgiveness.

"I love you, Red. There's no one else for me." He kissed her passionately on the lips, then pulled up, looking down at Queenie. "Don't you believe me?"

Queenie reached up and tried to push Linden away, but he grabbed her arms and pulled them to her sides.

"Don't resist. I promise to love and cherish you always. If marriage is what you want, I'm prepared to do so now."

"You're a joke, Linden. What kind of fool do you think I am?"

"I hope you're a fool who still loves me. I may not be as refined as some of the men you've been with. And no, I don't have a college degree, but I have a GED that's worth its weight in gold. I make good money working for the cable company."

"I want a man who has a larger vocabulary than yours," Queenie said dreamily. "I want a man who loves me for who I am and appreciates me with all my shortcomings. I want a man whose every thought isn't on making a sexual transaction; my coochie is worth much more."

"If you wanted a résumé, you should've asked me. But I do know that that Jheri Curl-wearing brother, with the old pimp walk, can't satisfy you like I can."

"First, what goes on between Joe and me isn't any of your business."

"Say what you want, Red, but your old man was at this bar I sometimes frequent, and he was bragging about how he was rolling with you in the sheets."

"You're lying, Linden. Joe Harris isn't that type of man."

"So, you're saying that you'd trust that country brother over me? I'm going to tell you straight up; his résumé doesn't sparkle either. I was told that the brother used to own a car dealership back in the day and bilked many of his welfare receiving clients out of their money. You work at the newspaper; I bet you could find a story or two on your Mr. Joe Harris, even if it is in small print and hidden behind the other twenty-thousand recorded thefts in the city of Durham."

Queenie was quiet, absorbing what Linden had said. Finally, voice less assured in spite of her words, she said, "This isn't a competition, Linden. It's my life; my story. I get to choose the road I want to travel, and it's not with you. We've come to the end of the line, and it's time for you to jump off."

Linden sat up and then stood up. "You want me, Red. I'm sure you can feel the tingling between your legs. I excite you; I make you say your ABC's backwards. You love the way my hands caress every part of your body while I get you ready for the climax of your life. Uhmm, I saw your body tremor…praying that I use my tongue on you so you can scream like a banshee."

"Enough; get out," Queenie yelled. She stood up and looked at Linden with disgust. "You don't deserve me. Your time is up."

Linden again scooped Queenie into his arms, assailing her with kisses. He bit her neck and left a purple bruise as a souvenir at the point of attack. With her hands, she pushed Linden away, but he held on to her, unwilling for the moment to end.

While he kissed her, he fumbled with the elastic on the pants of her lounging pajamas. Before he changed his mind about what he wanted to do, he slid the pants down. While he shouldn't have been, he was surprised that Queenie had nothing on. He cupped his hands over her glorious helping of buttocks and squeezed, panting rhythmically, as the heat of his passion was in an uproar.

"Stop," Queenie said, her voice faint, her will weak.

Linden pulled her close, the pants of her lounging pajamas now circling her feet. Lifting Queenie slightly in the air, Linden kicked the soft material away and concentrated on pleasuring her.

Surprise was plain on his face when Queenie leaned into him and kissed him back with equal force. He felt her quiver as he let her feel his erection against her naked body. With his teeth, Linden loosened the buttons on her top and released her breasts.

A large extended nipple fell into his mouth like a ripe, black olive and he sucked it gently for several minutes before plucking the other and delighting himself with a second helping.

They moaned and groaned, passion pulsing through their bodies. Pausing only to take off his clothes, Linden picked Queenie up and carried her to the bedroom. They fell back on the bed, loving each other as if they were the last two people on earth—kissing, hugging, and sucking until there was nothing left to do but bring each other to the ultimate climax. And they did.

Linden wasn't sure if he saw the Almighty, but he'd definitely climbed to the top of the mountain. It was the first time in a long time that he didn't need the help of the blue pill.

He held Queenie tight and squeezed, stopping to kiss her breasts in thanks for such a magnificent experience. Linden couldn't get enough. There was so much warmth and tenderness in the midst of their lust for one another. It had been a long time, and if he were to describe it, Linden would equate it later to an out-of-body experience. It was that good. It held passion and fire. For him it was also love and devotion. In the real, Queenie was the woman who brought out the best of him.

Queenie wasn't sure what had happened. The one thing she could say for sure was that Linden satisfied her sexual appetite like no other. Maybe she was hungry—that wouldn't be far from the truth. But there was more to it. There was passion and a true desire to please. He was attentive to all of her erogenous zones. The love making made her feel insatiable. At that moment, Queenie realized she wasn't ready to throw in the towel—it wasn't the end of the line yet for her and Linden.

As they lay together, they couldn't stop feeling, touching, kissing each other. Each time Linden touched Queenie, the longing for him intensified. She begged him to fill her cup again as she wrapped her legs around his waist in anticipation.

Then the doorbell rang. What a terrible way to come down from a high.

Knock Out

"Is that your doorbell?" Linden asked, lifting his head.

Queenie sat up, pulling the covers over her exposed breasts.

"No, baby, don't cover up my joy sticks. I'm going to be playing with them for a while longer."

Whoever was at the door was persistent.

"Damn, were you expecting somebody, Red?"

"I wasn't expecting you and yet here we are."

Linden smiled. "Let me go to the door and see who it is." Linden reached down and covered one of Queenie's plump nipples with his mouth. He sucked; she smiled. "I'll be right back."

Linden quickly put his pants on and halfway sprinted to the front door. Without looking through the peephole, he opened the door to find Joe Harris standing there, dressed in a brown, silk suit and an off-white hat with a tan, silk band. Wet curls extended below the hat.

Joe stared at Linden and Linden stared at Joe. Linden leaned against the doorframe, his tall, lanky and shirtless body on display.

"Where's Queenie?" Joe demanded.

"You mean Red?"

Joe rolled his eyes at Linden. "Queenie...Red, you know who I'm talking about."

"And what do you want with her?"

"Who are you?"

"My name is Linden Robinson. I'm Queenie's boyfriend…and have been for the past five years."

"Well, I've been with her for the past month."

"That's what I've heard, but I'm back now, partner. Actually, you're interrupting our make-up session. Red is waiting for me to come back to bed and give her the pleasure she deserves."

"You rat-face, buffoon, I don't know who you are and I don't give a damn. Go and tell Queenie I want to talk to her now."

"Old man, you need to jump back in your old-ass Caddy or whatever it is you're driving and get the hell up out of here."

"I want to talk to Queenie, now. I've invested a lot of time, money and energy in her, and I'll be damned if I'm going to be out talked by some slick-talking jerk like you."

"So, Joe, I'm an investment?"

Both men turned when they heard Queenie's voice.

"Look, Queenie, I didn't mean it like that."

"I don't have any problems with giving you back the necklace and bracelet…"

"Look, it's apparent that I've made a mistake about you. You can have the necklace and the bracelet. Consider it payment for my time in the hay with you."

Shock registered on Queenie's face. "I'm not some hoe, Joe. I'm a good woman. I'm the one who made a mistake falling for your swindling ass. It's time for you to go; it's over."

"You don't have to worry about that, sister. You weren't that good anyway."

"Get your ass out," Linden hollered, following behind Joe. Linden slammed the door as hard as he could. It shuddered and felt like a locomotive had knocked the house off of its foundation.

What Am I Going To Do?

T he week went by in a blur. Queenie and Linden had rekindled their on-again, off-again relationship. They couldn't wait for their work days to be over so that they could spend time together. Their romance appeared to be here to stay—this time.

It was Saturday, and all Queenie wanted to do was sleep, but she had to get up sooner or later to meet up with her sister friends for a girl's night out. She couldn't wait to watch their faces when she told them her good news.

Queenie quickly changed her linen and fluffed up the pillows on the chaise lounge. Next, she ran her bath water and poured in her favorite bubble bath. She raised her arms and stretched and thanked God for his many blessings. Things were looking up for her, and for the first time in a long time she felt happy.

Although she and Linden were hitting home runs, she was slow to give him the key to her house. She allowed him to stay over a couple of nights, but Queenie still preferred her privacy and wasn't in any rush to let a man rule her castle.

Luxuriating in the tub, Queenie closed her eyes and ruminated over the last few days with Linden. She felt that he was really in the relationship for the long haul. He was attentive to her needs. He fixed a few things around the house that needed attention and bought groceries so there would be some things he liked in the house whenever Queenie felt like cooking. Today, she was going to fix him a nice breakfast—grits, eggs, bacon, waffles with strawberries on top, and her. She smiled at the thought. She couldn't stay in the tub too much longer as Linden was due in an hour.

Feeling great, Queenie prepared to step out of the tub. As soon as she slung her leg over the side, her cell phone rang. She felt a pang in her chest and prayed that it wasn't Linden calling to cancel.

She ran butt naked into her bedroom and grabbed the phone, clicking the ON button without looking at the caller ID. "Hello?" she said out of breath.

"Umm, what a pleasant hello," the caller said in response.

"Who's this?"

"I can't believe you've forgotten my voice already."

Queenie grabbed her chest and sat her wet body on the bed. "Anthony, is this you?"

"Yes, it is. I told you I'd be calling."

"But it's been almost two weeks since we last spoke…since I last saw you. I figured…"

"You figured that I was one of those slick-tongue devils that had run a line on you to make you feel good."

"Well, I wasn't going to say all of that…"

"But that's what you were thinking."

"Close."

"So, how are you, Queenie? I really did enjoy your company in Vegas."

Queenie grinned in spite of herself. "I'm doing fine, working hard."

"I'd love to see you again. I'm going to Hawaii in a few weeks. I'd love for you to join me."

"Hawaii? In a few weeks? Wow, I'd have to think about it."

"What is there to think about? It's going to be paradise—fun in the sun. I am going out there for business, but there will be plenty of time to play."

"I'm flattered that you'd ask."

"Think about it and give me your answer when I call later this evening."

"I'm going out on the town with my girls tonight. Why don't I call you?"

"It'll be better if I call you. I'm in so many business meetings, and I would hate to miss your call."

"Okay, I'll look forward to hearing from you. I'll have an answer for you."

"Sounds like a plan. I'll talk to you later."

Queenie hung up the phone and lay on the bed longer than she'd planned. Why did Anthony have to call now and complicate matters? She closed her eyes and dreamed that she was in Hawaii drinking Mai Tais and eating fresh pineapple.

The doorbell rang and she flew from the bed, stopping to put on her silk robe. She composed herself, deactivated the house alarm, and opened the door. Linden stood on the porch with a bouquet of red and yellow roses. She wanted to die for allowing herself to even think about Anthony.

Breakfast At Queenie's

Queenie tossed Anthony's call to the wayside and gave all of her attention to the man standing in front of her.

Taking the roses from Linden, she walked to the kitchen to get a vase in which to put the fragrant smelling flowers.

Queenie stopped abruptly with Linden right on her heels. Linden twirled Queenie around and held her in a close embrace. He reached down and passionately kissed her as she returned the favor, roses forgotten.

It felt like they were in a bubble of their own, the world spinning only for them.

Queenie pulled back, catching her breath. "I was getting ready to fix breakfast, if you're hungry," she said.

"Oh, I'm hungry," Linden said, taking the roses from Queenie. He put them in a vase she had sitting on the counter and added water. "And I hope you're on the menu."

Queenie laughed. "Well, of course, I'm on the menu." She peeled her robe from her shoulders and let it slide to the floor. Linden nearly dropped the vase.

"Oh, Red, I don't know if I can wait for the eggs and bacon." He pulled Queenie to him and kissed her neck and held each breast in his hands. Linden reached in his pocket and pulled out a vial. "Let me toss one of these blue pills down my throat. I've got to have you now."

Queenie took Linden's hand. "This morning, you're going to learn the art of seduction. There will be no touching; you will make yourself comfortable on that stool by the counter." Linden started to say something, but Queenie raised her finger to her mouth to quiet him.

Linden complied and watched Queenie work. The only material thing on her body was a pair of satin slippers with a fluffy, clip-on bow attached.

Queenie moved about the kitchen in an organized fashion. For a plus-size woman, she had enough curves to make a man slobber. She cracked eggs and placed raw bacon in the microwave, but it was the movement of her arms and breasts when she beat the waffle mix together that excited Linden beyond his wildest imagination.

"Jesus, Red, you're making it hard…for me to concentrate. I hear the microwave browning the bacon and the grits boiling on the stove, but all I see is you in all of your glory. I can't think about nothing else. Whip that batter, girl."

Walking up to Linden, Queenie kissed him hard on the mouth. He slid off the stool and grabbed her buttocks and pulled her close to him. She felt the heat, too, as he nuzzled up against her. Then she abruptly pushed him back, watching him beg for more with his eyes.

She poured batter on the waffle iron and closed the lid. It hissed, and Queenie looked up and saw Linden wiping his brow. She went to the stove and stirred butter in the grits and then crossed over to the refrigerator and pulled out a pitcher of orange juice. With a small motion of her wrist, Queenie slowly moved the glass pitcher so that the liquid twirled gently inside.

Linden slid off the stool again and stood behind Queenie, gyrating like the juice in the pitcher. She moaned when he cupped her breasts and squeezed them tenderly, taking her ripe nipples in between his fingers, squeezing them until Queenie moaned with pleasure.

"You're ready," she said, pushing her body into his. "We'll eat this other food later. All I want is you."

Linden didn't have to be told a second time. He kissed her with all the passion within him.

Linden made love to Queenie, laying her out against the cool sheets she'd put on earlier, taking his time and making each moment last. The foreplay was so erotic and intimate that Queenie begged for the climax. She couldn't stand him kissing another nipple; the fire department was about to hear her scream. Linden flooded her gates with his manhood, which, thanks to her seduction had no problem rising naturally, and gave her everything he had.

They collapsed together, huffing and puffing. Queenie wiped Linden's bald head and kissed his nose, while Linden couldn't quite stay away from her breasts. Queenie laid there with Linden's sweat pouring on her, feeling the love she'd craved for so long.

Linden lifted his head. "Do you smell that?"

"It's the waffles. I forgot to take them off the waffle iron. I'm sure they've burned up."

"No, Red, it's burning up in here. And after we eat, I'll be ready for round two and three. I want to be with you forever."

Queenie smiled. She wanted to be with Linden, too.

Innocent Until Proven Guilty

Franklin O'Neill had been shaken from his foundation. After his wife received a telephone call from a stranger, a man she had met in Las Vegas, he'd wanted to strangle Jackie and ask God for forgiveness later. But he was a man of the cloth and realized that God sometimes administered these tests to shift his faithful out of their comfort zone .

Yes, he was blessed and highly favored, but every now and then it was good to be knocked off the top of the mountain so he would remember how he got there in the first place. Franklin recalled one of his associate ministers preaching on the purpose of the valley. He said that to get from one mountain to the next, you have to go through the valley. The valley experience was where you were strengthened for the journey ahead, and if it took you to the top of the mountain, you knew that God was with you.

Franklin got up from his knees and opened his bible to the Twenty Third Psalm. He found peace in that passage of scripture. King David was one of Franklin's favorite characters in the Bible as David was favored by God. King David had many highs and as many lows, and when he found himself in the valley, he got on his knees and cried out to God.

Looking the scripture over again, Franklin knew what he had to do. Although he had no plans to ever leave his wife, especially for a small indiscretion, he had yet to forgive her. The love they shared was being tested. Franklin hadn't touched Jackie since the day of the telephone call, and he barely spoke to her. That was not of God, and he certainly couldn't teach his parishioners about forgiveness and turning the other cheek when he failed to do so himself.

One thing Franklin hadn't admitted to himself was that he missed making love to Jackie. She was a dutiful lover and knew what buttons to push. And while he was a humble man of God, he enjoyed making his woman happy. He missed their role play. Jackie had even showed him new tricks to stimulate their lovemaking and put it on a higher plateau. Franklin shook his head at the thought. What Franklin didn't like was his wife's influences—those silver-haired demons, who happened to be part of his congregation. But he had to love them, too.

He went into their bedroom and found Jackie putting on her clothes. "Going somewhere?" he asked.

She sighed. "Yes, I'm meeting Queenie, Emma, Yolanda, and Connie for a girls' night out. I'll be gone a few hours. We're going to Bone Fish Grill."

"That's a nice pantsuit. I don't believe I've seen it before."

"I purchased it when I was in…Las Vegas. The girls and I went on a shopping binge, something I hadn't done in ages."

"The off-white looks good on your skin color. Jackie, the reason I came in here…"

"Franklin, baby, I did something stupid. It was all so innocent…"

"Calm down, baby. I'm not here to judge you. I do want to ask you for forgiveness for the way I've acted. I never gave you a chance to explain, but in my heart I believe that you weren't trying to establish a relationship with this person."

Jackie went and stood in front of Franklin and held his hands. "Baby, I love you. You have to know that without a doubt. The gentleman approached me while I was at the pool, and I only gave him my card in the event he was in the area and wanted to stop by our church."

Franklin wanted to believe Jackie, but he found it hard to accept her explanation. Jackie was a little naïve, but her explanation didn't make any sense, given that the man called. She looked sincere as she offered her account of the situation, and since he'd prayed about it and asked God to forgive his actions, Franklin's only recourse was to forgive. Still, Franklin wasn't sure that he could trust Jackie totally. Why would a married woman—a pastor's wife, give her information to a man she didn't know while lying out at the pool?

Franklin shook the negative thoughts from his brain. There was no doubt in his mind that he loved his wife, even with her shortcomings. This was a one-time act of indiscretion, at least that's what he believed. "Do you forgive me?"

"The question is do you believe me? Yes, I forgive you, but if you're harboring ill feelings underneath your forgiving spirit, I'm not sure I can forgive you. Please believe me when I say that I only saw the man when I was sitting by the pool for a few short minutes. The extent of our conversation was exchanging pleasantries, and, of course, me giving him my…no, our, number for a reason that sounds idiotic to me now."

Franklin sighed. He drew Jackie to him and kissed her on the nose and then planted a sweet and tender kiss on the mouth. "I love you, Jackie, and yes, I believe you."

Tears of joy sprang to Jackie's face. "Thank you, Franklin. I'd give my life for you."

Franklin wiped her face and kissed her forehead. "Now run along and have fun at dinner. Don't let those crazy women lead you astray."

Jackie looked at Franklin thoughtfully. "I'm my own person. I've never let anyone steer me to a place I don't want to be. However, I'll be mindful to act as a first lady should." Jackie picked up her keys and handbag. "I'll see you in a few hours."

"Have a good time."

Franklin watched Jackie walk out of the door, looking fine as ever. He had a priceless jewel, and he wasn't going to let a telephone call from another man trip him up and cause him to lose the best thing in his life. No matter that his mind was in turmoil, he loved Jackie O'Neill.

It Takes One To Know One

Everyone was cackling like hens in a hen house when Jackie arrived at Bonefish Grill. She was glad that the atmosphere was light, although her thinking changed when everyone became quiet as she neared the table. She smiled and took a seat next to Connie.

"Hey, Jackie," everyone said in unison.

"You're looking snazzy in that outfit," Connie said, reaching over and giving Jackie a pinch. "You were serious about your shopping."

Jackie gave her a fake smile. Maybe it hadn't been such a good idea for her to come. She wondered what each person was thinking or what Queenie and Emma had told the others about her situation. Plus they had all witnessed Franklin's sermon

"How are you all doing? I see that everyone is in a festive mood."

"Why don't you have a drink, Jackie," Queenie suggested. "It may calm your nerves."

Jackie waved her hand. "No, I'm not indulging in the bitter fruit. I've got to keep my faculties in a good state of mind. I don't want to make the same stupid mistake I made in Vegas."

"You didn't do anything wrong," Emma chimed in. "You're only guilty of looking so hot that the brother had to stop and say something to you. There's nothing wrong in that."

Jackie bowed her head and raised it back up. She swiped at a tear that had formed in the corner of her eye. "No, there's nothing wrong with someone paying you a compliment, but as you and Q so eloquently put it the other day, it was the dumbest thing I could've ever done. Franklin asked for forgiveness for the way he acted toward me."

"That's great," Queenie said.

"While it's great, I don't believe Franklin is ever going to trust me again. I've betrayed that trust, and from here on out, he's going to be looking and judging although I told him I was faithful. And I can't blame him. I would've been pissed to high heaven if a woman called my house looking for Franklin."

"Yeah, that's a tough call," Connie added. She rubbed Jackie's back. "This too shall pass. You and the reverend will be whole again."

Jackie smiled. "I hope so."

Queenie smiled, preparing to turn the tide of the conversation. "Well, I've got some good news," she said.

"Your guy from Vegas called and wants to see you again," Yolanda said, breezily.

"Yes, he did. In fact, he wants me to go to Hawaii with him in two weeks."

"You go, Q," Yolanda said, giving Queenie a high-five. "You picked a winner this time."

"Not so fast. I haven't said I would or wouldn't, yet."

"What's wrong with you?" Emma asked, giving Queenie a wicked look. "Tell me you didn't fall in love with the old man with the Jheri curl."

Everybody laughed, including Queenie. "No, I won't be seeing him again. I...I gave him his marching papers last week."

"Good for you," Yolanda added. "You were too good for him, Q. Now, I'd be packing my suitcase with the hottest bikini I could find. Hot pink would look good on you, Q."

"Not so fast, YoYo. I'm not sure that I can go. You see…" Queenie took a deep breath. "Linden and I are a couple again."

Not a sound could be heard from the group of women. They sat there and stared at Queenie for minutes on end. Emma, Connie, Yolanda, and Jackie took turns rolling their eyes in disgust. Then all of a sudden Jackie erupted in laughter. She laughed so hard, it made the others laugh.

Queenie gave Jackie a hateful look. "And what's so funny, First Lady?"

Jackie tried to contain her laughter. She put pressure on her throat and finally breathed in slowly. "And you called me a dumb fool? I don't get you, Queenie Jackson." Jackie started laughing again.

Queenie shot up and pointed her finger at each of the ladies. "You can say whatever you damn well please, but Linden is the man I'm in love with. Take it or leave it. I don't know Anthony from a sack of potatoes. He could be a serial killer."

"Uhm," Emma said, "Could've fooled me. In Vegas, you stayed out with your serial killer until four in the morning. I'll let you slide on that one, but Linden? Girl, you are a damn fool."

Queenie grabbed her purse and headed out of the restaurant without saying a word.

"Well, what are we eating?" Jackie asked. "I'm famished."

Oh No He Didn't

Queenie was pissing mad. She was in love with Linden and couldn't care less what everybody else thought. It was her life, and she was going to live it the way she damn well pleased.

Queenie took off for home and called Linden on the way. Right now, all she wanted was his loving touch, his loving caress to take the sting out of the rejection she felt from her girlfriends. They were supposed to be there for her no matter what—it was the Silver Bullets' code. Not an articulated code, maybe, but the truth of the matter. Queenie had been there for Connie and Jackie, but no one was there for her.

She dialed Linden's number four times; no answer. For sure, she thought Linden said he was chilling out tonight. Maybe his battery was dead, but the call didn't automatically go to voice mail.

Queenie pulled into her garage. She went straight to her bedroom and pulled off her clothes. After a moment, she sat on the edge of the bed and picked up her phone and dialed Linden's number one more time; still no answer.

The house was too quiet, and Queenie didn't want to be there alone. She put her clothes back on and decided to go to her favorite jazz club and get a drink. If she was going to be a good Christian, she had to stop hitting the juice, but tonight she needed something to soothe her nerves.

Zipped and ready to go, Queenie made one last phone call to Linden. No answer. Queenie got in her car and drove the ten miles to her destination. Inside, the music was soothing to her ears.

Queenie took a seat at the bar and ordered a Long Island Iced Tea. A local jazz band was headlining, and the music was hypnotic. Queenie swayed to the music, taking sips of her drink ever so often. It was refreshing to be away from the wannabe divas she called her friends.

Scanning the room, Queenie didn't see anyone she knew. She sighed and ordered another drink.

She felt her phone vibrate. It had to be Anthony calling to see if she'd made up her mind about Hawaii. Any other time, she'd be packing her suitcase, but her heart was somewhere else. The phone continued to vibrate and then it stopped.

"Chuck," Queenie said to the bartender, "I'm going to powder my nose. Don't let anyone take my spot or my drink."

"I got you covered, Q."

Queenie made a quick trip to the restroom and returned to her perch on the bar stool. Normally, she didn't hang around the bar area, but tonight she wanted to be incognito and feel the groove by her lonesome.

That's when she spotted him.

Queenie downed the last bit of her drink and eased her behind off the bar stool. She weaved her head back and forth, following the outline of what appeared to be familiar faces. Her eyes hadn't deceived her. No more than a few feet in front of her were Linden and Drema D. They were seated at a table and engaged in intimate conversation.

Without thinking twice, Queenie moved forward to make her presence known. Her body moved with the music—the vision of a lover scorned. She was mad as hell, and someone was going to give her some answers.

Disregarding all else around her, Queenie stopped at Linden's table and parked herself on the edge of it. She tapped Linden on the shoulder and then slapped him on the side of his head.

"Tell me what's going on?"

"What's your problem?" Drema D asked, since Linden was still stunned from the blow to his head.

Queenie threw her arm out and pointed her finger in Drema D's face. "Hussy, I'm not talking to you. See that you stay out of this conversation."

"Now hold on a minute, Queenie. I don't know what's up with you. This isn't the first time you've seen Linden and me together. In fact, you were with someone else."

"I told you that this wasn't about you, Drema D."

"I heard you, but I don't understand what you want with my man. You didn't want him, but now that he's with me, you want to reclaim your spot. Heifer, you need to back away before you get hurt."

Queenie reached over Linden and tried to grab Drema D's hair. Linden stood up and pushed Queenie back. Queenie lunged again, sweat pouring down her face. Linden grabbed Queenie by the arms and asked Drema D to stay put.

The manager came out of nowhere to see what the commotion was all about. "Look, we run a respectable establishment here, and if you're not going to conduct yourselves accordingly, you'll have to leave. I have other paying customers who came to enjoy the music."

"Red, it's not what it looks like," Linden said, ignoring the manager.

"Oh, it isn't? You told me that you and Drema D weren't serious."

Linden looked from Queenie to Drema D. "Calm down, Red. This isn't the place to have this discussion."

Queenie pounded Linden in the chest while tears flowed from her eyes. "Oh now you don't want to discuss this…this…whatever it is. You made this the place for this discussion. You're a sorry excuse for a man, Linden Robinson." Then she turned to Drema D. "Do you know where Linden has been the past week?"

Drema D's lips trembled while one of her hands was balled into a fist. She looked from Queenie to Linden without saying a word.

"He's been in my bed making love to me."

Those who were sitting nearby gasped. The manager gave the trio another warning.

"He came to my house, banged on the door, and begged me to take him back," Queenie continued, totally committed to the conversation. "I see that it's all been a lie; I should've never trusted his sorry ass. And do you know what else he told me, Drema D? This fool said he wanted to marry me."

Drema D got up from her seat and hit Linden on the other side of his head. "You can have him, Queenie. I don't like to be humiliated, and I certainly don't take sloppy seconds. I don't want a man who doesn't know how to be one." Drema D picked up her drink and threw it in Linden's face. Then she walked out without taking a second look back.

Queenie bucked her eyes and put a hand on her hip. "I don't want you either. You are dead to me, Linden. Dead."

"Come on, Red. Drema D arrived in town this morning and called to see if I would take her out to the club tonight. She was relentless about me taking her out and I didn't see any harm since you were with your girlfriends, and…"

"You figured what exactly, Linden? Do you know how to form the word *no?* It's easy. It's a one syllable word that doesn't take any energy to pronounce. You don't need a GED to know how to say it. You told me you loved me and wanted to be with me, but you couldn't formulate that one word in your brain that would've saved your ass. You're history, partner. I'm out."

"Don't go, Red. I do love you."

Queenie walked away without a glance backwards. She hated that she had to go there. At that moment, she hated herself for being so gullible and needy. Her girlfriends were right about Linden, but she hadn't listened.

Her phone vibrated in her purse. She stopped to see whose name appeared in the caller ID. It was Anthony. Queenie dropped the phone back into her purse, got in her car, and drove home.

The Battle Is Not Yours

Three weeks passed with no word from Connie. Yolanda sat in her living room, her face soaked with tears. Her worst fears had been realized; her only sister had gone into the Witness Protection Program with her husband.

Fear gripped the city every time a new announcement was made about a new arrest related to the drug trafficking ring. The drug war had become even more gruesome; six dead over the last weekend. Even prosecuting attorneys were wearing bullet-proof vests.

Yolanda had spoken to Illya only a few times since he'd left Raleigh. Their conversations were short and cryptic. Yolanda knew that Illya had information about Connie and Preston's whereabouts, but as a good soldier of the law, he wasn't at liberty to divulge any information—that is if Yolanda wanted to see her sister alive in the distant future.

Yolanda scratched her head and sighed. She couldn't find solace anywhere. She had no idea as to the day or the hour Connie disappeared from her life. The only thing she did know was that her heart ached.

It was Sunday morning, and the only thing she could do was turn to the Almighty. Yolanda hadn't been to church since the last time she and Illya, Connie and Preston were together. Different ones called to see about her, but she didn't have it in her to respond.

Yolanda looked at the clock on her living room wall. It was nine-thirty. She still had time to make it to church if she pushed herself. Today, she needed a word from the Lord, and there was no one place like Shiloh Baptist Church to get it.

She ran through the shower and put on her Sunday best. Yolanda unwrapped the silk scarf from around her head, pleased at how good her hair looked. There were a few stray strands of silver hair out of place that she took care of with the swipe of her flat iron. Mascara and a little lipstick completed her look, and she was off to church.

As Yolanda drove to church, she thought about her sister friends, the Silver Bullets. They'd become disjointed since Vegas. Everyone had something going in their lives—Connie and Preston's dilemma, Jackie's fall from grace with her husband, and Emma. Emma's life seemed to be the only one without a flaw. Then Yolanda thought of Queenie. The last time she saw her was when she ran out of Bone Fish Grill. She hadn't even called Queenie to see if she was all right.

Yolanda turned into the church parking lot and turned off the ignition. She sat for a moment and reflected on the past few weeks. Life had thrown her a curve ball, and she wasn't coping very well. She needed the Word to soothe her broken heart; she got out of the car.

The faces of familiar people lit up when they saw her walk through the door. First Lady Jackie O'Neill was at the piano and Emma stood in the choir stand, waiting for the moment to usher the choir in.

Yolanda caught a glimpse of Queenie as she marched by, her voice raised high above the others. Queenie had a beautiful voice and was the reason why Emma gave her all of the good songs.

Yolanda missed her sister girlfriends; she needed them more than she was willing to admit.

Now that all the preliminaries were done, Pastor O'Neill got up to bring the morning message. Yolanda sat with uneasiness, praying that the pastor would deliver a good word.

"Saints, the enemy is busy. Many of you have read the paper or heard the television accounts about the drug trafficking ring that has got the cities of Raleigh and Durham on lockdown."

Yolanda fidgeted in her seat.

"No one knew that a major drug ring was operating in our own backyard. One day we were going about our business, mowing our yards and running to the grocery store to purchase ingredients for the night's supper. And boom," Pastor snapped his fingers, "we hear that our city is under siege and that federal and state level law enforcement are dropping nets everywhere to try to secure and reclaim it.

"The drug ring came like a thief in the night to destroy our city and its citizens with the poison of drugs for the love of money. People that we held in high esteem, some who held prestigious jobs within our communities, were some of the perpetrators of this heinous crime. No doubt, some of you have been touched in some way or another to the extent that you have loved ones or are a victim yourself of the war on drugs.

"I'm here today, church, to tell you that while the federal agents, marshals, local and state law enforcement are doing what they can to fight this horrific crime, I'm here to tell you that the battle is not yours; it's the Lord's. I've been talking about King David for some time now, and we know that with all that David went through, he would get on his knees and cry out to the Father. You don't have to fret or sweat it; God is on the case. He knows the desires of your heart, and He will honor your request if you believe."

People jumped up from their seats and praised the Lord. Yolanda couldn't contain herself and cried out with the rest.

"Sister Queenie Jackson, please sing 'The Battle is Not Yours'.

Queenie rose from her seat and went to the microphone. She began to sing the verse as Emma brought the choir to their feet. Queenie was consumed with the words of the song, however, as she neared the end of the first verse, Queenie burst into tears, crying out to the Lord to help her. No one had seen Queenie get as emotional as she did that day.

When the song was over, Queenie marched down to where the congregation sat and went to Yolanda and hugged her. They hugged for more than a few minutes, and before long, the whole church were up on their feet hugging one another. Pastor O'Neill prayed for everyone.

The heart of the people was stirred. The tears that flowed down Yolanda's face weren't tears of sadness; they were tears of joy. At that very moment, her spirit knew that God was going to take care of her sister, Connie, and her brother-in-law, Preston.

That's What Friends Are For

Church services ended on a high note. Love bounced all over the building as various ones hugged each other. There wasn't any idle chit chat at the end of service. Everyone smiled and exited the building with a new type of humility.

First Lady Jackie waved to her girlfriends. She and Pastor Franklin were again of one accord. He put his arm around her shoulders and gave her a peck on the cheek. They exited toward the church offices and were soon out of sight.

"Lunch, ladies?" Yolanda asked, looking between Queenie and Emma. "Any place but P. F. Chang's."

Emma and Queenie laughed.

"You all go on," Emma said. "I'm fixing dinner for my husband today. Last night, Billy and I had a soul searching moment, and I realized that we were lost souls in our own home. These are our twilight years, and we should be enjoying them together. Our kids are doing well, and we don't have want for anything. Billy said he wanted to take me on a cruise—get away from it all."

"That is fantastic, Emma," Yolanda said. "You do have an amazing man. He's been a model husband…"

"Now, I wouldn't say all of that, but I wouldn't trade him for no one else. I love myself some Billy Wilcox, and if I have to eat fried chicken on Wednesdays for the rest of my life, I'll do it, so long as I don't have to cook it." The ladies laughed.

"But you know what, ladies?" Emma continued. "Pastor put a word out today. We take so much for granted. All I've ever wanted was a peaceful home, a good husband, and a good job. The Lord has blessed me with all of the above. I had the desires of my heart all along, but I didn't know how to treat it."

Emma turned to Queenie and took her hand. "Queenie, I have to apologize for how I acted...reacted to your announcement about being back with Linden. Who am I to judge? I don't know who and what is best for you. God may have a plan that I don't know anything about."

Queenie held up her hand. "There's no need to apologize, Emma. You ladies were right. Linden Robinson is a fraud and the truth isn't in him. I can't believe how gullible I've been. I let my heart rule my head. Any man who halfway gives me a parting glance, I jump at their feet without thinking about the consequences or what's best for me. I'm like a homeless person who'd take any old handout that's dropped in my lap."

"You're not that bad, Q," Yolanda said. "You're a beautiful person...a beautiful friend. You were needy, and you sought refuge..."

"What Yolanda is trying to say, Q, is that we love you and we're here for you whenever you need us. We're not here to judge."

Queenie tried to hold back the wall of tears, but they sprung forth like a busted dam. "I'm sorry guys; I can't seem to be able to control my emotions. I heard what you said, and I appreciate it. I'm done with Linden. From now on, I'm going to do me. I'm going to do what's best for Queenie Jackson...no compromising."

Queenie stopped when she felt her phone vibrate. "Hold on a minute." She took her cell out of her purse and looked at the caller ID. She sighed.

"Who is it?" Emma asked.

"Anthony…the guy I met in Vegas."

"Didn't he ask you to go to Hawaii?" Yolanda asked.

"Yeah, but I never responded to him. I was so caught up in what I thought was a new lease on life with Linden that I ignored all of Anthony's calls. I'm sure he's been to Hawaii and back. If I had said that I wanted to go with him after Linden and I had our final falling out, it would've looked as if I was on the rebound. Rebounds are out for me. I'm going to go on hiatus and get Queenie together."

Both Emma and Yolanda gave Queenie a hug.

"Before you go and take care of Billy, Emma, I need to tell you and Q something. Connie is gone."

"What?" Emma screamed, clutching her heart.

"Not so loud. I don't want everyone to know."

"Are she and Preston together?" Queenie asked, her eyebrows arched as high as they could go.

"Yeah." Now it was time for Yolanda to push back the tears. She drew her hands together and wiped the tears that had formed in her eyes. "They entered the Witness Protection Program. I haven't spoken with them in several weeks, but the last thing Connie said to me was that she was going to be with her husband. And apparently that's what she did."

Emma and Queenie hugged Yolanda.

"I'm sorry, YoYo," Queenie said. "We're going to miss them, too."

"Look, I'm going to call Billy and tell him that I'll make it up to him later," Emma said. "My girls need me. Let's go and get something to eat."

It's All About The Queen

The trio walked into Bahama Breeze, chattering about everything from what the pastor spoke about that morning to the price of gas. Queenie, Emma, and Yolanda made a pact to always be there for one another, holding up the sisterhood—a special bond among friends.

Queenie loved the Caribbean cuisine at Bahama Breeze. Her mother used to make a lot of jerk chicken when she and her siblings were growing up. She settled for the Jamaican chicken wings and opted for a Margarita instead of her usual Long Island Iced Tea.

Yolanda ordered the lobster and shrimp quesadilla—her favorite.

Emma settled for the jumbo lump crab stack. She should have gone home to be with her husband and fix the meal she promised, but she was happy to be with her sisters; they lifted her spirits.

Besides, Billy might as well have been there. She talked on and on about how much she loved him and revealed their plans to renew their vows before leaving for their cruise.

"Oh, Lord, these wings are the thing," Queenie said, taking a bite as soon as the waitress laid the dish on the table. She unselfconsciously licked her fingers. "These wings are nothing but the truth."

"My crab isn't shabby either," Emma said between bites. "I haven't been here in a year or so, but this meal reminds me how much I've missed it."

"You all are right about that. My lobster quesadilla's practically melting in my mouth," Yolanda said.

The ladies ate and enjoyed. For the first time in a long time, there was no drama. They ate and laughed and ate some more.

"Oh, hell no," Emma said, looking toward the ramp that was used to access the lobby. Your favorite boyfriend and Drema D are coming this way."

"Suck it up, Q," Yolanda was quick to say. "Put on your big girl panties and kick those misfits under the rug."

"Done," Queenie said without missing a beat. "My heart doesn't beat for Linden Robinson anymore. It's all about the Queen.

"It's funny how fast we change our minds. Drema D said she was through with Linden…didn't want any sloppy seconds, but here she is with that lying bastard. They're both liars, and if Drema D wants that sorry ass need-to-take-a pill-to-get-it-up, it's on her. No man is going to hinder me from doing what I've got to do.

"Silver Bullets, next Saturday, I'm going to the beauty shop and get this weave cut out of my hair. I'm going to go all natural. I'm going to rock my new look with every bounce of my hips."

"You go, girl," Emma said, high-fiving Queenie. "Linden isn't worth your time."

"The old geezer is looking this way," Yolanda said.

"Let him look. He's had all the banana pudding he's going to get from me."

The ladies laughed, and Queenie laughed the hardest.

"It was fun kicking it with my sisters," Emma said. "I'm going to run home and give my baby some love. If he hasn't already fixed himself something to eat, I think I'll put something together."

"Why don't you get him a plate to go?" Yolanda said. "That's the easy thing to do. That way you can spend more time loving him up. I don't know why I have to always think for you all."

"Good idea. Thank you for the suggestion, YoYo. I'll call the waitress over here and order another plate of what I had. It was especially good today."

"Do you think Connie and Preston will ever return to Raleigh?"

Yolanda dropped her head, pondered Queenie's question, and then lifted her head. "I pray that they do, Q. I miss my sister so much. She was all that I had. Mama and Daddy are gone, but as long as Connie and I had each other, we were all right."

"Look at the bright side," Emma interjected. "They're safe wherever they are. I believe in due season, you'll see them again."

Yolanda smiled. "You're right, Emma. I will see them again. Here's our waitress."

Thirty minutes later, the waitress brought Emma's food. They paid their bills and prepared to leave.

Queenie brought up the rear, as the trio began to depart the restaurant. Out of nowhere, a strong arm grabbed Queenie.

She was stunned and temporarily speechless. Her heart pounded in her chest, but she relaxed when she saw Emma and Yolanda head back in her direction.

"Red, I need a word with you. I don't like how we left things the other night," Linden said, his free hand shaking.

Very calmly, Queenie peeled Linden's hand from around her arm. "There's nothing to be said, Linden. I'm through. You are free to be with whomever. I can't do this anymore."

Linden reached for Queenie, but Yolanda threw her arm in between them. "Back up, buster."

"This is not about you, Yolanda. You and Emma can run along. My business is with Red."

"Maybe you didn't hear what the lady said," Emma barked. "She's through."

"Red, you better tell your girls to back off."

Emma grabbed Yolanda and pulled her aside. Then she went for Queenie and pulled her away from Linden. Putting her arm through Queenie's, the trio walked out of the restaurant, leaving Linden by himself with his hands in the air, looking like the fool he was."

"I'll never go back," Queenie growled. "Never."

"You better not," Emma said, waving goodbye. "I've got to take this hot food to Billy. Love y'all."

The ladies waved back. "You're going to be all right, Q. You stumped that devil in the ass. And I bet before long, Drema D is going to leave his sorry behind on the side of the road."

"I'm not ever going back to him."

Yolanda put her arm around Queenie and walked her to her car. "Never is a strong word, Q, but I like the way you say it."

Dinner Is Served

Emma smiled as she pulled into her garage. She carried the food into the house and set it in the kitchen before crossing to their bedroom to slip into something more comfortable.

The basketball game was on—Lakers vs. the Sacramento Kings—and Billy was asleep in his favorite recliner. She couldn't believe he'd fallen asleep on his favorite pastime. She let him sleep while she transferred his food from the restaurant container to one of her best china plates.

"Billy," Emma said, when she brought the food to him. "Wake up. Dinner is served. I brought you something good to eat from Bahama Breeze." She knocked his knee with her knee and his head slumped further in his seat.

"Billy," Emma called again, her eyes bulging from their sockets. "Billy, wake up."

The tray of food crashed to the floor. Food splattered across the hardwood floor and the china plate shattered into pieces. Emma screamed.

"Billyyyyyyyy."

There was no response, and when she grabbed Billy's hand, it was cold.

Emma stood in the middle of the floor and held her hands to her head and screamed again. Suddenly, as if she had come out of a trance, she took deep breaths and rushed for her landline. She dialed nine-one-one.

"Nine-one-one, what's your emergency?"

"I think…I believe my husband may have had a heart attack. I don't know," Emma cried.

"Is he breathing?"

Emma looked at Billy slumped over in his seat. "No, ma'am," she cried. "He's not doing anything."

"Ma'am we will send an ambulance right away."

The nine-one-one operator verified the address and tried to talk to Emma. The phone dropped from Emma's hands as she sank to the floor.

Fifteen minutes passed before there was a knock on the door. "Paramedics," the voice on the other side of the door shouted.

Emma pulled herself up from the floor and walked wearily to the front door. She opened it, her face stained with tears, stepped aside and pointed toward the living room.

The paramedics rushed to where Billy lay, side-stepping the food and china that was splattered across the floor. They checked him for pulse and breathing. "He's gone," one of the two paramedics said.

Emma watched in horror as they prepared to take Billy away. She tried to push the hurt and pain away, but she couldn't. Her emotions were too close to the surface.

"Is there someone I can call for you?" the female paramedic asked.

All Emma could do was cry. She never answered the paramedic and soon they were gone to the hospital with Billy's body. She slumped into a nearby chair and stared blankly at the recliner for several minutes and then at the mess on the floor. Seeing the telephone, Emma got up from the chair and picked it up. The numbers were memorized in her head, and within seconds, she had Pastor O'Neill on the line.

"Sister Emma, what's wrong?" Pastor O'Neill asked.

"It's Billy. Billy is dead."

"Jesus," Pastor O'Neill said. "Jackie and I will be right over."

"Thank you," Emma said and hung up the telephone.

Emma looked all around her and continued to cry. Folding her arms around her waist, Emma rocked back and forth. "Billy, I'm sorry I didn't come home. Maybe if I had been here, I could've saved you. I'm so sorry, baby."

Taps

The family processional nearly filled the middle section of Shiloh Baptist Church. Billy came from a large family. His mother, who was in her eighties, didn't look a day over seventy, and his five brothers and two sisters were all an attractive lot.

Emma, dressed in a white, two-piece seersucker suit, was followed by her three children, Erin, Richard, Reece and their families. Emma looked stunning, although grief hung on her. Her eldest son, Richard, had to hold her up during most of the service, but she needed him most when it was time to say her final goodbye.

Pastor Franklin O'Neill preached a homegoing message that resonated with everyone. Family members jumped up from time to time and shouted hallelujah and told the preacher to preach. Pastor O'Neill admonished the audience to let their light shine as Billy did, so that men would see their good works and glorify God.

Billy was laid to rest in a local cemetery. He received a full military escort—the pallbearers wearing their military Class-A dress to a tee. Emma watched as the soldiers meticulously folded the flag with such precision that you could almost count the seconds between each fold. And when the flag was handed to Emma, the tears flowed relentlessly. And then the soldiers lined up, their rifles at their sides. And they fired in unison—a twenty-one gun salute. Following the salute, a small military band that had assembled played "Taps"—a final farewell to a fallen soldier.

Emma lost it. She didn't hear Pastor O'Neill's final words. In fact, she didn't hear what anyone had to say. Everything was a blur.

Emma's girls—Queenie, Yolanda, and Jackie—had been with her throughout the week. Queenie had stayed with her until Emma's family arrived from out-of-town. Yolanda had filled in where needed. Jackie prayed with her, asking God to give Emma some peace in the midst of her sorrow.

That sorrow hit her hardest the morning after the funeral when she realized Billy would no longer occupy their bed, hold her, and give her his usual morning kiss.

Emma lay in bed for the next three days and cried until she was bone dry.

Smells Like Fried Chicken

There seemed to be no words that could console Emma. Queenie, Jackie, and Yolanda gave up their daily lives to help revive a friend. They tried to feed her, sing to her, and be the friend Emma needed, but there was no response.

Today was going to be the day that Queenie knocked some sense into Emma. She wasn't about to watch her best friend die. She was aware of the hurt and pain Emma was in over losing Billy, but it was time for her girlfriend to pull herself out of the funk.

Wednesdays were usually very busy at the newspaper, but Queenie took the day off to sit with Emma. Emma's daughters, Erin and Reece, had to go home and tend to their immediate families.

Emma had given Queenie an extra key to her house, and she let herself in. The house was eerily quiet and Queenie jumped when she thought she heard a noise. She had stopped at the store to buy some groceries and went to the kitchen to deposit her load in the refrigerator. Her plan was to cook Emma a good meal today and start putting some fat back on her bones.

Tiptoeing into Emma's bedroom, Queenie found her friend lying in bed with the covers pulled over her head. "It stinks in here," Queenie said out loud. She crossed the room, opened the blinds and windows."

"Shut the windows," said a somewhat muffled voice.

Queenie turned around so fast, she almost fell down. "So you're talking today," Queenie teased. "Now that I have your attention, you're going to hear what I have to say."

"Go away, Q. Leave me alone."

"I'm going to leave you alone when I get good and ready. I had to take a vacation day to babysit your behind."

"Q…"

"Q, nothing. You're going to get your stanky behind up from this bed and get in the bathtub." Queenie came and sat by Emma and held her nose close with her fingers. "Whew, you stink, girl. Now, I'm going to run you some bath water so you can soak awhile. You need it."

There was no response from Emma. She lay facing the wall, probably to shut out Queenie's nasty insults.

Queenie rubbed Emma's arm and then got up to draw her bath water. She poured in Emma's favorite bubble bath and stuck her finger in the water to test it. Queenie nodded her head in approval.

"Hey, baby," Queenie said, rubbing Emma's arm again. "I know you're hurting like hell. We all miss Billy. But you've got to be here for your children and grandchildren. Don't you want to see your grandbabies grow up, go to college, and get married?"

Emma squirmed a little and stretched her arms, but remained silent until Queenie pulled back the covers and pinched her on the butt.

"Damn you, Q. Why won't you leave me alone?"

"Because it's my duty to help you mend. As your best friend, my task is to help you get back to normal. Now get your ass up out of that bed."

Emma didn't move, not right away. But after several minutes, she shifted the covers on her body and exhaled. She lifted her head up slightly from the pillow and squeezed her eyes together, trying to focus them. When she saw Queenie hovering over her, she dropped her head and collapsed back onto the bed.

"Come on, Emma. You're making this harder than it should be. I'm here to help you, babe. I'm here as your friend and confidante; I love you and want to see you get well."

Emma continued to lie on the bed. Queenie turned and walked to the window, shedding tears for the first time since Billy's death. Grief was rough, and she hated to see her once vibrant friend wasting away. "God, help me," Queenie cried softly.

"Q, I need some help."

Queenie dried her tears and turned around. "Jesus." Emma was trying to sit up in the bed. Queenie rushed to Emma's side and brought her legs around.

"Who were you calling?" Emma asked weakly.

"I was calling one-eight hundred-on-my-knees-4H—the hotline to the master. He answered my prayer. Now hold on to my neck."

Queenie lifted Emma from the bed and took her to the bathroom. She hiked up Emma's gown and lifted her into the tub. She pulled the gown from Emma's upper torso and threw it on the sink.

Emma sat in the sudsy water with her knees pointed upwards and her arms flopped down, a blank stare on her face. Queenie got on her knees and took the washcloth she had laid on the side of the tub and began to wash Emma's back.

After a few moments, Emma's head fell backwards, her eyes closed. She seemed to be enjoying Queenie's massage and groaned with contentment ever so often.

"Okay, sister, you've got to scrub your own vajay-jay. Queenie don't scrub windows or private parts." She handed the washcloth to Emma.

"Thanks, Q. Thanks for having my back and for being a real friend."

Queenie kissed Emma on the top of her head. "I'm lucky to have you as a friend. I love you. Now hurry; I've got some more surprises in store for you. I'll go so you can feel free to…"

"Don't go, Q. "

So Queenie obliged her friend and stayed while Emma finished scrubbing her body. She witnessed when, for the first time in days, a smile crossed Emma's face. It was a sad smile. "I miss him, Q; he's probably having a ball frying chicken up there in heaven. It's Wednesday; Billy wouldn't have it any other way."

Queenie started laughing and couldn't stop. "Girl, I got the visual of Billy and his fried chicken, serving folks in a line a mile long. First in line are Jesus and the eleven disciples. I'm not sure Judas made it to heaven."

Emma laughed. "You are so crazy, Q. Only you would come up with that scenario."

"And guess who else is in line?"

"Who, Q?"

"My mama and daddy; my cousin, Tony, and his ratchet mama, Gloria; my grandma, Mattie, and…"

"I get it, Q. Your whole family and mine. I see Billy with a big smile on his face. He loved it when people complimented him about his fried chicken. He had a secret chicken recipe that tasted better than Colonel Sanders."

"You're right about that, Emma. I can't count how many times I purposely stopped by your house on a Wednesday so I could steal a chicken breast that Billy cooked. That's a memory I'll store away for life."

"I'm ready to get out of the tub now. If my best friend could hand me a bath towel, I'd appreciate it."

"You're back, Emma. I'm so glad you're coming around."

"So what is the next surprise you have in store for me?"

"We are going to the hairdresser. I'm cutting my hair and going natural. I'll probably have some highlights put in it."

"I like my blond hair."

Queenie handed Emma a bath towel. "We aren't called the Silver Bullets for nothing."

"I don't need silver hair to be called a silver bullet."

"You don't have to change your hair color, but after you see mine, you're going to wish you switched."

"We'll have to see about that." Emma dried herself and pulled the towel tight around her. ."

"Okay, go and get ready. I'll fix us a quick lunch."

Emma went to her bedroom while Queenie made a mad dash for the kitchen. She took her package out of the refrigerator and went to the sink. Queenie washed the chicken wings, seasoned and floured them, and put them in the hot grease she heated. She quickly peeled four medium-size potatoes and put them on to boil. Spinach was Emma's favorite vegetable, and Queenie fixed it the way Emma liked it—butter and onions swimming on top.

Queenie knew that Emma could smell the concoction, but she busied herself until the chicken was fried, the mash potatoes were whipped, and the spinach ready to be served.

Queenie looked at her watch. An hour had passed, but she'd wait patiently for her friend to come into the kitchen. Without notice, Emma appeared from behind the wall with her hands on her hips and stared at the spread Queenie had made.

Tears streamed down Emma's eyes. "Fried chicken day. Thanks for honoring my husband."

Nothin' But The Truth

The Shiloh Baptist Church ensemble played some contemporary numbers on their instruments, while Deacon Phillips and one of his helpers tended the barbeque pits. The sisters of the church covered picnic tables with red and white plastic tablecloths and then set bowls, crock-pots, and pans of homemade potato salad, baked beans, macaroni and cheese, corn-on-the-cob, salads, assorted cakes and pies on top of it. What a feast they had.

"A nice day for a picnic," Pastor O'Neill said, pausing at the table where his wife and girlfriends sat as he gnawed on a piece of barbeque rib. "Isn't that right, Sister Emma?"

"It sure is, Pastor."

With a light squeeze of her shoulder, Pastor O'Neill moved on.

It had been two months since Billy Wilcox had been laid to rest. With the help of her friends, Emma was working through her grief. Today was especially hard; Billy was the designated barbeque pit master for all of their church picnics, or, he used to be. The church picnic was like a family reunion. Old members who had left the church for one reason or another would always make their way to the annual church picnic, especially to get some of Billy's barbeque.

"There's nothing like Billy's barbeque," Queenie said cautiously. No one commented right away.

Then Emma spoke up. "You're right about that, Q. Deacon Phillips' barbeque is all right, but it can't touch Billy's. Billy used to say it was in the marinade and the sauce. Whatever it was, that man of mine could throw down."

"Lord knows he could," Yolanda said, stuffing a piece of barbeque chicken in her mouth. "But I'm not going to complain. The fellowship is what it's all about." Yolanda put her arms around Emma.

"Don't get any barbeque on my cute top," Emma said. Everyone laughed.

"I'm not sweetie. It's so good to see you here with us having a good time."

Emma smiled. "I'm happy, too." She choked back a tear.

"I was thinking," said First Lady Jackie O'Neill, as she wiped her face with a napkin. "Why don't we take a trip to Hawaii? Summer is right around the corner. It would do us some good to get away."

Queenie looked at Jackie with questioning eyes. "Are you sure the good Pastor Franklin O'Neill is going to let you traipse across the United States—to Hawaii at that, especially after what happened in Vegas?"

"Franklin and I are of one accord. We've worked through that issue and have moved on. When Franklin forgave me of that stupid transgression, the subject was over."

"It may be over, but he hasn't forgotten, Jackie. Deep down inside he still may have some trust issues."

Jackie chewed on Queenie's comment for a moment. "Maybe you're right, and I'm not saying that you are. However, that's my business. The one thing I do know is my husband loves me unconditionally, and I promised myself...I promised him that I wouldn't do anything as stupid as what I did in Vegas. I was naïve, but I'm not any longer."

"Whatever you say, First Lady."

"That's what I'm saying, Q. You can take it or leave it. Right now, I'm going to enjoy this rib I'm sucking on. Deacon Phillips put a hurting on these ribs."

"I'm all for going to Hawaii, Jackie," Yolanda said. "Emma, Queenie, don't you want to go? Hawaii sounds like the perfect place for us to go and have some fun, although I may have to lose a couple of pounds so I can look good in my bikini."

"I'm in," Emma said. "I need a getaway…someplace far away."

"I was planning on going to Jamaica," Queenie said.

"When are you going? Do you have your ticket?" Yolanda asked, with her hands on her hips. "The answer is probably no. Well, you can stay right here in Raleigh while the rest of us go on to Hawaii and have a good time."

Queenie caved. "You heifers aren't going anywhere without me. But, if I go to Hawaii, I'm eating everything that isn't nailed down and that includes any drink that comes with an umbrella."

"All right now," Yolanda said, giving Queenie a high-five. "Let's decide when we're going and let's do this thing." The ladies threw their hands in the air in agreement.

Hearing all of the commotion, Pastor O'Neill waltzed back over. "So what are you ladies so happy about?"

"Are you pretending to be checking on all of your parishioners to see if they're having a good time or are you being nosey, Franklin?"

Pastor O'Neill gave Jackie a big kiss on the forehead. "A little of both, dear."

"Since you want to know, Queenie, Emma, Yolanda, and I have decided to go to Hawaii. We need a little fun in the sun."

Pastor O'Neill looked from his wife to her girlfriends as they stared back at him. "Sounds like a great trip. Baby, you deserve it.

I want you and the ladies to enjoy the island paradise but behave like the women you are."

"What does that mean, Pastor?" Queenie asked, with her hands on her hips and her lips stuck out like a snake's fangs ready to strike.

"If I have to explain it, Sister Queenie, then all I can do is pray for you. But I'm going to do something that may come as a surprise to you four women."

The tension eased somewhat from Queenie's face.

"I'm going to pay the airfare for all four of you to go to Hawaii." There was a moment of silence. "You don't have to say anything. Now, I'm going to enjoy the rest of the picnic."

"Thank you," the ladies said in unison as they jumped up from their seats. Pastor O'Neill waved his hand, although he had already moved on.

"Is he for real, Jackie?" Queenie asked. "My ears didn't deceive me?"

"I'm as stunned as you are," Jackie said with the biggest grin on her face.

"Well, Pastor O'Neill has my vote. I'll have to take back everything I said, Jackie. You all must've made up real good."

"I'll accept your apology, if that's what that was, Q. The Pastor and I are in a good place, and I'm not going to threaten my standing with him ever again."

"Look, whatever you're doing, keep on doing it," Emma said. "I thank you; Billy thanks you. I truly need this trip."

Jackie got up, stepped behind Emma, wrapped her arms around her neck, and squeezed real tight. "All of us, the Silver Bullets, will always be here for you. It's going to be all right."

Emma leaned into the hug, accepting the comfort offered, before being distracted by an unexpected sight. "Oh Lord," Emma pointed. "Look who has the nerve to be stepping up to the bar-beque?"

Everyone turned their heads in the direction Emma pointed.

"Can't even enjoy a church picnic on holy ground," Yolanda said. "And he's got the nerve to drag that wench around with him. When was the last time Linden darkened the doorway of a church?"

"You all are making a fuss over nothing."

"Come on, Q, you hate Linden's guts and I'm sure you're upset that he's brought his junky mess with him."

"I have no love for Linden, YoYo. If he wants Drema D, he can have her. If she's stupid enough to want to be with that sorry excuse for a man, she's welcome to him. I'm finished."

"I'm proud of you, Q; my girl," Emma said. "Linden is nothing but trash that you've buried. Now, if a dog pulls it out of the trash and decides to claim it as their own, more power to them."

Queenie laughed. "I couldn't have said it better, Emma. Nothin' but the truth." They gave each other high-fives.

"He's looking this way...he's coming this way," Jackie said. "I don't want any mess, Q."

"And forfeit my plane ticket to Hawaii? You've got to be crazy." Everyone laughed.

Linden strolled up to the table with Drema D on his arm. He turned and looked at Queenie. "Hey, Red," Linden said in a low, sultry voice. "I want you to meet my new wife, Drema D. Robinson."

Best Friends

There were no words that could console Queenie Jackson or make her feel better. She felt like she'd fallen onto a beehive and had been stung by a thousand bees. There was no laughter in her large, brown eyes or love in her heart, only hate. She hated Linden Robinson with a vengeance.

When Queenie looked up, Drema D was cocked under Linden's arm. All was quiet on the church grounds, and those who were nearby waited for Queenie to make her move.

Queenie got up from her seat and stood in front of Linden. From the bowels of her throat, she ushered up a mouth full of saliva. Her hatred for Linden was so strong that her legs nearly buckled. And then Queenie took one more look at him and spat right in his face.

Linden wiped at his face and pushed Drema D behind him. "You ugly, fat bitch, you're going to pay for that."

Pastor O'Neill rushed to where Linden and Queenie stood. "You get out of here right now, Linden," O'Neill said. "We aren't going to have this at God's house. This is holy ground."

Linden pushed Pastor O'Neill with his hand and then balled his hand into a fist. "Old man, I'm not talking to you. Be gone. That fat bitch spit in my face and she's not going to get away with it."

"If you don't get off this property right now, I'm going to call the cops and have you thrown off."

"Call the damn cops; see if I care."

"Come on, Linden," Drema D said, pulling his arm.

"You got what you deserved," Queenie interjected. "I feel sorry for you, Drema D."

"Don't worry about me, Queenie. The best woman won."

Queenie's lip began to quiver and she started gritting her teeth. "Nobody wants that piece of trash you got, Drema D. Have a happy life taking care of a man who has nothing, ain't about nothing, and is going to use you until there's nothing left." And with that Queenie walked away without looking back. Linden began shouting curses at Queenie that had people covering their ears. Queenie kept walking with Emma running behind her. They jumped into Queenie's red jag and sped away.

"I'm sorry about what happened, Q," Emma said, trying to calm Queenie down. "Linden is a worthless nobody; he'll get his."

Tears streamed down Queenie's face. "Emma, the fact that Linden was with Drema D didn't bother me. It was the fact that this same fool asked me to marry him a couple of months ago, declaring his undying love for me. Today he had the audacity to show up and flaunt Drema D on church grounds, a place he hasn't been in almost a year, to make me look like a fool. I don't want his sorry ass. What man tells one woman that he's in love with her and turns around and marries another in less time than it took me to tell his sorry ass *no*? He made me look like a fool and I believed he really loved me. I walked away from that relationship only after I saw him with Drema D the moment I took a break to be with my girls. It's crazy bull crap. I'm rambling but I can't help it."

"It's all right, Q. Close this chapter of your life so you can begin to live again. It's really over."

"Emma, will I ever find Mr. Right?"

"If it's meant to be, Mr. Right will come along. Why don't you ask God to send you someone?"

"God doesn't know what I want."

"Why don't you ask Him? He said He'd give you the desires of your heart. I'm sure He'll be happy to take your order."

Queenie wiped her face and smiled. "That's been my problem. I've being driving through the fast food lane so long giving my orders to the wrong people. But…do you think God will do that for me?"

"He'll give you what you need. Now don't go asking God for some big Hollywood hunk that has a bank account that doesn't have your name on it. He'd probably ask for a pre-nup anyway."

"Why can't I ask God for that?"

"Queenie, God might honor a request like that, but from where I sit, that isn't the prescription you need. You need to ask Him for a man who will honor, love, and respect you. You want a man who's sensitive to your needs and who'll give you his all. But most of all, you need a man who loves God."

"Is that how you and Billy felt about each other?"

"Truthfully, we did. We had our ups and downs; all marriages do, but for most of our marriage, we were together…worked together as one. I loved some Billy Wilcox."

"You've always said that, even when Billy would get on your nerves. I've always admired that about you and yours—in fact, I think I was sometimes jealous of your relationship."

"We were true soul mates who worked hard to make our marriage work. But we did it." Emma smiled.

"You know what, Emma?"

"What, Q?"

"Today, I realized that God has tried to warn me so many times about my fruitless relationship with Linden. I was so stubborn. I wanted that man for my own selfish reasons—the wrong reasons. I'm really the lucky one. Poor Drema D saved me from hell."

"Hello. Yes, she did. Now let's go and get some pastries with a lot of fat calories in them and talk about our trip to Hawaii. I can't wait."

"Thanks, Emma." Queenie patted Emma's leg. "Thanks for being the best friend a girl could have."

"Love you too, Queenie."

Up, Up And Away

"Hawaii, here we come," Jackie shouted in the car.

It was early, seven a.m., but the Silver Bullets were in high spirits. No one was bringing any baggage except their suitcases that contained plenty of loungewear, swimsuits, shorts, and sundresses. Although the Hawaiian Islands were a lot further away than Las Vegas, they were going to be on their best behavior.

Pastor O'Neill smiled as he drove his wife and her friends to the Raleigh/Durham (RDU) airport. "Pastor, thank you for being so kind and generous in paying for my airfare," Queenie said. "You're the first man to ever treat me like a real queen."

"You're welcome, Sister Queenie. You all have sparked life into my Jackie that I can't describe. Your friendship has meant a lot. It has given her an opportunity to explore some new things like travel outside of Raleigh and have some fun. Jackie has and always will be dedicated to the church, but I'd like for her to have an outlet that doesn't always cater to me."

"We'll take good care of Sister Jackie," Emma said. "I also thank you for my trip and for being the kind of man who's upstanding, a hard worker, God-fearing and exemplifies what a good man is."

"I think she meant that for me, Pastor," Queenie said. "If the Lord has someone for me, I'll wait until He sends him."

Everyone laughed.

"He will send you what you need."

"I want to thank you also, Pastor, for what you've been to me and my family," Yolanda said. "I feel so alone without my sister, but I do understand why she and Preston did what was best for them. Your messages over the past months have given me strength."

"Thank you, Sister Yolanda. I'm glad that God has given me the right messages to give to you. Now I want you ladies to lighten up and have a great time in Hawaii. Go and get a richer tan and eat all the pineapple you see."

The ladies laughed.

"Be good. I love you, Franklin."

First Lady reached over and gave Pastor O'Neill a big wet kiss, while the others made faces from the back seat.

They sat together, with plenty of snacks and enough games on their iPads between them to stay entertained for the entire trip. Queenie pulled out her Kindle so she could finish a mystery she was reading.

"Don't wake me up until we land in Dallas and have to change planes," Yolanda said. "I was too excited to sleep last night. I'm going to catch some shut eye before we reach Hawaii. I want to see everything the island has to offer."

"The first thing I'm going to do when I get to Hawaii is buy one of those grass skirts and coconut booby holders," Emma said, eliciting a laugh from the group. "I'm going to shake my hips and see what the north wind brings."

"Gila monsters are going to be nipping at your butt," Queenie said, laughing at her own attempt at humor.

"They don't have Gila monsters in Hawaii, but they do have a lot of lizards crawling on the island," Emma countered.

"They have those…," Yolanda snapped her fingers, "those…the GEICO lizard."

"Gecko," Jackie said, also snapping her fingers. "A girlfriend of mine was stationed in Hawaii and she said they would come into her living quarters all the time. She and her roommate made a contraption called a gecko buster."

"What does a gecko buster look like?" Emma wanted to know.

"Don't laugh when I tell you," Jackie said. "Gecko buster is a fancy name for vacuum cleaner. When my girlfriend would see a gecko in the house, she would turn on the vacuum cleaner, run after it, and suck it up."

"Damn," Queenie said, wrinkling up her face. "That's nasty."

"A gecko moves fast, but it can't outrun a moving vacuum cleaner that has good suction."

"That is too funny, Jackie," Emma said, laughing. "I can see all of us in a room trying to catch a Gecko with a vacuum cleaner."

"Do you know what they'd call us?" Jackie asked.

"The Silver Bullets Gecko Busting Service," Queenie said. Everybody laughed.

"This is your pilot speaking. Flight 1997 to Dallas-Fort Worth has been cleared for takeoff. Flight attendants, prepare for take-off."

All the jokes and laughter subsided. Takeoff was serious business and everyone on the plane wanted the pilot to make a safe ascent into the sky. Jackie said a prayer for safe arrival at their destination, while Yolanda studied the flight attendants, making sure they followed proper procedures before the plane took off—as if she was an expert. Queenie's eyes were shut tight in silent prayer, and Emma sat back in her seat like a seasoned, frequent flyer with no cares in the world.

When In Hawaii

"Are we there yet?" Queenie asked as she opened her eyes. "It feels like we've been traveling all day."

"Darn near all day," Yolanda quipped. "I'm excited."

"I want the plane to find land," Jackie said, unbuckling her seatbelt so she could go to the restroom. "All this water is getting too much for me. If the plane went down, I'd be out of luck. I can't swim a lick."

"I can't believe I'm flying over the Pacific Ocean," Emma said, nibbling on peanuts.

"This is your pilot speaking. Our estimated time of arrival is one-thirty p.m., Hawaii time. We will prepare for landing in approximately thirty minutes."

"Yeah," screamed the crowd.

"All right," Queenie yelled, throwing her hands up in the air, before launching into a rendition of Elvis Presley's "Blue Hawaii." Other passengers joined in, cranking up the volume.

Jackie smiled as she listened. "This is a wonderful way to begin our vacation."

Thirty minutes later, the American Airlines jumbo jet hit the tarmac at Honolulu International Airport. Rays of sunlight streamed in. Everyone was anxious to get off and get their vacations started; the Silver Bullets were no different.

The tour company that was to meet the ladies upon their arrival held a sign high in the air with their company name on it. The head of the company greeted the ladies and placed a wreath of plumeria flowers called a lei around Queenie, Emma, Jackie, and Yolanda's necks, as is customary when someone arrives in the Hawaiian Islands.

The ladies were giddy and excited about all the attention, but it wasn't until they'd exited the airport and were being whisked away in a limo that they acknowledged how beautiful the island was even though they hadn't seen much of it yet.

"I could stay here forever," Emma said, taking in the scenery. "This is so breathtaking." She paused for a moment. "I wish Billy could've seen this." No one said a word.

"I want one of those thick Samoan men to squeeze me tight and rock me all night long," Yolanda said, trying to lighten the mood. "And I bet they know how to make a woman feel good."

"What about Illya, your FBI boyfriend who seemed to have disappeared from the face of the earth?"

"Q, I was really feeling him, but he's too mysterious. His job has him going undercover most of the time, which means he may have to move from place to place more often than I'd like. Besides my gut feeling tells me he's not over his ex."

"The one you said took him for everything?" Queenie asked as she gazed out of the window of the limo.

"One and the same." Yolanda puckered her lips and then popped them. "He's distracted. His telephone calls have been very sporadic. But as for me, I believe I'm ready to make a fresh start. Who knows when Illya will show up again? I can't wait around forever. I've got things to do."

"Hmph, so that's your excuse to go messing around with the natives," Queenie said.

"Q, I don't care what you think; it is what it is." The limo driver pulled up in front of the hotel. "Look at that hunk of a bellhop waiting to greet me and my lei?"

Queenie began to snicker. "Oh, yes, we're going to have fun."

The Hilton Hawaiian Village was the only true oceanfront resort in Waikiki. It had everything—five pools, water slides, dining, shopping, beautiful gardens, animals and twenty-two miles of beach. The ladies got situated in their double suite of rooms, refreshed themselves and headed outside.

"I want a Mai Tai," Jackie said, giving the girls a wink and running her tongue over her teeth. "Of course, I'd want more pineapple and orange juice than rum."

"Uhm hmm," Queenie said, wagging her finger at Jackie. "You've barely touched ground and you want to get into trouble already. I don't want the good reverend to come over here and snatch your butt home. Behave."

"The saying is, when in Rome, you do as the Romans."

"I don't think the natives are the ones throwing Mai Tais down their throats, Jackie. It's the foreigners who truly believe that Hawaii is a playground for adults where they can get buck wild and do everything they wouldn't do at home."

"Look who's talking. Emma, didn't I hear you say that you wanted a strong, sexy Samoan to squeeze your little butt tight?"

"No, that was YoYo, but if our bellhop wasn't so young, I might have jumped his bones."

"Emma, you're crazy," Yolanda said. "A while ago you were wishing Billy was here."

"Well he's not here, YoYo. The sky is the limit. I'm a widow."

"Well. help yourself, darling. If the right one steps in my path, I might have to drink a couple of Mai Tais to get up enough courage to go home with him."

"Yolanda, you're talking trash."

"Jackie, for the first time in a long time I truly feel wild and free. I'm going to enjoy this Hawaiian vacation and throw caution to the wind."

"Well, I'm ready to stuff my face with something good to eat," Queenie interjected. "We have seven days on this island, and it's not going anywhere."

"All hail to the Queen. Let's go and eat," Jackie said.

I've Got A Date

The trip to Pearl Harbor was meaningful. None of the ladies had yet been born when the Japanese attacked Pearl Harbor. They'd read about it in their school history books and reflected every December seventh on how it had changed America.

From Pearl Harbor, the ladies took the tour bus out to the Dole Pineapple Plantation on Hawaii's North Shore. They were surprised to learn that the Dole Pineapple Plantation was still a working pineapple field. The ladies elected to go through the Dole Maze, a maze made of large shrubbery and plants. It took them an hour and a half to get through the maze.

"I'm going to take home two pineapples," Jackie said, clutching her souvenir box.

"You'll be lucky to get that home with four women vultures standing around," Yolanda said.

"I'm not threatening anyone, but I'm going to say this loud and clear. Get your own pineapple."

"It sounds like a threat to me, Jackie," Emma said. "But I feel you. I'm going to purchase two of my own. This is only the second day of our trip, and I didn't want to have fruit hanging around for five days in the room, but I'm going to get it anyway."

The women were scattered throughout the gift shop and visitor's center, purchasing trinkets and pineapple. All of a sudden, there was a lot of chatter. A group of African-American men, alone and without female companionship entered the premises. They were like them—Queenie, Emma, Jackie, and Yolanda. Their hair was salt and pepper and had to be in their mid-to-late fifties; well, not all of them.

Queenie ran to where Emma stood and pointed out the obvious. "It's raining men in here, and they're without females tagging along. I counted ten all together, and that means there's enough for us to have two apiece, with two left over."

"Q, you are crazy, but believe me, my eyes are in good working order. Lord Jesus, we've got to be some bold sisters and see what's going on."

Emma looked around as Yolanda came up behind her. "Do y'all see what I see?"

"Yes, we see, YoYo," Emma said.

"There are ten stallions ready to be ridden. Get my drift?"

"Get a hold of yourself, YoYo. We can't act as if we're desperate and hard up. Act natural like God gave you some sense."

"Emma, may I pinch you. I don't know what's gotten into you, but…"

"Cool it, YoYo," Queenie said, putting her finger over her mouth to hush her up. "I think they've spotted us."

"Lordy, Lordy," Emma said. "They're coming over. Where is Jackie?"

"Who cares?" Queenie stated matter-of-fact. "We don't need her over here messing with the groove that's up in this place."

Queenie jumped when the tall, dark-skinned gentleman with the gray temples said hello.

Standing face to face with the gentleman, Queenie offered him a smile. He smiled back. "Uhh, hello. My name is Queenie and these are my very dear friends Emma and Yolanda."

"Hello, everybody."

"That's our friend, Jackie, who's coming our way."

The gentleman stuck out his hand. "My name is Donald Griffin."

"Has anyone told you that you look like Richard Roundtree when he played in *Shaft?*" Queenie quizzed flirtatiously.

"No, they haven't. So what are you beautiful ladies doing in Hawaii?"

"I'd ask you the same."

"Queenie…"

"You can call me Q." Emma and Yolanda gave Queenie the evil eye.

"Well, Q, my brothers and I…"

"Your brothers, as in blood brothers?"

"Not the whole lot of us, although three of those guys are my biological brothers," Donald said, pointing in the direction of the men. "We're here on a spiritual mission."

"So are we," Jackie said, stepping closer to get a good look at Mr. Griffin. She shook his hand. "We live in Durham, North Carolina and are members of Shiloh Baptist Church where my husband, Reverend Franklin O'Neill, is the Pastor."

"Well, we have something in common," Donald said, turning back to Queenie. "How long are you ladies going to be in Hawaii?"

"Seven whole days," Yolanda said, flashing her broad smile and stepping slightly in front of Queenie. "Maybe we can get together while we're here."

Donald noticed Yolanda for the first time and gave her an extra looking over. It was apparent he liked what he saw. Donald turned and waved to the group of men he'd come with and invited them over.

They came in various sizes and shapes—tall, medium, short, plump, and thin. "These sisters are here on a spiritual retreat as well."

The men observed the lot of them—Queenie, Emma, Yolanda and Jackie. Some looked longer than others. They gave their names and shook the ladies' hands.

"So, what kind of spiritual mission are you on?" Emma asked, speaking for the first time since Donald ventured over.

Donald took Emma's hand in his. "Emma, right?"

Emma blushed. She even found herself squeezing Donald's hand. "Yes, that's right."

"The brothers and I recently dedicated our lives to be the best men that we can be...for ourselves, our families..."

Queenie's eyes rolled in her head when she heard the word families. "Families, as in wife and kids?" Queenie asked, cutting to the chase.

Donald nodded. "For some of us that's true. Rico, Damien, John, Ray, and my brother Wayne are married and have been for a number of years. Marriages have their obstacles as you may well know, but married or single, we've dedicated our lives to being better men and we're attending a retreat that allowed us to get away and meditate."

"And your wives allowed you to come all the way to Hawaii where there are plenty of distractions like fun, sun, beach, bikinis, and beautiful women?"

"For some of us that might be a concern," Donald said, still playing spokesman for the group. "Trust is one of the factors that we are addressing at the retreat."

"So," Yolanda began, as she pushed in front of Queenie. "So, as a single man, what do you plan to get out of this retreat?"

Donald gave Yolanda a healthy smile. "I'm looking to settle down. When I do make that step, it's a one-time deal for me. I want to make sure that I have what it takes to be deeply grounded as a man and in my faith so that my path with whomever I choose to be with forever is the right one. I'm human, I've made mistakes and will continue to make them, but I want a divine authority to be head of my life, my heart, and my home."

Jackie clasped her hands together and brought them to her mouth. "That was so beautiful. I need you to come to my church and speak to the young husbands and couples."

"I'd be glad to do that, Jackie. I live in Atlanta, and Durham isn't too far for me to come."

"Thank you, Donald. It was a pleasure to meet you. I think our tour bus is getting ready to leave, but I hope you'll stay in touch."

"We're staying at the Hilton Hawaiian Village."

"Ohh, that's where we're staying," Jackie said. "For sure, we'll see you all again."

"Here's my number," Yolanda said, handing Donald her business card. "My cell number is the last number on the card."

"Thank you. Maybe we can all get together for dinner."

"That sounds nice," Emma said.

They waved to the guys and they were gone.

Queenie couldn't wait to get outside and read Yolanda. "You're a snake in the grass, Yolanda Morris. You saw me talking to Donald, but you had to bogart your way into our conversation and take over."

"Out-strategized you, did I? The only thing I did was inject myself into the conversation. You were being selfish by trying to commandeer the discussion toward yourself."

"You are tripping, YoYo. Nobody was trying to commandeer the conversation."

"Well, don't get mad with me for offering my ten cents."

"And that's all it was worth."

"Queenie and Yolanda, we're not going to have any fighting on this trip," Emma said. "Donald may not be interested in either one of y'all. You guys don't know how to work it anyway." Emma held up a business card. "You see, while you two were haggling over Donald, the other tall, fine brother with the green eyes was ogling me. And he's thirteen years my junior. We traded business cards, and I may or may not be joining you for dinner. Don't hate." Emma switched her behind and got on the bus with the biggest smile on her face.

"Whoa, Emma has gone and hit on a young man. She pulled one over on you," Jackie said to Queenie and Yolanda, who looked like they had been punked.

Queenie rolled her eyes at Yolanda. "You can have him. I'm waiting on God to send me a man."

"Yeah, right. You darn near killed me with that attitude of yours over Donald. Get your ass on the bus, Q, and let's act like ladies. You remember what we promised Pastor."

"You were the one acting desperate. I'm through with this conversation, YoYo. I'm ready to shop."

The ladies spent a lot of money at the Ala Moana Shopping Center. All the big stores were there, and Yolanda couldn't restrain herself at Neiman Marcus. The bus tour returned them to the hotel where they freshened up and prepared for the luau that evening.

"Whose cell phone is ringing?" Queenie yelled, acting as if she were annoyed.

"It's mine," Jackie said, as she hit the TALK button. "Hey, baby, how are you doing?"

"I'm calling to ask how you and your lady friends are doing. Did you have a good day?"

"Franklin, Hawaii is so beautiful. We went to Pearl Harbor and to the Dole Pineapple Plantation. I'm bringing you some fresh pineapple."

"Great, baby. Have fun. Are you still going to the luau tonight? It was on your schedule."

"Yes, the ladies and I are getting ready now. I wish you were here."

"I wish I was, too. Anyway, I do have a surprise for you tonight. Call me back later and tell me all about it."

"Can you give me a hint?"

"It wouldn't be a surprise if I did now would it?"

"You're right. Okay, baby, I've got to run. Love you. Kiss, kiss."

"Back at you, baby. Tell everyone I said hello.

Okay. Bye."

"What was Franklin squawking about?" Queenie asked, as she squeezed her body into a fitted, low-cut, strapless sundress.

"He said he had a surprise for me—at the luau."

"Surprise at the luau?" Yolanda asked with a puzzled look on her face.

"He's probably on the island spying on Jackie," Emma added. "He didn't trust your butt after all."

"That's not fair, Emma. Franklin and I are good. We're in a good place with our marriage."

"I'm sorry, Jackie," Emma said. "I was being a little insensitive. I'm still mourning Billy's loss."

Jackie went to Emma and put her arm around her. "It's okay, Emma. There are no hard feelings. Oh, look, your cell phone is ringing."

Emma picked up her phone. A smile lit up her face. "Hello, Terrance." Pause. "Sure, I'd love to join you at the luau. That's where the girls and I are headed." Pause. "Okay, I'll meet you in thirty minutes in the hotel lobby." Emma hung up the phone. "I've got a date."

What God Has For You Will Be For You

Queenie, Yolanda, and Jackie, dressed in their colorful sundresses, sauntered down to the lobby to wait for the tour bus that would take them to their authentic luau. Queenie glimpsed Emma standing off to the side with a gentleman; a tall man, a little over six feet, medium brown with a box-cut fade. From her vantage point, Queenie could see that he had a moustache, something she wasn't that keen on; and was very good looking, but a little too young for her taste. She was surprised she hadn't noticed him before. She wouldn't mind being a cougar for a minute.

The lobby became crowded with other tourists who also had tickets to attend the luau. And then the brothers from earlier in the day appeared with Donald leading the pack.

"I wonder what spiritual word they received after leaving us," Yolanda whispered in Queenie's ear.

"I really don't care. All that I'm interested in is feasting on the roasted pig that they've been cooking all night and day. A man and his thoughts are the last thing on my mind."

"Whatever, Q."

"Why don't you go over there and ask Donald what spiritual guidance he received, since you're so concerned."

"You're still mad from this afternoon. I can't help that Donald seemed to be more interested in me."

"I'll make sure the next time I see Illya to tell him that you have eyes for someone else. There's no loyalty with you."

"You're a killjoy, Q. I'm not talking to you for the rest of the evening. Jackie, are you excited about the luau?"

"I am, although I keep looking around expecting Franklin to pop out from behind a palm tree any minute."

"I understand having a surprise for someone, but did he specifically say that the surprise was going to be at the luau?"

"That's what he told me, YoYo. I agree it was strange, and I haven't stopped thinking about it since Franklin called.

"Maybe, it's nothing. I'm going to try and have a good time."

"That's the spirit, Jackie," Queenie said, butting into the conversation.

An extremely attractive Polynesian woman, holding up a stick with banana leaves attached to it, asked for everyone's attention. She gave instructions on boarding the buses and what the tourists would see and do once they arrived at the luau. Once she was finished, the crowd followed her through the double doors of the hotel and to the buses.

As the ladies approached the bus, a strong hand tapped Queenie's shoulder. Donald Griffin stood behind her.

"Good evening, Queenie. Would you mind if I sit next to you on the bus?"

Queenie was going to ask about Yolanda since Donald seemed to be paying her a lot of attention at the pineapple place. Then she thought better of it, looked back at Yolanda and Jackie who were paired off behind her, and nodded her head. "Yes, I would love for you to sit next to me."

Donald helped Queenie onto the bus and they sat down. Queenie smiled when Yolanda glared at her as she and Jackie passed by on the bus. Yolanda and Jackie didn't even sit in the seat behind them.

"I was hoping you were going to the luau."

"Before we go any further, I have to ask you a question, Donald."

"Sure, Queenie. What is it?"

"This afternoon, you seemed to pay more attention to Yolanda, and so I thought…"

"You thought I was interested?"

"Well, yes, that's what I thought."

"Yolanda is a good looking woman, but I picked you out as soon as I saw you. Yolanda seems to be a nice woman…but you seem gentle and unpretentious."

Queenie smiled. Her eyes looked toward heaven. *God, is Donald the one?* "That was nice of you to say, and I'm glad that you asked to sit next to me. ."

Donald reached over and took Queenie's hand. He interlocked his fingers with hers and Queenie wanted to melt.

"There's something I like about you," he said. "I feel it in my spirit. I look forward to enjoying the luau with you."

Queenie couldn't contain the smile on her face. She gloated in the fact that Donald chose her, and for the first time in a long time, she felt as if this might be the making of something that was meant to be. She held Donald's hand tight and settled in for an enjoyable ride to the beach.

When the bus arrived, it unloaded its passengers. They walked to the luau staging area. The ocean was calm and inviting and made Queenie think about the old Brooke Shields movie, *The Blue Lagoon.* Hula dancers dressed in their grass skirts and colorful leis did a traditional dance. Three bare-chested Hawaiian guys accompanied them on ukuleles. Each tourist was welcomed with an "aloha" and a lei made of cowrie shells.

Benches were provided for them to sit, and Queenie and Donald sat together still holding hands. Queenie saw Emma and her man off in the distance, getting acquainted. Jackie and Yolanda sat together but far away from Queenie and her date.

Cameras flashed every few seconds—the tourists capturing the event as it unfolded. Off to one side, a whole Kalua pig sat in a pit where it had been roasted earlier. The host for the event explained the tradition of the luau and what dishes accompanied the feast. They were shown how poi, the underground stem of the taro plant, was made into paste for eating. Each tourist was given an opportunity to taste the poi, but Queenie spat it out discreetly. She wouldn't be eating it again.

After the entertainment and demonstrations, everyone was invited to eat. Besides the pig, there were sweet potatoes, shredded salmon diced with onions, tropical fruit that consisted of diced pineapple, mango, and papaya that sat in a carved out pineapple shell. Raw fish was also served. Best of the all were the unlimited glasses of Mai Tais that not only quenched everyone's thirst but gave them a good buzz.

"Queenie, I'd like to get to know you better," Donald said, taking a bite of his salmon. "I've wanted to settle down for a long time. It has been twenty years since my wife and I divorced. We didn't have any children, but sometimes I wish we did. I won't lie, I do have a couple of sons that I produced out-of-wedlock."

"I've been divorced almost the same length of time as you have but I've been in some turbulent relationships. I wasn't sure that I could ever love again, but I said if I did, the Lord would have to send that man to me. I feel that God sent you to me."

Donald squeezed Queenie's hand. "I asked for the same thing, and here we are. Let's make the most of our time here and see where things go. I don't want to play with your emotions, so when I tell you that I'm serious about us, know that it comes from the heart."

Queenie smiled as she squeezed the sand between her toes. "That's the nicest thing anyone has said to me in a long time.

"My girlfriend, Emma, who's holed up with one of your other brothers, recently lost her husband. This outing today was good for her."

"Your friend, Emma, is with one of my biological brothers. His name is Terrance."

"Oh my God, Emma and I may be dating brothers. Who would've thought?"

"God is in the matchmaking business."

Queenie smiled. "He sure is."

Miracles

Flame throwers and fire eaters rounded out the night, showing off their artistry. A good time was had by all, and it was getting near time to return to the hotel.

"Well, it doesn't look as if I'm getting a surprise tonight," Jackie said to Yolanda.

"Maybe he said that to keep you on your toes."

"Well, that's crazy and doesn't make a bit of sense. Franklin must have had something to drink that made him delirious."

"I wouldn't worry about it, Jackie. We had a good time, even though Queenie and Emma didn't hang with us."

"Sometimes I worry about Q, YoYo. She says one thing and she does another. She said that she was going to wait on the Lord to send her a man, and the minute someone looks her way and pays her some attention, she falls under the spell."

"That's Q for you. She's a slave to the penis."

"That wasn't nice, YoYo."

"It's the truth and you started it."

"You're right, but I hope she doesn't get her heart ripped to shreds, again."

"If she starts looking for the right thing in a man instead of the bull crap he's giving her, maybe she would find true love."

"I can't worry about what everybody else is going to do. My

priority is my husband and my marriage. Even though I didn't get the surprise Franklin was talking about, I still love him."

"You've got a good man, Jackie. If I were in your shoes, I'd be acting like you."

"Is there anyone in the audience by the name of Yolanda Morris?" the host announced.

Yolanda's head jerked around.

"They're calling your name," Jackie said to Yolanda. "Get up."

"Did you say Yolanda Morris," she asked, standing up so that she could be seen.

"Yes. I need you to come up front."

Yolanda frowned. "I wonder what this is all about?"

"Go on up there, silly. Give me your purse. I'll keep it safe for you."

Yolanda passed her purse to Jackie and slowly walked to the front of the group. There was a low tide, but you could hear the water as it rolled onto shore. The evening had gotten cool, and Yolanda wished she had brought a jacket with her.

When Yolanda approached the host, the host smiled at her. Yolanda was even more puzzled and her body tensed.

The host brought the microphone to her lips. "I have a special presentation to make to you, Yolanda. Why were you chosen? You'll find out in a few moments."

Yolanda stood there in front of everyone. She looked out into the audience and located Jackie. She needed her for moral support. The host put the microphone back to her lips and began to speak.

"Tonight, we have a special gift for you and I hope you'll be as excited as my staff is."

Two figures appeared from the tent that served as a kitchen, dressing room, and whatever else. As the figures came near and the light of the moon reflected on them, Yolanda gasped. Queenie,

Emma and Jackie all stood up when they realized what was going on.

Yolanda began to cry and couldn't hold back the tears. Her arms were outstretched as Connie and Preston reached her. They held each other.

"Ladies and gentlemen, Ms. Morris hasn't seen her sister and brother-in-law in months. It was arranged for them to be here to surprise Ms. Morris on this day. You all enjoy each other and with that I'll say to the rest of you, I hope everyone had a great time and I hope you'll return to our beautiful island again so we can make a feast for you."

Yolanda wiped the tears from her face. "Connie...Preston, what are you doing here?"

"We're no longer in the Witness Protection Program," Preston said. "The feds said there shouldn't be any reason to be in fear of our lives. There's plenty of evidence to take down Dr. Cole without my being involved. I was a small fish in the whole scheme of things."

"I'm so happy," Yolanda wailed.

"We're happy, too," Connie said. "We've known for over a month about the release, and Preston wanted to go to Hawaii to celebrate his release from the program and to give me the honeymoon I didn't get."

"But I will still be on probation. I broke the law and didn't report what was going on. I've cooperated with the feds, and with what little information I had about the whole operation, they've given me a deal. Time served with probation."

"God is good. By chance did Pastor O'Neill know anything about your being here?"

"Yes. He set up the surprise," Connie said.

"He called Jackie earlier today and told her he had a surprise for her. This must've been what he meant."

"Probably so," Preston said. "Here are your friends now."

Queenie along with Donald, Emma and Terrance, and Jackie were out of breath when they approached the trio.

"Give me some love, newlyweds," Queenie said, stopping long enough to give Connie and Preston a hug. "You all are a sight for sore eyes. It's a miracle."

"It is a miracle, Q," Connie said. "A real miracle."

"We're so happy for you," Jackie said, taking her turn to give the couple a hug. "This must've been the surprise Franklin was talking about."

"You're right, Jackie. As I told YoYo, your husband was instrumental in setting this up."

"That's my baby."

Emma reached in and gave Connie and Preston a hug. "I'm so happy for you, too. This was the best part of the luau."

"Thanks, Emma. This will always be a special night. Now who is the man hanging on your arm?" Connie whispered the last part.

"Someone special I met on the trip. His name is Terrance Griffin. I'm really digging him. Terrance, I want you to meet a dear friend. This is Connie, Yolanda's sister, and Connie's husband, Preston."

"It's nice to meet you all," Terrance said.

"Likewise," Connie said, then whispered in Emma's ear, "You go with your bad self." Emma winked.

Sunday Brunch

A trip to Fayetteville for Sunday Brunch was what the crew needed. Connie had heard about this wonderful place called The Hilltop House that catered the most fabulous Sunday brunches. Reverend O'Neill had adjourned Sunday services early in order to catch a flight to Nairobi, Kenya, along with the assistant pastor and several other members of the congregation. They were making a yearly sojourn to visit several churches that Shiloh Baptist supported in their Foreign Mission program.

They were all there—First Lady Jackie, Connie, Yolanda, Emma, and of course, the Queen. Some lives were blossoming, while others were back on track. The girls looked like a bunch of sorority sisters who couldn't live without each other, while they sometimes fought like real sisters do.

"I don't know why we had to come all the way from Raleigh to Fayetteville to get a bite to eat," Queenie began, as she plopped into a chair.

"Q, can we enjoy the day without you complaining about everything?" Emma asked.

Queenie gave Emma the evil eye. "I believe I can do that since the food is looking mighty good. And it better be worth my while."

"So, Q, is Donald the one?"

"YoYo, Donald is the one. He's nothing but the truth. I've learned a lot from him and about myself in the month since we've come home from Hawaii."

"And what have you learned?"

"To love myself...love the skin I'm in. I've located that thing down inside of me that gives me purpose. I don't have to go over the top to get someone to notice me, although Donald didn't complain about the big, baby doll smile I gave him when we first met. YoYo, I've finally found a man who loves me for who I am. Donald listens to what I have to say. The biggest thing I learned though is that I don't have to sleep with a man to get him to stay."

"Thank you Jesus." Jackie said, raising her hands toward heaven.

"Damn, she really did learn something," Emma interjected, laughing. "If Q had realized that in the first place, she wouldn't have had to change her sheets every day when her Jheri curl man tried to set up permanent residence."

"I'm going to let you slide, Emma, but you're right. Joe Harris thought he was going to be a permanent fixture at my house, but I knew well in advance that his time was limited. I thought that if I shared my bed with Linden and gave him my everything, he wouldn't stray. I'm not even sure that I really loved him."

"Like Franklin said, sometimes when we go through hell, we come out on fire."

"Ohhh, listen to Jackie quoting the pastor, her husband, the Reverend Franklin O'Neill," Yolanda said teasingly.

Jackie smiled. "I've lived with that man a long time, Yolanda. I've got plenty of good word from him and the Lord."

"Well, ladies, you can talk about what you learned after we get some food in our bellies. I'm starving," Connie said, easing up from her seat and leading the pack to the buffet. "I'm going to get my eighteen dollars and fifty cents' worth today."

"Married life must be comforting," Queenie said. "Why is it that when the marriage is good, the husband and wife gain about twenty pounds?"

Everybody laughed. "Let's eat," Emma said, pushing Queenie along. "You don't have to worry about that for a while. It's too early in the game to push Mr. Donald Griffin into a corner and beg him to marry you."

"Shut up, Emma. You don't know what in the hell you're talking about. Stay in your lane and don't worry about me and mine."

"I got a marriage proposal."

Queenie stared at the back of Emma's head as she moved away and began putting food on her plate. "A marriage proposal?" She couldn't wait to get back to her seat to interrogate Emma further.

"Oh my God, this food is divine," Yolanda said, shoving a spoonful of shrimp and grits down her throat. "I wasn't sure what I wanted to eat with all the choices." Yolanda took her fork and cut the end of her French toast. "Oooh-wee, this Bananas Foster French Toast tastes good. Did you get some, Emma?"

"Girl, I'm trying to keep my figure, but I couldn't pass up the prime rib, mac and cheese, and corn casserole."

"What's on that salad plate?"

"Plenty of fresh jumbo shrimp and smoked salmon. Where's your sister? She was the first one to jump out of her seat."

"Emma, I think Connie and Preston starved themselves to death when they went into hiding. I went over their house last weekend, and Preston barbequed everything that wasn't nailed down. I'm so glad my sister found love."

"Me too, YoYo. It was a long time in coming."

"So what's this about Terrance asking you to marry him? You pissed Q off; she's looking for a wedding ring like a vulture looking for food."

"Shhhhh, here she comes now."

Queenie put her plate on the table. She said grace and turned away from Emma's and Yolanda's staring eyes.

"You got a little taste of everything, huh Q?"

"Mind your business, YoYo. I'm not eating to stay slim. I love myself. Anyway, I'm not the one you should be concerned with. Your sister is balancing two plates. Now that's greed."

Connie finally found her way to her seat. She said a silent prayer and went straightway to eating. Connie didn't raise her head for conversation; she was too busy shoveling food in.

She looked up after demolishing her second plate to find her friends staring at her in awe.

"Where in the world did you put all of that food?" Jackie wanted to know.

"Are you sick?" Emma asked.

Connie raised her head and smiled. "I'm pregnant. I'm going to be a mommy and I'm eating for two."

Hands flew up in the air. Tears of joy started flowing. Yolanda got up and gave her sister a big kiss and a hug.

"I'm going to be an auntie. Why didn't you tell me?"

"I wanted it to be a surprise. Everybody knows you can't keep a secret, YoYo."

"But I'm your big sister. I deserved to know before the rest of these women."

"Hold your thought, big sister. It's dessert time. I saw a peach cobbler and some bread pudding out there."

Everyone began to shake their heads in disbelief. Connie was pregnant and going to have a baby.

"This is cause for celebration," Emma said.

"What are you celebrating?" Queenie asked. "Your engagement or that Connie's pregnant? You're always trying to steal the show."

"You better sit back and act like an adult, Queenie Jackson, before I have to beat your fat ass down. You are so jealous that it makes you look ugly. You said you learned some things since you've been with Donald, but I see that you're still the same self-centered, all-about-me wench you ever were. Why don't you try patience?

"Anyway, I told Terrance I couldn't marry him. My heart will always belong to Billy. I want the memories that are now intact to stay that way. Terrance and I will probably continue to go out, but our focus is our soul. If I'm going to see my baby one day, I've got to get things right on this earth. Now stop being a piss-in-the-mud and celebrate Connie's good news."

Queenie put her knife and fork down and twisted her lips. "I'm sorry, Emma. I'll try to do better. It isn't all about me all the time."

The ladies laughed.

"Well, I've got some news…sort of," Yolanda said, twirling her fork in her hand. "Illya and I are still seeing each other, although this long distance romance is hard on a sister. We'll keep going as we are and see where it leads. I'm like Emma; I'm not interested in getting married, even if our reasons are different. Someone to keep me company—go to the movies, out to dinner, the park or on a fabulous vacation is all I need."

"I'm in a good place with Donald," Queenie interjected. "I love him, although we've only been together for a little over a month. He's the most respectable man I've met in a long time. And if he asks me to marry him, you all can be my bridesmaids. Emma, I hope you'll be my maid of honor."

"Q, are you really asking me to be your maid of honor? This isn't a trick, is it?"

"No, Emma. You are my best friend. We're hard on each other, but I won't be able to do it without you by my side."

"That's the kindest thing I've ever heard you say, Q."

"Connie, you keep eating and stay out of this conversation." Everyone laughed.

"I'm happy y'all," Connie said. "I finally got the man of my dreams. And I've always wanted to be a mother. I'm sure that there's going to be those who'll be talking behind my back, saying stuff like I'm too old for childbearing. But I don't care who says what, this is my body.

"Speaking of my body, I found a gray hair in a place I don't want to talk about. I plucked that sucker out right away. I don't want my baby to come into the world thinking that his mama is some old chick trying to prove something to the world. Yeah, baby, I plucked that sucker."

"You are a real Silver Bullet now," Queenie said as she burst into laughter. The others followed, hardly able to contain themselves. "You are a bonafide Silver Bullet."

About the Author

Suzetta Perkins is the author of several novels including *Behind the Veil; A Love So Deep; EX-Terminator, Life After Marriage; Déjà Vu; Nothing Stays the Same, Betrayed, At the End of the Day* and *In My Rearview Mirror.* She is a contributing author of *My Soul to His Spirit.* She is also the co-founder of the Sistahs Book Club. Suzetta resides in Fayetteville, North Carolina. Visit her at www.suzettaperkins.com, www.facebook.com/suzetta.perkins, Suzetta Perkins' Fan Page on Facebook, Twitter @authorsue, and nubianqe2@aol.com.

Book Discussion Questions

It is part of the normal course of life when one ages and hits the half-century mark that one thinks about mortality more than ever. For some, fifty is the new thirty...or new forty, depending upon whose view it is. In *Silver Bullets*, four women show that age is just a number by seeking out new forms of pleasure, love, and romance.

1. Queenie Jackson, Emma Wilcox, Connie Maxwell, Yolanda Maxwell Morris, and First Lady Jackie O'Neill deserve their own Housewives of Raleigh franchise with *Bravo* television. Who is most grounded and who do you feel is most insecure with their life? Why?

2. Queenie hasn't had good luck keeping a man. She sometimes goes to the extreme in trying to please a man. What are some of the things she does to try and keep her man happy, although her friends aren't sure she's being truthful about all she tells them? Which was your favorite?

3. Linden Robinson, Queenie's on-again, off-again boyfriend, knew how to work her buttons. Do you think Queenie took him for granted and would you have taken him back after knowing that he'd been sleeping around with someone else? Why do you think Queenie didn't want to let him go?

4. Emma Wilcox was married to Billy for thirty-six years. What did Billy do every Wednesday? What other things did he do for Emma? Was she ungrateful?

5. After a divorce or breakup, some women will opt to be out of the dating game. Yolanda Morris was happy to be single and free. Enters the fine and handsome Illya Newsome. What does Yolanda do? Is this a sign of weakness?

6. Connie Maxwell, Yolanda's sister, has always wanted to get married and have a baby. She's forty-nine and still waiting for the "love of her life" to put a ring on it. How long is too long to wait for your significant someone to ask for your hand in marriage?

7. There are women who have babies late in life. What are your thoughts?

8. Preston Alexander finally asked Connie to marry him. Why was he inattentive to Connie's needs?

9. Considering Preston's situation, would you have married him?

10. Connie was finally getting married and her sister, Yolanda, gave her the bridal shower. What happened at the bridal shower that turned it into an afternoon the ladies wouldn't soon forget? Have you ever attended a party like that?

11. Do you feel that First Lady Jackie O'Neill was too naive about sex? What do you feel about her actions in Las Vegas? Do you feel it was innocent?

12. Pastor Franklin O'Neill received a wakeup call. First Lady Jackie's indiscretion almost caused Franklin to lose his religion. Was he justified in his actions?

13. This over-fifty quartet gave us plenty of demonstrations on how to please your man. They pushed the limit and our imagination to get their point across. Each day brought about a new revelation. Do you believe the ladies learned anything about themselves?

At The End Of The Day

BY SUZETTA PERKINS

AVAILABLE FROM STREBOR BOOKS

1

Rain threatened the New York sky. Rain or shine, there was going to be a wedding. It had been postponed six months because Denise Thomas wanted to share her special day close to her family and in the city of her birth rather than in Birmingham, Alabama, where she now lived with her fiancé, Harold, and their daughter, eight-year-old Danica. New York in December would not lend itself to the fabulous venue she'd chosen for her nuptials; however, on this June day that still held promise, she was going to marry her lover, the man she adored, and the cousin of her ex-husband.

Denise sat in the white Rolls-Royce limousine with its spacious, luxury interior flanked by her mother, grandmother, daughter, and two sisters. She watched as her guests arrived dressed in their finest, although it was the middle of the day, taking in the splendor of the crabapple trees, the beautiful violet flowers, and the rest of the floral extravagance that comprised Central Park in the Conservatory Garden. Conservatory Garden was said to be one of the hidden wonders of Central Park and a favorite place to have a wedding.

And then she saw them, Sylvia and Kenny Richmond—Sylvia dressed in an emerald green lightweight wool and silk skirt-suit with faux-jewel buttons; Rachel and Marvin Thomas—Rachel dressed in a stunning red Italian wool crepe suit that boasted a stand up-collar on her raglan-sleeve jacket over a matching classic skirt; Claudette and Tyrone Beasley—Claudette dressed in a Caroline Rose mushroom-colored long jacket of Italian polyester with an oversized collar and a matching scoop-neck tank and black silk slacks; Trina and Cecil Coleman—Trina in an ultra conservative charcoal skirt-suit with a classic V-neck collar and embroidered front panel; and the ever classy Mona and Michael Broussard—Mona dressed in an Albert Nipon onyx polyester and wool skirt-suit that looked absolutely fabulous on her. They were her special family, and they strolled in the garden like they were New York elitists, each lady's arm seductively looped in the arm of her husband. They blended well with the movers and shakers that were New York. It was Harold's family that brought the 'Bama with them, however, it didn't matter to Denise because this was her day.

Everything was planned down to the minute. The ceremony was to take no more than forty-five minutes, according to Denise's wedding planner. Then it would be on to the Roosevelt Hotel for the fabulous reception that would rival any platinum wedding that was showcased on television.

It was time. At the direction of the wedding planner, the bridal party was ushered from the limousine to the elaborate makeshift staging area to await their cues. Denise could hear the beautiful melodies of the string violinists floating in the air and could feel the anticipation of the guests as they waited for her to come down the aisle. Her mother and grandmother were escorted to their seats. Her sisters, who served as maid of honor and bridesmaid, respectively, glided down the aisle, each in knee-length, strapless lavender satin dresses and diamond lily brooches that served as hair accents placed in half-moon clusters in their upswept hair. With long, Shirley Temple curls that hung past her shoulders, Danica, dressed in a beautiful white satin cream dress with ruffles at the bottom, waited to walk in before Denise so she could sprinkle lavender rose petals on the ground.

And then they were playing her music. All eyes were on Denise as she floated down the aisle as if walking on air, savoring every minute and in perfect time with the musicians. Her bronze-colored skin was radiant in a sleek satin organza strapless gown that conformed to her body, accentuating her curves like a fine piece of sculpture. The sweetheart neckline wrapped in a beaded overlay draped her shapely breast and her manufactured one like a freshwater mermaid, while the satin skirt was embellished with a beaded lace overlay accentuated with freshwater pearls, Swarovski crystals and rhinestones with sleek satin-covered buttons that ran the length of the entire back of the gown. A ten-carat diamond Eternity necklace decorated Denise's neck. Setting it all off was a bouquet of lavender roses mixed with sweet peas and parrot tulips that Denise clutched tightly in her hand.

Denise's thin lips stretched into an elongated smile when she finally looked ahead and saw Harold waiting for her and Danica standing beside her aunt holding the satin basket that was full of rose petals only moments before. Denise was the happiest she'd be in a long time.

"I pronounce you man and wife," the minister finally said, clad in his black and purple ministerial robe after a twenty-minute heartfelt ceremony that had guests dabbing at their eyes two or three times. "You may now kiss the bride."

Harold held his bride and kissed her passionately, Denise not shy in reciprocating. Loud claps erupted from the two-hundred guests who gave their approval of what they had witnessed. And when Harold and Denise finally parted their lips, the clapping intensified, sounding like thunder. The bride and groom turned to the audience, Denise waving her hand for all to see. They jumped the broom, the fairly new tradition in African-American wedding ceremonies, and walked up the aisle arm in arm, ready to start their brand-new life together. As if on cue, the sun peaked and immersed itself fully from behind the cloud that had threatened rain all morning, lighting up the New York sky in a blaze of glory.

"Denise is absolutely gorgeous," Sylvia said, as she and Kenny, along with the other four couples, filed out behind the wedding party to offer congratulations to the new bride and groom.

"Denise? Shoot, this place is fabulous," Mona said, still gazing at the floral splendor that made the Conservatory so popular among prospective brides. "Yeah, Denise looks pretty, too. Doesn't she, Marvin?"

"Okay, Mona, no need to press Marvin's buttons," Michael said, giving his wife a tiny jab in the ribs.

"It's okay," Marvin said. "Yes, Denise is beautiful and she looks happy, too. See, my boo," he winked at Rachel, "knows that I love her and only her."

"Mona, you did comprehend what my boo said?" Rachel countered, flicking her hand in Mona's direction. "Now shut up and let's get through this and enjoy the rest of the festivities. We know that Denise is going to show out because she wants us Southerners to know how they do it in the Big Apple. That's why she didn't want to get married in Birmingham."

"Hmmph, I think we look better than the rest of her guests," Claudette chimed in. "Maybe Denise doesn't realize that Atlanta is right next to New York when it comes to bourgeoisie."

Everyone laughed.

"You tell them, Claudette," Mona said, trying to quiet the laughter.

"Well, New York has a flare of its own that trumps Atlanta, L.A...." Trina began. Sylvia, Mona, Rachel, and Claudette threw their hands on their hips and twisted their bodies to look Trina in the eyes.

"Says who?" Mona huffed. "I'm from New Orleans, and I know we have a zest for the flare, but since I claim Atlanta as home, I'm here to tell you that it rivals all those big cities you named. Why else would everyone want to move there? You can't tell me that we don't entertain, that we don't live in fabulous houses, have as much disposable income, and can rock fashion right along with these wannabe New York socialites. Look at me. I catered an event for then Senator Barack Obama, who is now the forty-fourth president of the United States. What black socialite in New York can say they've done that?"

"All right, you've made your point," Trina said. "It's that..."

"It's that...nothing," Mona said, cutting Trina off. "I can compete with anybody, no matter where they come from...Los Angeles, Milan, Paris, and New York."

Trina rolled her eyes at Mona, while the others stifled a laugh.

"Girl, Mona isn't going to change," Denise said to Trina.

"Tell me about it."